hookin' up

The H Books #2

TRACY BROEMMER

Hookin' Up

The H Books, Book 2

by

Tracy Broemmer

Contemporary Romance

Published by Tracy Broemmer

Edited by Lexie Broemmer

Cover by Designed with Grace

All Rights Reserved

1

———

S weat glued his shorts to his ass cheeks. Parker Moore swatted at some flying little demon, but he missed. Figured it would be back to bite something before he was done here. He tugged his earbud out and then, Blake Shelton singing in his right ear only, he swiped the side of his face on his shoulder.

Wasn't September supposed to be cooler? Well, okay, not necessarily, but the humidity today was so bad, Parker felt like he was breathing with his head stuck in a pot of his grandma's vegetable soup—chock full of every vegetable known to mankind, thick enough to stand without a bowl.

He eyed the brick house warily and then looked back at the mower.

The summons this morning had left him on edge. Parker snorted and pushed the mower closer to the spigot on the side of the house. He unwound the hose from the reel and turned the water on. On edge, hell. He was jumpy as a gigolo sneaking out of a convent the morning after.

He and the lady of the house—Vanessa Mayne—had texted a bit last month, but that had been strictly about her landscaping, and it had all been texts.

This morning, there had been a new text message on his phone when he got up.

Please check in with me when you're finished with the yard. Need to discuss something with you.

Okay, yeah, it was impossible to read the tone of a text, but it sounded pretty uptight and bitchy to him. He'd dressed quickly, downed a cup of coffee—because why not be boiling on the inside as he headed off to work in sweltering temperatures all day?—and headed to his first stop without dwelling on the text. Or so he thought.

Turns out, he had been dwelling on it all morning long. His phone was in the console of his truck, but he'd been watching the damned truck all morning, as if the phone might sprout legs and jump out the window to join him while he mowed. Maybe beat him over the head for a while.

Earbud still on his shoulder, Parker heard a siren in the distance. The quiet growl of another mower somewhere nearby. He eyed his truck again as he sprayed the mower off. Shifted his gaze to the house—his one bedroom, one bath, bungalow would fit inside Vanessa Mayne's house three or four times—and then looked down at his shoes. Beat-up, grass-stained work boots. Socks that were once white scrunched down around the tops of the boots. Blades of grass stuck to the hair on his legs. Sweat dripped off the ringlet curls in the back of his hair. He had been sweating since seven this morning; he smelled pretty ripe already.

And Ms. Mayne wanted to speak with him about something?

He sighed and squatted down to eye the spray of water over the mower chassis. Normally, he used his own equipment, but there were certain clients who specified that he should use theirs. Vanessa Mayne was one of them. Satisfied that the mower shined brighter than his truck had in weeks, he considered turning the hose on himself. It would sure as hell feel good. Couldn't hurt the visual package, either. The only thing that stopped him was the thought of squelching water out of his boots as he stepped inside the house.

He'd never been inside, but he assumed it was pretentious and fancy and—well, honestly, he figured it looked a lot like his brother's house back when he was married to Kiara. Something to be featured in an interior design magazine, but certainly nowhere Parker would ever be comfortable living.

Once he wrapped the hose around the reel, he went back to the garage for the weed eater. Never one to shirk any responsibility, never one to cut corners, today, he wanted to quit now and see what that text was about. He wondered if he should take his socks and boots off, and slip on flip-flops when he did go inside to talk to her. That would be gross, though, wouldn't it?

Or maybe she wouldn't invite him in. Maybe they would have a conversation on her front porch. He stuck the earbud back in and tried to relax back into his Wednesday playlist, but as he trimmed along the east side of the house—she really did need some attention to her landscaping—he found himself worrying about the text again. The topic that she needed to discuss with him. Was she going to fire him? What the hell had he done to deserve that?

He was as conscientious with his clients' yards as he was his own. Never left a mess when he was finished. Every lawn he cared for was so green and luxurious, it could have been carpet. And if it was about him looking at her? Really? The woman was here every time he worked in her yard; she knew when he would be here, and she chose to sit outside and sunbathe.

She wore a bikini. One he was sure his ex-sister-in-law would find offensive to womankind everywhere. *Parker* liked it. Liked what was in it, though he never ventured close for a really good look. Not his fault if she let her girls get a bit out of control and he got an eyeful when he trimmed around the patio. Definitely not his fault when she shifted her legs or bent her knees, giving him a peek at smooth, lean inner thighs and the sweet spot between them that the tiny scrap of orange material didn't really cover.

If you asked Parker, it was more of a neon arrow pointing all eyes to that particular part of Vanessa Mayne's body.

He held his breath as he rounded the corner of the house. Yep, there she was in all her glory. She never unhooked the top. Didn't seem to care about tan lines on her back. But somehow, she was always *on* her back when Parker was in the area. He looked now—the curves of her breasts spilled out the top of the suit, as always. Eyes closed, she seemed oblivious to him.

Determined to finish the job—even if Vanessa Mayne was going to fire him, he would walk away today after finishing a job he was proud of—he turned his back to her and continued trimming around the patio.

When he was finished, he mopped the sweat off his face again and carted the weed eater back to the garage. Time to face the music. He didn't usually worry about his appearance; he cleaned up fine when he had reason to. He and his brother had both been fortunate with looks handed down from their parents, who had made a damned good-looking couple. Nick and Parker shared some of the same physical attributes—same eyes, though their blues tended to change by mood, same basic build, though Nick was harder and more compact, compared to Parker's ranginess.

Women found them both appealing; occasionally the same woman found them both appealing. They liked different types, though. Well, Nick had gone from bohemian to stick-in-the-ass uptight and back to a more free-spirited woman with Mercedes. Parker just liked women.

He wasn't terribly concerned about impressing Vanessa Mayne. But he wasn't crazy about the idea of stepping inside her castle dressed like a homeless guy, either. He would have preferred a shower and a change of clothes for whatever this confrontation was about.

He wasn't a coward, either, so he found himself on her front porch wondering if she was still out back. With a sigh and a shrug, he tugged both earbuds out and let them rest on his shoulders. Rang the doorbell and swung his gaze back to his truck out front. Wasn't so much worried about the phone or text anymore, not now. Maybe counting steps for when he walked out, maybe just admiring a job well done.

Would she really fire him? But for what reason? No, it wasn't a big deal. Her retainer wasn't going to make him or break him. But logically, there was no reason for her to fire him, and that drove him nuts.

"Hey." She pulled the door open and nodded for him to come in. Disappointed that she'd put some clothes on—though the white t-shirt and skimpy denim shorts didn't cover too much more than the bikini—Parker stepped inside, frowning at the white marble tile. "Thanks. For taking a few minutes to talk."

Parker watched her close the door. Catalogued her bare fingers—even her ring fingers. Her neatly filed, but bare fingernails. The bright red polish on her toes. A very fine gold ankle bracelet on a very fine-looking ankle.

"Would you like something cold to drink?" she asked when she turned back to him. So, she was going to fire him over a glass of sweet tea? Her warm, genuine smile was totally at odds with what he assumed was coming. Parker looked around the cavernous living space. All white marble flooring, white and slate gray furniture, white walls. Air conditioning set at North Pole. Even more uncomfortable now in his sweaty clothes, Parker suppressed a shiver and nodded as he swung his gaze back around to her.

"Would you rather me wait outside?"

"What?" She frowned. "Why? It's gotta be at least the sixth circle of hell out there right now."

While Parker followed her reference to *Dante's Inferno* and definitely agreed with her, he noticed she didn't appear to have sweat at all. Her cheeks were a healthy sun-kissed color, and the rest of her—that he could see—

was a golden tan. She had twisted her hair up in a messy bun, but she certainly didn't look hot.

Well.

Parker coughed and made a show of checking out his grass-stained boots again.

Vanessa Mayne was smoking hot, but that had nothing to do with Dante or an inferno or the mercury pushing ninety outside.

"I'm not really dressed to be in your house."

"Oh." Vanessa shook her head and waved her hand at him as if to dismiss his concern as silly. "Come on back to the kitchen."

Parker answered with a slow nod and fell in step behind her when she turned and walked the other way. He cast a few doubtful looks behind him, but he didn't notice that he was leaving a trail of green, so he decided if she wasn't worried about it, he wasn't, either.

"I'd offer you a beer, but I assume you have more appointments to keep."

"You would be correct." He studied her carefully, still completely lost as far as her motives or his reason for being in her house right now.

"I know you don't do a lot of landscaping." She turned her back to him and took a glass pitcher of tea from a double wide stainless-steel refrigerator.

Parker stood near the end of a long peninsula counter that jutted out from the main counter along the southern wall of the kitchen. When sweat dripped in his eyes, he lifted his t-shirt up to wipe them dry. Vanessa Mayne was eyeing his abs when he dropped the shirt and looked at her again.

His overactive imagination immediately slipped into

overdrive. Which made his dick perk up, which was not convenient when the lady of the house was watching him with a curious, pensive look on her face. What if she had asked him to come inside to service her? What if she suggested a cool shower and steamy sex on the bathroom floor? Or a little dessert here on the counter?

"Do you like sweet tea?"

He didn't. Not particularly. But it was cold and wet, and he was dry and hot and getting hotter by the second.

"Thanks." He nodded. Waited until she turned her back to him again to fetch two glasses from a cabinet to adjust his dick. He moved quickly, fixed it—though there wasn't much that felt comfortable when his shorts and briefs were plastered to his balls and his legs—with one quick move, unlike any major league sports professional who ever adjusted his cup on live TV.

"Would you be interested in doing that for me?"

Parker coughed when he took the glass from her. Thank God her fingers didn't touch his, or he might have dropped the glass and picked her up. There was a long stretch of counter perfect for an afternoon quickie, and if the counter didn't work, she had good wall space.

"I've been looking at some magazines," she continued, and Parker almost squirmed under her wide, innocent gaze. "Getting ideas."

He didn't need magazines to give him ideas of things he would love to do for Vanessa Mayne. With Vanessa Mayne.

Landscaping, he reminded himself. She was talking about landscaping.

"Absolutely." His voice sounded funny, but she didn't seem to notice. He took a big swallow of the tea, so desperate to douse the fire in his groin that he didn't notice the overly sweet taste that usually made him gag.

"Good." She smiled and sipped from her glass.

"You could have just texted me that," he said with a quick grin. "I know you're home on your lunch hour."

"Mmm." She swallowed more tea and nodded. Parker watched her set her glass on the counter, admired the firm shape of her upper arm, her long, elegant fingers. "I actually took the rest of the afternoon off."

"Oh." He nodded. "Did you wanna get started on that today?" Why else had she taken the afternoon off and invited him in? She sure as hell wasn't going to show him the rest of her house. Or the rest of her.

"No." Her little burst of happy laughter lit up her eyes. "No, I know you're busy. I just...do you have a minute?"

"Sure." He nodded. "Is something wrong?"

"No." She took a deep breath and backed up a step to stand in the corner of the counter, a stainless-steel sink to her left and another short counter space with a coffee maker to her right. "I...um. Well, Parker, I have a proposition for you."

"Okay." He shifted on his feet. The sweat had stopped rolling over his skin, but now his stiff, wet shirt hung on him and made him want to shiver. His nipples felt a bit chafed. He wondered how women could stand a wet t-shirt clinging to their breasts, their nipples.

The thought brought his dick to a full salute. He felt a rush of heat in his face, but thankfully, Vanessa's gaze was on the floor between them. Her upper teeth tugged nervously at her lower lip. Odds were his balls were purple right now, either from the damp chill in her refrigerated house or from the rush of blood pounding there at the thought of Vanessa Mayne in a wet t-shirt and nothing else.

"I want you to get me pregnant."

Forget his dick. His jaw dropped so hard, he heard it click and wondered if it was his teeth breaking on the marble floor.

"I'm sorry?"

"I want a baby, Parker Moore. And I've decided yours would be the perfect sperm."

2

The poor guy looked like he swallowed his tongue. Vanessa felt a stab of guilt, but her nerves were wound so tight, she had nothing to offer to ease his discomfort. Not even a hard whack on the back to make sure he was still breathing. Eyes wide and mouth hanging open, Parker Moore gaped at her like she had summoned the voice of Satan from deep within.

"You want—? What?" He tipped his head and looked to his right for the counter. Vanessa winced when he crashed the glass of tea hard enough to break, let out a sigh of relief when it only skidded over the counter and sloshed tea around.

Maybe she should have approached this differently.

Maybe you shouldn't have done this at all, Vanessa.

Giving herself a mental shake—that inner voice had led her astray one too many damned times for her to listen to it again, no more of that—she sipped her own tea and stared at Parker with what she hoped was a cool, remote expression.

"I want a baby, Parker," she repeated as if she was only asking him to fertilize the lawn.

"And you think I—?" He blinked, apparently still stunned by her grand announcement. "Me? What?"

"Yes. I do."

"You don't even know me," he argued.

"I've asked around about you."

She had. She'd asked a lot of people about Parker Moore. And she had found that most people who knew him thought he was charming, responsible, and easygoing. Add those qualities to all of his very nice physical qualities and her positive qualities; seemed like a no-brainer to her.

"You've asked—?" He groaned and scrubbed his hands over his head. Apparently remembering he was still sweaty and dirty from working in her yard, he lowered his hands and frowned at them with disgust. "That doesn't mean you know me."

"Well," she nodded and rushed on before he could put up a real fight, "I've given this a lot of thought. We could get to know each other while we wait for our labs. Once we're both given that clean bill of health…"

Parker stared at her with wide eyes, hanging on her words, waiting for her to finish her thought. This part was a bit trickier. She had practiced it, but those times she'd said this into a mirror, looking into her own face were easy peezy compared to standing here in the same room with all six foot and one hundred and eighty pounds of potent male, telling him the same thing.

"We can…" She shrugged and wagged her eyebrows, praying that he got her meaning without her actually having to say the words.

"We can—?" He shook his head. "Wait." He growled and then shoved his fisted hands into his eye sockets. Turned his back to her and stood for a moment. Vanessa watched anxiously as he finally moved his hands, though the move from his eyes to the back of his neck where he dug his fingers in didn't seem terribly positive. "You wanna have sex? With me? To get pregnant?"

"Yes." She almost lunged for him, gratitude for him putting the words out there so she didn't have to almost oozing from her.

"Oh my God." Parker chuckled. "Are you kidding me right now? Is there a hidden camera in here?"

"No!" This time she did move toward him. Maybe not a lunge. Well, almost, but she caught herself. Zipped up the desperation and offered him a smile. Professional, courteous, but not sultry or sexy. That was laughable. Greg hadn't found her smiles sexy. Why would this guy?

Parker sighed and groaned again.

"I just…" She shrugged when he turned to her and met her eyes. "I mean…I don't wanna have conception stories that involve turkey basters."

"There are places you can go for this." He tipped his head. "You know that, right?"

Certain now that he was going to say no, she nibbled on her lip and raised an eyebrow.

"I'd like something a bit more…" Romantic? No. Nope. She was done with that. Over it. Physical, she supposed. If her child ever asked about his or her father, Vanessa at least wanted to say they had a whirlwind affair that created a child and then they went their separate ways. It would be a bit of a stretch, but it sounded so much better than words like *sperm bank* and *fertility clinic*.

Besides.

Parker Moore was a fine male specimen and while she was very much over romance, she missed sex. A lot.

Parker huffed out another big sigh.

"You're gonna say no. Aren't you?"

He reached for his abandoned tea glass and gulped the rest of the cold liquid down.

"I am so…" He shrugged and let his words trail off. "I thought you were gonna fire me, and while losing you as a client wouldn't break my piggy bank, it was making me nuts trying to figure out what I did that you didn't approve of. And now, you're telling me you wanna have sex with me because you want me to get you pregnant, and I don't even know a damned thing about you."

"Why would I fire you?" She narrowed her eyes at him.

"Beats me," he mumbled. He stared at her silently; Vanessa felt his eyes crawling over her skin.

"Can we talk about it?" she asked when the quiet dragged out too long and the sensation grew unbearable.

"Um." He cleared his throat and made a show of looking at his work boots and grass-stained socks again.

"I know." She nodded. "You have to get back to work."

"I do," he agreed. "I also feel at a distinct disadvantage. I've been working outside since first thing this morning. It's hotter than hell out there."

"I know." She took a deep breath and smoothed her hands over her hips. "Would you come back here for dinner? Tonight?"

"Dinner." He smacked his lips together and stared at her like she was a riddle to be solved. "Tonight."

"Do you have plans? We could do it a different night. We could—I could—"

"Tonight's fine." The fierce stare didn't let up, but Vanessa sagged with relief at his words. No, he hadn't agreed to her plan, but he was at least willing to come back and listen to her pitch. She had her foot in the door anyway.

"Good." Her smile stopped far short of professional this time. Hovered closer to uncertain. "Is six too early?"

"Six works." He took a step toward her, his gaze dropping to her lips. Vanessa's heart skipped and hammered double hard when it beat again. She heard the rush of blood in her ears, but Parker didn't seem to notice it.

Was he going to kiss her? Mouth dry, she struggled to swallow. Lost the battle to keep her eyes on his. Parker barked a harsh laugh and stepped back.

"I'm not gonna kiss you." He said it like a promise. A vow, maybe. Vanessa felt a rush of heat in her face, a little bit hurt by his tone. What if he wasn't into her? What if he told her no because he didn't want to have sex with her? Here she thought she'd worked out the perfect situation. She was going to offer him money. She had a figure in mind; in fact, she had discussed her plan with an attorney, a friend of a friend. She would pay to have a contract drafted, put everything in writing. No strings attached. Money and sex for him. A baby for her. Okay, a baby and sex for her.

She had assumed it was a win/win situation, but maybe she was wrong. Maybe Parker Moore wasn't attracted to her and had no desire to have sex with her.

"Of course not." Her tone was clipped and cool, but thankfully, she found her professional smile and glued it back in place. "I'll look forward to seeing you tonight."

"Right." He nodded and turned away from her. Rooted

to the spot, Vanessa watched him disappear from the kitchen. She folded her arms over her chest and stood, paralyzed, until she heard the quiet click of the door closing behind him.

"Not your best sales pitch, Van," she mumbled. Frustrated, she unclipped her hair and ran her fingers through it. She should have practiced more. She should have just invited him to dinner and plied him with a beer or two. They could have had a little conversation and maybe some laughs, and then she could have laid out her plans to him in a simple, logical way.

Her timing had been all wrong. While she had no qualms about standing in the same room with him when he was all sexy, sweaty hot male, he was uncomfortable, and she should have thought of that. Then again, if he wasn't interested in her, if the idea of no-strings-attached sex with her wasn't appealing to him, then there wouldn't be a right time.

"Not a big deal, Van," she told herself. "Just dazzle him tonight."

She checked the time on her stove and huffed out a tired sigh. Time to get moving if she was going to wow him in a few short hours.

3

A *baby.*

Vanessa Mayne had summoned him this morning via text message to discuss getting pregnant. To discuss *him getting her pregnant.*

Two hours later, he was still poleaxed by the whole conversation. Head in the clouds, he had nearly mowed a few toes off his foot at the Pattinson's house. That damned incline was hell on a good day; on a day when his entire world had shifted—shifted, hell, how about rammed out of orbit—the incline in the backyard could damned well be fatal.

He wanted kids. Sure, he did.

Some day.

But. Not yet. *Not like this.*

Right?

Vanessa Mayne had offered up sex. Damned if he hadn't fantasized about that very thing a hundred times or more this summer. But not like this. Not with the end result of her getting pregnant.

And then what, anyway? What would happen then? They hadn't gotten that far, and honestly, Parker had been thrilled to haul ass out of her place and down the road. His cold, damp briefs stuck to his balls had been ten kinds of uncomfortable, and his shirt was wet and gross. He could smell his own sweat. He had probably shivered a time or two while he was standing in her kitchen. What if she thought he was a pussy, afraid of what she had proposed? Or what if she thought he wasn't into her?

She thought he was going to kiss her earlier in her kitchen. Hell yes, he would love to lock lips with her, but not looking and smelling like he did. He would kiss her. No matter what was decided about this baby thing, Parker was going to lay one on Vanessa and leave her with some steamy thoughts that made sleep impossible. But not until he had showered and put on respectable clothes and brushed his teeth.

No matter what was—

"Really, man?" he grumbled. "You're really considering this?"

He finished trimming the Pattinson's yard and then carried their newspaper and mail up to the front door for them. The older couple didn't get around too well anymore. Now and then Mr. Pattinson was sitting out on the front porch while Parker worked—fully clothed, no bright orange bikini for him—but Parker hadn't seen either of them today. He surveyed the butterfly bush he had planted in front of the Pattinson's garage window last summer as he headed back to his truck. Satisfied that it was blooming and looking good, he climbed up into his truck and started it.

Done for the day at half past four. He wanted to talk to

his brother, but Nick was rarely home by six, let alone four thirty. Parker did a mental shrug and turned the truck toward 42nd, the biggest thoroughfare on the east side of town. If Nick wasn't around, Parker would hang out with his girlfriend and the kids for a few minutes. Not quite the same as the heart-to-heart he needed right about now, but good enough.

Parker was crazy about Nick's kids. Pretty crazy about Nick's fiancé, too. Watching his big brother *now* made him want all those things for himself. But he hadn't intended to really go after them just yet.

He shifted in his seat now and pulled his ancient iPod from the pocket of his shorts. The damned thing had been dropped, almost run over, immersed in rainwater and then in a bowl of rice, and it kept right on playing. The screen was a scratched, pocked mess, and there were times he had to just tuck it in his waistband depending on what shorts he wore for work, so it was often greasy-looking, all covered in sweat. He tossed it on the passenger seat now, mind back on Vanessa Mayne.

In that damned bikini.

She had already mind-fucked him. No matter what happened tonight, this wasn't just going to go away. He could already imagine the dreams he would have after today's discussion. Maybe he could take care of it in the shower later. Before he went to dinner at her house. It would be easier to talk to her if he didn't have to worry about his dick poking a hole through the fly of his pants during dinner.

Then again, could he do that and then look her in the eyes when they talked? About having sex. Making a baby.

He pulled his truck to the curb in front of Nick's

house and climbed out. Still in desperate need of a shower, he tugged his sweat-soaked shirt over his head and tossed it on the floor of the passenger side. He always had a spare shirt or two in the truck, so he grabbed a clean one now from the passenger seat and pulled it on quickly. Not perfect, but it was a bit better.

Mercedes had started parking her car in Nick's garage. Ever since the group proposal. Parker chuckled as he loosened his shoestrings and tugged his boots off one at a time. Nick and Mercedes had fought the cliched daddy/nanny romance for a little bit, and then one or both of them had given in—Parker didn't know the particulars and didn't need to—and then, naturally, they'd blown up. The first big fight had led them to a breakup and Nick's ex-wife had been involved somehow. Parker shivered now at the thought. That woman was an ice princess. So cold, she had frozen his brother's emotions over time, and Nick hadn't even realized it was happening.

Thankfully, Nick and Mercedes had worked out what-ever issue they had. With some help from the ice princess herself, apparently, and then there had been that morning when Mercedes said in front of him and the kids that she loved Nick, and Maisy—Nick's five-year-old—had announced that her daddy and Mercedes were gettin' hitched. Parker had helped Maisy dig through her trea-sure chest of kiddie junk for a gaudy, plastic ring, and Nick had put it on Mercedes' finger. Worried that it would break, and Mercedes would run or something, Nick bought her a real ring.

Nothing elaborate. No channel diamonds. No giant thick band. Just a simple diamond solitaire. Fearing that the real ring might be too much, too fast, Parker had high-tailed it out of his brother's house when he popped the box open. Apparently, Mercedes was okay with it, since she had been wearing that ring faithfully.

She wouldn't move in, though. Sensitive to what the kids were thinking, she wouldn't move in, and to Nick's frustration at times, she wouldn't stay the night, either. But she did park her car in his garage now.

"Uncle Parker!"

Parker caught his niece as she ran down the driveway and threw herself at him.

"Hey, Mase." He kissed the tip of her nose and then offered Mercedes a smile as she moseyed out of the garage.

"Hi." She tucked her hands in her hip pockets and scrunched her bare toes over the drive. Parker noticed the messy green polish on her toes and peeked quickly at Maisy's fingers. Same color. Better paint job. Reminded of Vanessa's bare nails and red toenails, Parker wondered if Vanessa would let her child paint her nails.

He would never make a play for Nick's woman. But he loved the hell out of her for the way she loved Maisy and Eli.

"Me 'n' Eli are gonna play on the swing set," Maisy told him. "You wanna?"

Parker grinned and set her down.

"How about I watch? I need to talk to your daddy."

"Daddy's not home." Maisy rolled her eyes, but she took off through the garage and the house to go out back.

"Nick gonna be late?" Parker asked as he fell into step with Mercedes through the garage.

"No, actually." She shook her head. "He texted. Should

be here in about ten minutes, but I didn't tell the kids. Just in case something comes up."

Parker nodded.

"You okay?" She eyed him suspiciously.

He laughed as he followed her into the kitchen.

"Yeah. I'm good."

"You need to talk to Nick?"

He watched her retrieve a couple of beers from the fridge and took one when she offered it to him.

"I do." He nodded, twisted the top off, and took a long pull.

He had always taken the girl stuff to Nick, rather than his dad. Probably his dad would have been okay to talk to about most things. Whether or not to ask Staci Kennady to the prom. If it was a bad sign that his girlfriend Nicole never wanted to see him.

But this was different. He couldn't imagine sitting down with his dad and asking for advice about Vanessa Mayne.

"Okay." Mercedes nodded. "You wanna sit outside? It's pretty warm out there."

It was, and the kitchen felt pretty perfect, but Parker had told Maisy he would watch her and Eli on the swing set, so he shrugged off the worries over the heat and led Mercedes to the deck.

"Set a date yet?" he asked as Mercedes perched on an Adirondack chair. He lowered to the edge of a lounge chair and watched Eli chase Maisy in circles out in the yard.

"Oh my God." Mercedes chuckled. "No. But Mase is all in on the search for a dress."

He grinned.

"She told her teacher the other day that we're gettin' hitched, so I can sleep in Nick's big boy bed with him."

Parker snorted. "That kid hears and remembers everything."

"Let's hope she doesn't hear everything," Mercedes mumbled. Parker noticed the pink in her cheeks, but she was laughing.

"So. You will sneak around when you're here, but you won't sleep with him. Until you're married."

"I just don't want the kids to see me in his bed," she answered simply. "Until we're married."

Parker nodded and turned his attention back to the kids, who were now climbing on the swing set. He wondered how Vanessa Mayne would feel about that. If he got her pregnant now, and she had a boyfriend five years from now, would she be sensitive to that stuff? Would she want her child to learn those same morals? Or was she looser with her sexuality?

Why was he even considering this? He took another long pull from his beer, his shoulders sagging in relief when he heard the sliding door open behind him and Nick joined them on the deck.

"Hey." Nick slugged his shoulder. Parker waited—eyes on the kids—while Nick moved over to kiss Mercedes hello. "Here for dinner?"

"No." Parker drew in a deep breath.

"Stay, Parker. I made—"

"I can't." He interrupted Mercedes. "But I do need to talk to you about something, Nick."

Nick tipped his own bottle up and tugged at his tie with his free hand. He frowned as he swallowed. "Okay. What's going on? You okay?"

Parker shot Mercedes a quick look.

"Oh." Mercedes nodded. "Okay. You want to talk to *Nick*."

She stepped around Nick to leave them alone, but he caught her by the belt loop and tugged her back to him.

"It's just…" Parker stood and rubbed his hand over his face.

"I mean, you can talk in front of me, Parker. *To* me, in fact. You've had your tongue down my throat, after all." Mercedes shrugged and offered him a playful smile. He chuckled.

"Is that what it felt like? Was it that bad?"

Mercedes trilled her cute laugh and shook her head.

"No. Why—"

"Really, Cedes. For other women, am I a bad kisser?"

"Um." Mercedes glanced over her shoulder at Nick. He answered her unspoken question with a lazy grin and an eye roll.

"Feed his ego," he mumbled.

"You're not a bad kisser," she told him. Parker flinched. He had kissed Mercedes. Before she was involved with Nick. They had become fast friends, and he had been stewing over Vanessa Mayne even then, trying to work out if it meant anything that the woman came home every time he was there to sit outside in that bikini. He had suggested a test kiss to determine if he and Mercedes were attracted to each other. The answer had been no for both of them, but it still rankled, wondering if she considered him a bad kisser. "I mean…" She laughed softly. "It was nice."

"Nice." Parker groaned. "Nice kissing is like saying

you're as turned on by it as you are by petting puppies and eating ice cream."

"Well." Mercedes blushed and laughed softly.

"I know." Parker let his eyes skate over his brother's face. They hadn't really discussed the fact that Parker had laid one on his girlfriend and Nick had seen it. He wasn't any more comfortable talking about it than Nick was. "Hot for Nick Moore. Not Parker."

"So, what's going on?" Nick asked, apparently done talking about Parker and Mercedes' kiss.

"Remember Vanessa Mayne?" Parker cut his gaze to Mercedes now and waited for the name to register.

"The one—?"

"Yeah."

"Wait." Nick shook his head. "The one what? Vanessa who?"

"The reason I kissed your girlfriend," Parker said irritably, but he kept his eyes on Mercedes. "She invited me to dinner tonight."

"Oh!" Mercedes grinned. "Parker, that's so cool."

"It's not, though." He shook his head. "It's not cool, because she wants me to get her pregnant."

Nick, bottle at his mouth, coughed and spewed a mouthful of beer.

"She wants what?" Mercedes looked first at Nick, concerned that he might really be choking, and then she turned her attention to Parker. "She what?"

Nick nodded and swung the hand that held his beer in Mercedes' direction as if to repeat what she had asked.

Parker hooked the fingers of his left hand around his neck and squeezed. He spoke haltingly, filling them in on the text this morning requesting that he speak with

Vanessa before leaving today. And her mention of land-scaping and then the proposition about getting pregnant.

"Doesn't she know she can go to a fertility clinic? Find an anonymous sperm donor?" Nick asked with a frown.

Parker shrugged. "Well, I would think so, Nick." He sighed and huffed, his body a knot of anxiety. "But she doesn't want any turkey baster stories about conception. She wants—"

Mercedes snorted. When both Nick and Parker turned to look at her, she covered her mouth, but it was obvious she was giggling.

"What?" Nick frowned. "And what does this woman have to do with you kissing Mercedes?"

"She comes home every time Parker's there to do her yard." Mercedes dabbed at her eyes, crooked grin on her face. "Sunbathes in a sexy bikini."

"And?" Nick looked from her to Parker.

"I wasn't sure if I wanted that to mean something. To mean she was into me," he mumbled. "So, I suggested a test-kiss with Mercedes."

"And you decided?"

"Parker, she wants sex."

Parker nodded at Mercedes. "She does."

"So, you're about to become a lawn boy in every sense of the word." Nick's lips twitched with amusement.

"No."

"No?"

"She doesn't just want sex. She wants me to get her pregnant." He drained his beer and peeked over his shoulder at the kids. Maisy was flat on her back on the sliding board. Eli was doing somersaults in the grass. "She specifically said she wants me to get her pregnant."

"She doesn't even know you," Nick argued.

"I know. She said she's asked around about me."

"Oh." Mercedes pursed her lips. "She's serious. You're serious about this."

"I'm so fucking serious," Parker groaned.

"So, you told her no. Because she's a nutcase. End of story. Stay for dinner." Nick turned to the door, fingers working the buttons of his dress shirt.

"She asked me to come to dinner tonight."

"Dinner." Mercedes' eyebrows shot up comically fast. At the same time, Nick shot Parker a look of disbelief. "And you're going?"

Parker cleared his throat. "I said I would."

"Dude." Nick drew back like Parker had smacked him. "Are you nuts? Some stranger says she wants you to get her pregnant? I wouldn't touch that with a ten-foot pole."

Parker snuck a peek at Mercedes, but he shrugged his eyebrows at Nick. "You might, man."

Mercedes snickered.

"I'm glad you find this so funny." Parker swatted at her.

"Guess you don't need to take any condoms to dinner." She folded her arms over her chest.

"Seriously? Did you say that?" Nick shot Mercedes a frown. "Parker, think with your brain, not your dick, man. There're women everywhere who would drop their panties for you. Why this one?"

Parker looked at Mercedes. Her struggle not to giggle drew a frustrated laugh.

"You wanna make a baby with someone you don't even know?" Nick rolled his eyes at both of them. "Babies are a huge responsibility. Look at mine. Once you've got 'em, you can't take 'em back, man."

Parker looked over his shoulder again, Nick's words like a fist pummeling his heart. Look at Nick's kids. Hell yeah, he wanted something so wonderful for himself.

But this wasn't what Vanessa had in mind, was it? She wanted a stud for the deed. She had said so herself. His physical attributes and whatever she had heard about him. A little sex. End of story. Hell, maybe she didn't even care if he was good in bed, as long as he left a sperm deposit.

"I gotta go." He shrugged.

"You're going? To dinner? So, like, you're gonna go shower and go to this woman's house and perform? Like a mating thing with animals?"

"No. This is just dinner," Parker argued. "She said she'd like to talk about it more. And she asked me to come for dinner tonight."

"I'm kinda worried about my little brother's virtue," Nick mumbled with a glance at Mercedes.

"There won't be any sex tonight," Parker assured them. "She mentioned blood tests. Making sure we're both clean."

"I don't get it." Nick eyed him uncertainly as Parker moved toward the door. "You seriously have women all over who would come running. What's the draw?"

"I don't know, man." Parker threw his hands up to ward Nick off. "I just…I'm gonna go have dinner with her. End of story."

Fingers still wrapped around the longneck bottle, he went back inside. Mercedes followed him.

"You think this is a mistake, too?"

She winced and tucked her hands in her pockets. "I don't know, Parker. I guess it doesn't hurt to have dinner with her. Hear her out."

Eyes on the table, Parker nodded and cut loose a long, tired sigh. He set his empty bottle down and met Mercedes' eyes.

"Perfect opportunity, right? For a guy like me? Free, no-strings-attached sex. And yes, it feels super weird to say this to you, but she is smokin' hot, Cedes. She's got the prettiest eyes. And her arms...so toned and tan."

He stopped when he saw the grin on Mercedes' face.

"I get it."

"No. I mean, I coulda told you...last month. In that bikini. The provocative poses." He groaned. "That would turn any guy on. Even Moses. But up close today? She's beautiful."

"Okay." She offered him a small smile. "I get it. Just..."

"What?"

"Be careful."

She hugged him. Parker was used to her hugs now. Totally sister-in-law sorts of hugs, but he liked them just the same. Mercedes always smelled good, and she was crazy about his brother and the kids, and Parker thought they were pretty good friends. Still, the warning grated on his nerves all the way out to his truck.

Vanessa Mayne wasn't his first rodeo. He knew his way around women, around female bodies, all the hot spots and pleasure zones. The only thing he didn't have much experience with was the heart, and he doubted that would be a problem here. Vanessa Mayne wanted his dick. No strings attached.

4

Vanessa turned music on earlier while she worked on dinner. But she was still jumpy, and the hard knock on the front door was so loud, she jerked her hands while she tossed the salad and nearly dropped it all over the floor. Was it Parker? She rinsed her hands and dried them on the dishtowel. She tossed the towel to the counter, smoothed her hands over the short skirt of her dress, and made her way through the living room to answer the door.

He rang the doorbell earlier. What if this wasn't him? What if it was Greg? Good God, she needed Greg Mitchell to show up right now like she needed this five thousand square foot mausoleum of a home.

What if it was Parker, though?

She hesitated now, one hand on the doorknob and the other flattened on the door itself. What if he was hammering on the door because he thought about her proposition, and he was angry? Offended or even just totally not into the idea of hooking up with her?

A second knock—this one a bit sharper and louder, maybe because she was standing right on the other side of the door now—revved her nerves to the breaking point. If it was Greg? Well, she would send him packing. Okay, he already did that. But he had walked out and left her a stupid house she didn't want, and she would just tell him she had a date. No need to give him any details.

It wasn't Greg. She knew that for certain.

And if it was Parker? Well, if he was angry, she would attempt to soothe him. Now that she knew he would sit down and they could discuss this over dinner, she could give him the very well-planned version of the idea instead of how she had just thrown it at him earlier. Most definitely not the way she had meant to handle it.

And if it was Parker, and he was on board? Well, then, she looked forward to finally peeling those clothes off that delicious-looking body and climbing on.

The thought made her fingers tingle with anticipation. The nerves wound through her belly and up into her chest and neck until her whole face tingled. Good grief. She was going to open the door looking like Mrs. Claus with rosy, red cheeks.

Reminding herself one last time that she could handle this no matter what Parker decided, she pulled the door open and drew in a deep, calming breath.

"Hey."

Well, okay, except she forgot that he would look like this. The guy worked sweaty T-shirts and khaki shorts and work boots like a model on a runway. Why hadn't she considered what he would clean up like? Five-alarm fire on her front porch is what.

Mouth dry, she let her eyes take a quick slide over his

thick dark hair—rakishly long with a bit of a wave around his collar—the white button-down shirt, and the dark wash jeans that molded thighs she would like to climb. Bare feet in flip-flops didn't usually do it for her. Parker's feet were tan and sexy, and she couldn't work up enough spit to swallow. Couldn't really breathe, either.

Hands tucked in his hip pockets, head ducked, he wore an amused grin when she forced herself to stop the ridiculous ogling and look him in the eyes.

"Hi."

She whooshed out a sigh of relief when he didn't call her out for the once over, and then realizing that he seemed to be reading her mind, she felt that damned blush creep into her cheeks again. *What's the problem, Mayne? Good grief, you're not some silly virgin, inexperienced with men.*

Well. Greg might say otherwise about experience. Or maybe he would just complain about her services.

Vanessa blinked. Parker was still standing on the porch, and now she was staring at him and thinking about her ex. The one who had dumped her for an older woman. Talk about a slap in the face.

"Come in," she told him. Much to her relief, Parker stepped inside when she gave him room. She leaned around him to close the door, catching his freshly showered scent. Something smelled decidedly masculine, outdoorsy and fresh.

"I'm sorry?" He looked at her over his shoulder. Had she moaned out loud? Just because he smelled good?

"Um." She shook her head and averted her eyes. She had asked this guy to get dirty with her and make her pregnant, and now she couldn't look him in the eyes?

Might be a problem. "Thanks." She shrugged. "For coming."

Parker nodded. She could swear he had another smirk on his face, but when she swung her gaze around to see him clearly, his face was a mask of innocence.

"Thanks for the invitation." He was being too polite. Vanessa's stomach twisted in on itself. Fear that he was going to say no. "Easier to enjoy a conversation after a hot shower."

She nodded, though the word shower brought to mind some very interesting images. Rather than struggle to look at him and not blush seven shades of red, she nodded and motioned for him to follow her into the kitchen.

"Can I get you something to drink?"

"Yes." He followed her to the counters, rather than parking at the table where she had arranged two place settings for dinner.

"Beer or wine?"

"You tell me, Vanessa Mayne." He tipped his head and folded his arms over his chest. "If you've asked around about me, surely you know which I prefer."

Fair enough. She did know he preferred beer. She nodded and turned her back to him to grab two long-necks she had stuck in the freezer about five minutes ago. She turned to hand him one, intent on turning the timer off that she set to avoid having the bottles exploding in the freezer. She bumped into a hard wall of muscle and tipped her head up to look him in the eyes.

"What—?"

Up close like this, Vanessa could see that his eyes weren't just one color of blue, but a mix of ocean turquoise and midnight skies. She wondered if he had shaved; dark stubble covered his cheeks and his chin, but she had seen him wear more scruff and a goatee at times, too. His body was solid against hers, and even in the air-conditioned room, she could feel his heat rolling off him.

She could feel something else, too.

Parker didn't seem inclined to answer her, and when she opened her mouth again to ask him what he was doing, he leaned in without permission to get closer and kissed her. The press of his warm lips to hers was such a thrill, she almost dropped the bottles.

"What're—?" She tried again, but Parker shook his head.

"Shhh." He rubbed his lips over hers again, and then before Vanessa could process how good it felt to have his soft skin pressed to hers, he parted her lips with his tongue and stroked hers intimately but tenderly before pulling away.

"What was—?" A little bit breathless, she cleared her throat and tried again. "What was that?"

"Did you ask me earlier to get you pregnant?"

Dumbfounded that he had just dived right in, she nodded silently. Weak in the knees, she wobbled a bit on her feet and squeezed the bottles harder, still worried she might drop them. Did he think they were going to start tonight?

Did he want to?

Because she certainly hadn't planned on it, but that one damned kiss, that one little wiggle of his tongue inside her lips and over hers, had left her greedy for more.

"I didn't—" She pressed her lips together, an arrow of longing hitting her low in the belly when he dropped his heated gaze to her mouth. "I didn't mean tonight."

His lips twitched and then spread up in a slow, lazy grin. Vanessa squirmed when that same arrow traveled further south. She could imagine being flat on her back, gazing up at that cocky grin.

"I know." He nodded. "But seemed like the thing to do if we're gonna be discussing procreation."

Pro—?

A surge of electricity raged straight down to her girl stuff, but at the same time, her brain waved a warning flag. Parker Moore had just kissed her and left her panting for more, and rather than looking even just a little bit hot and bothered, he looked amused. At her. And he had referred to what she wanted to do with him right now—he could easily slide her over and back her up against the refrigerator for traction as he drove into her— as procreating.

"Right." Her voice sounded a bit too high, too strained for normal, but the good thing was Parker didn't know her well enough to know that. "You're right. Good thinking. Because we should make sure we're compatible if we're going to pro—"

His arms shot around her when she took a step back. Fingers still curled around the damned bottles, she ducked her chin to look. Shirt sleeves rolled, his forearms were tan and thick with muscles, covered with enough dark hair to look very masculine. He linked his fingers behind her back and hauled her up against him, against the proof that kissing her, thinking about procreating with her, had some kind of effect on him.

"Vanessa." The low timbre of his voice drew her gaze back up to his. Chills climbed her spine and broke out over her bare arms. She hoped that if he agreed to this, if agreed to take her to bed and try to make her pregnant, he would say her name like that. Preferably while he had that big hard erection buried inside her and his balls tucked up snug against her.

"Parker, I'm gonna drop—"

His kiss cut off her confession. This time, there was no tenderness. It was wet and greedy. Parker's hands roamed her back possessively, though unfortunately they stayed above her waist. But his mouth? Damned bold and demanding. His lips were open over hers, the pressure firm and unyielding, though still so soft on her skin. He flicked his tongue over the tip of hers, teasing, licking her until finally, she reacted and went after him. Desperate to capture his tongue in her lips, her teeth, she feasted on his mouth, sliding her tongue over his teeth and around his tongue.

The timer went off, and Parker's hands finally slid south to rest on her butt. Another surge of heat shot through her. Vanessa struggled to remain upright. To hold onto the bottles. To talk her beaded nipples down. Not gonna happen tonight, girls.

Unless he brought condoms.

"What the hell is that?" Parker finally drew back from her. "Is that a fire alarm? Is the kitchen burning up?" He stepped back. Mumbled something that sounded a bit like *I thought it was just me.*

Vanessa slipped around him, praying he didn't notice she was trembling. A wave of warmth slipped over her, and she nearly lunged for the counter to put the beers down.

"It's a timer," she answered, but she kept her back to him.

"Why do you have a timer set?" he asked.

"I put these bottles in the freezer, so they would be chilled when you got here." She felt his gaze burning a hole in her back, but she took a deep breath and then opened the drawer where she kept kitchen utensils and pawed through everything looking for her bottle opener.

"Here." He moved up behind her again and twisted the tops off both bottles. Close enough she could feel his heat but nothing else. Vanessa wasn't sure if she should be disappointed or relieved at the reprieve.

"Thank you." She turned away from him and reached to stop the microwave timer. "I have a fruit salad in the refrigerator. Tossed salad. And I have steaks to grill."

"Sounds good."

She chanced a peek at him, unnerved again when he tipped his head up, bottle at his lips.

"Can I do anything to help?" he asked, apparently unaware of her distress.

"Um." She raised her eyebrows hopefully. "Would you mind grilling the steaks?"

"Not at all." He shrugged and set his bottle down, ready to get to work.

Vanessa took the steaks from the refrigerator and handed the plate to him when she turned.

"Grill's out back."

"Oh, I know." He nodded. Because she knew he knew the backyard well—the patio, specifically—she ducked her head to hide the blush. "You gonna come out with me?"

She looked up at him as the blood in her face rushed south again. Not quite to the girl parts, but it pounded through her body, leaving her feeling pumped and ready to move.

"Sure."

She carried his beer, followed him outside, still barefoot. Parker put the meat on her patio table and went about pulling the cover from the grill. Vanessa tugged her dress down and then settled into a chair. Parker turned back as she crossed her right leg over her left.

"So." He sat in the chair next to her and eyed her with interest. "While we wait for the grill to heat up, let's talk."

Already? He wanted to talk about *that* already? Vanessa had hoped for some time, maybe another beer or two, before she launched into her argument for him sleeping with her and getting her pregnant.

She tried and failed to stifle a giggle when it hit her that it sounded like she was a little kid, preparing her argument about why she needed a puppy.

"What's funny?" He took another drink.

"I know you don't wanna know about biological clocks—"

"I do, actually." He sounded sincere. "I honestly want to know the whole thought process you've had going on."

Okay, so she hadn't expected him to be...interested. In the sex, yes. In the reasons why and the what came after, no.

"Well, I'm getting older, Parker, and I'm—"

He shook his head. "Not yet. Just talk to me. Tell me about yourself. Tell me about this house."

She pursed her lips. Okay, this was good. Getting to know each other was a good thing. She wanted to know more about him. If this smoking hot guy was interested in her biological clock and not just the equipment that it encompassed, she most definitely wanted to get to know him. She could even understand why he wanted to know more about her.

But why did they have to start with the house?

Talking about the house would inevitably lead to talking about Greg Mitchell, and Greg was the last damned thing she wanted to discuss with anyone, especially Parker Moore.

5

Kissing her was the perfect start to the night, but not really. Because instead of giving him the upper hand, it had lit him up and primed him for more. More of her hot, wet mouth. More of that lithe, warm body pressed up against his.

Now he was grilling their dinner, listening to her talk about the house like she was a realtor working hard for her commission. He didn't much care about the house, how many bedrooms and bathrooms there were. He didn't care that she found the sectional sofa and the chairs for a steal. Didn't care about the appliances. He wanted to know why she was living in this dream house by herself.

"What do you do?" he asked, interrupting a long monologue on the long debate over a walk-in shower or a claw-footed tub or both. Brain fogged, and his dick particularly interested in Vanessa in either a walk-in shower or a claw-footed tub, he poked at the steaks for a second. He shot a peek at her over his shoulder, found her looking at him, and prayed she wouldn't notice his hard-on when he turned toward her.

"What?"

"What do you do?" he repeated the question.

"Do—where?" she asked with a frown. "In the shower?"

He blinked at her, barked a laugh, and swung back around to the grill.

"No." He counted to ten, imagined his own house, the mess he left in his wake after his shower. He had almost called Mercedes to ask her for fashion advice. What to wear. What not to wear. In the end he hadn't called, but his man card would be in jeopardy if anyone saw the current state of his bedroom.

When she didn't say anything, he used the tongs to turn the steaks and then turned to look at her again.

"For work? What do you do?"

"Oh." She looked embarrassed. Again. Interesting. She had blurted out earlier today in her kitchen that she wanted him to get her pregnant, but tonight, she had blushed so often, he felt like he was with a skittish high school girl. "I own a salon."

"You what now?" He sat down again, though he dragged his chair close enough to hers that their knees bumped.

"I own a salon." She shrugged. Lifted her hand and waved it at her head. "Hair studio. Speaking of which, you could use a trim."

"A—?" He frowned and shook his head. She owned a hair studio? He assumed she was in corporate America. In some high-powered eighty hour a week job—minus the time she spent sunbathing when he was around—and a posh corner office.

"That long, unruly look is sexy," she continued, "but you could still use a trim."

"What salon?"

"The Mayne Studio." She frowned at him as if she couldn't believe he hadn't heard of it, hadn't put two and two together.

"Oh." He shrugged his eyebrows. He had never heard of it. But then, he didn't have any one woman in his life long enough to know much about salons or spas or any of that other girl stuff. His relationships usually burned hot and bright for a few weeks. They were deep enough to offer some incredible sex, good times out and about, and some good laughs. End of story.

Parker avoided Vanessa's eyes and fidgeted with the tongs. Had she heard that about him? Not sure how he felt about that, he climbed to his feet and made a show of checking the steaks again.

"What?"

"Nothing." He shook his head.

"No, what? You're thinking something."

Parker shifted on his feet and looked down as she sidled up to stand by him.

"How do you like your steaks? Pink? Medium well?"

"Done."

"Ruined?"

"No, but no pink, either." She shivered in disgust. Parker noticed the jiggle of her breasts, but his eyes were drawn to her face. She looked a little deflated now.

"So, where's your salon? Here in town?"

"On Maine Street." She spoke quietly, nodded, but refused to meet his eyes.

"What's wrong?"

"Nothing." Now she sounded too happy, a little bit chirpy. "I'm gonna go inside and get the salad and the fruit on the table."

Parker nodded. "Okay. I'll be a minute or two."

He watched her. She leaned over to snag her beer from the table and then slipped inside quickly, like she couldn't wait to get away from him. With a long, frustrated sigh, Parker turned his attention back to the meat on the grill. *Women.* He would never understand them. Why couldn't he find one like his brother's new fiancé?

Cute. Sexy. Okay, no, he did not think that. Not about his brother's woman, but still. Everything about Mercedes was perfect, including how she fit into his brother's life. Was it too much for Parker to want the same thing?

The direction of his thoughts startled him. Since when did he want what Nick had? Well, he did, but he was in no hurry for it. It wasn't as if he had been stewing over it before Vanessa proposed the baby thing earlier today. So why now? Why was he turning an offer of no-strings-attached sex and some extra cash into a big life decision?

And what was her deal? Vanessa had been upbeat and cute and a little thunderstruck after that kiss, if he did say so himself. She had looked a bit uncomfortable when he asked about the house, and then rather than tell him anything personal, she launched into a sales pitch for the property. And when he asked about her job, she really clammed up.

Took a shot at his hair. Did he really need a trim? Should he ask Mercedes? Have Vanessa cut it? Maybe if that was his plan, he should do it before he took her to bed. No need for her to rate his sexual prowess with a haircut. What if she scalped him?

Before he took her to bed.

Parker groaned as he lifted the steaks from the grill one at a time and placed them on a clean bright red plate. Not *if* he took her to bed. *Before.* Seemed like his brain was trying to tell him something. As he grabbed his beer, he thought of Nick and Mercedes earlier, looking at him like he told them Vanessa had asked him to sell his house and join a cult. Nick most definitely didn't like this idea; Parker was less than certain what Mercedes thought.

He stood for a moment, eyes on the long, open yard behind Vanessa's house. Plenty of room for a swing set. For whiffle ball games. To toss a football. Put up a trampoline. He imagined what it would be like to stand here on the patio and watch his kid play ball. Maybe he and Vanessa would toss a ball around with the kid.

Nope.

She hadn't gone too far into her plans earlier, but Parker assumed that this wasn't going to end with them as a couple. Vanessa Mayne wanted him to ride her bareback until she got pregnant, and then she was going to give him a deposit of her own and ask him to walk away. Somehow knowing that he might have a kid out there and be expected to walk away from him or her was worse than worrying he might never have the chance, the relationship, to make a baby.

Okay, so it wasn't his brain talking. Or his heart. Nope. His dick led the way back inside. He scanned the kitchen, saw Vanessa around the counter, phone in her hand. She didn't look much happier now than she had a few seconds ago. Her teeth tugged at her bottom lip so hard the skin was white; she frowned at her phone and then hurriedly typed something.

Was she texting someone?

What if she was—? Was she married? She wasn't wearing a ring, and Parker had never seen a man around the house, but that didn't mean anything.

When she heard the tap of the plate on the counter and the rattle of the tongs on the plate, she glanced up quickly and dropped her phone on the counter. Guilt written all over her face, she offered him a quick, uncertain smile.

"You okay on your beer?" she asked him. "Need another?"

"I'm good." He might need another later, but for right now, it seemed like a good idea to keep a clear head.

"Water?"

"Thanks." He nodded.

He watched her for a moment, and then feeling awkward standing there as she did all the work, Parker moved to lend a hand. He took the salad bowl and the fruit salad and put both on the table and then grabbed the steaks and set them on the table also. Vanessa carried two glasses of ice water over and sat down. Parker joined her, but he couldn't help a peek in the direction of her phone.

"Can I ask you something?"

"Four chairs. Currently renting out two. I have a nail salon, too. I've considered other services. I would *like* to add other services," she shrugged and continued, "but it takes time. I don't wanna half-ass anything. Right now, it's a really classy salon. Our clients expect nothing less."

Parker stared at her silently across the table. Vanessa

stared back with wide eyes, as if she was waiting for him to launch an attack.

"Are you married?"

Nothing. Just that deer in the headlights look.

"Vanessa?"

"Am I—?" She finally stirred, tipped her head, and shot him a frown. "What? Why would I ask you to get me pregnant if I was married?"

Parker's relief was probably obvious in the way the tension drained from his shoulders and he slumped forward.

"Thank you for not saying stud services."

"What?" She shook her head, the frown easing a bit. However, the intensity of her stare didn't; if anything, she appeared to be studying him as if to memorize his face.

"Feels like we're going to breed thoroughbred horses," he mumbled.

"That's kind of a cold way to look at this, don't you think?"

"Honestly, I don't know what to think," he admitted. "It's not every day that I'm approached by a beautiful woman and asked to donate sperm."

"And the offer of sex doesn't tempt you?" She cleared her throat and rested her elbows on the table. "Wow. I'm sorry. That must sound incredibly conceited. You're a sexy guy, and from what I hear, you're also one of the good guys. I'm sure you must have women lining up for a chance to get in your bed."

While he did have his choice of women to spend time with, Parker wasn't sure he liked the way Vanessa phrased it.

"I didn't say I wasn't tempted," he reminded her. "I said I don't really know what to think."

She considered his answer and finally nodded.

"Eat." She waved her hand at the food on the table, but she only picked up her beer to take another drink. "Might as well eat while it's hot."

"You're not married?"

"No." She groaned.

"Ladies first," he told her with a nod at the steaks.

"Is that your philosophy in bed, too?"

"Yes."

She huffed a quick breath and then poked her fork in the steak nearest her.

"That's yours."

"Do you wanna have sex with me?"

"Of course, I do." He rolled his eyes. "What kind of question is that? You've been torturing me all damned summer in that skimpy orange bikini."

"Melon."

"Yes." His eyes dropped to her breasts for a second and then he looked her in the eyes again. "I like 'em."

She laughed softly, but she shook her head. "The color. The bikini. It's not orange. It's melon."

"Right." He laughed, surprised that she didn't blush again.

"Why would you ask if I'm married?"

"I don't know."

"Because of the house," she assumed.

"It's a big house for one person." He stabbed the remaining steak with his fork and hefted it to his plate. It was at least a fourteen-ounce slab of meat. Parker wondered if she thought he ate like a horse.

"I lived with someone," she mumbled.

"The Brady Bunch?" he suggested, relieved when she met his eyes and grinned.

"Well. Greg." She nodded.

"You lived with Greg Brady?"

"I lived with Greg Mitchell, and he was nothing like Greg Brady," she answered. Parker watched her serve herself some of the salad with yet another pair of tongs.

"And so, you and one guy lived here."

"Yep." She licked her lips. "We built the house two years ago. He walked out about ten months ago."

"I'm sorry."

No wonder she had acted weird about the house. Maybe it felt like a mausoleum because it was home to bad memories.

"Don't be." She slipped her fork into her mouth and then covered her lips with her fingertips while she chewed.

"Were you planning to fill it with babies?"

Her loud bark of laughter almost made him jump.

"No. Greg didn't want kids." She dabbed at her mouth with a napkin and then sipped her water. "Well, I guess he didn't *not* want kids. But he wasn't in a hurry about it. It's not why he built the house."

"So, he had a small penis."

Vanessa snorted and turned her head, but not before Parker saw the look of surprise and amusement on her face.

"Well." She nodded her head back and forth. "He liked to make an impression. I'm just gonna leave it at that."

Somehow it made Parker feel at ease that she hadn't just jumped on his comment and slammed her ex.

"Why did he leave?"

"Amanda Sorenson," she answered simply. "Forty something mother of three. Newly-divorced."

Parker winced. Vanessa watched him cut a bite of his steak and then lifted her eyes to his.

"Never thought I'd lose a guy to an older woman," she said quietly. "I mean, I thought that worry was only for junior high days when your high school crush goes out with high school girls. Greg's thirty-five. Left me for her. She doesn't even have good boobs."

"You know her?"

"Know of her."

Conversation ebbed for a few moments as they focused on their dinner.

"You do."

"I do what?"

"Have good boobs."

She chuckled. "You haven't even seen them."

"I've seen a lot of them when you're flat on your back in that lounge chair," he reminded her.

"I'm sorry I tortured you like that."

"No, you're not," he challenged her. "You wanted my attention."

"I did," she admitted.

"So. Tell me."

"What?" She cringed again. Parker studied her for a second. He had been about to lead her into the reason she had invited him over, but he changed lanes as he opened his mouth.

"Who were you texting?"

"What?"

"When I came inside," he reminded her in a gentle tone. "Who were you texting?"

"Um." She pressed her lips together and lowered her gaze to her plate.

"Greg?"

"No." Her whispered answer was heavy with relief. And truth. "God, no. I promise you Greg is so out of the picture."

"Do you still love him?"

"No." She sat back in her chair and folded her arms over her chest. "I'm not sure we ever had that. We liked each other. In the beginning. We had mutual friends. Liked a lot of the same things. So, we started dating."

"Was the sex good?"

"If I say yes, you're gonna assume I'm lying about not loving him. If I say no, you're gonna hold it against me for throwing shade at my ex."

Parker set his fork down and then picked his bottle up to drain it. Under her heavy stare, he rubbed his fingers over his mouth and his chin and finally shrugged.

"If you say yes, I'm gonna take it as a challenge and give you the best sex of your life."

There it was. That cute little surge of color in her cheeks.

"And if I say no?"

"I'm gonna give you the best sex of your life anyway," he said simply.

"It was okay," she answered. "Sometimes it was good."

"Now tell me who you were texting."

"Journey."

"What?"

She chuckled and repeated herself. "Journey."

"Are you bullshitting me?"

"Nope. She's my best friend."

"Is that a stripper name?"

Vanessa snorted. "No. But I'll be sure and tell her you asked."

"Don't do that!" He shook his head.

"Her mom was high most of the time when she was younger. She was...deep. Philosophical. All about the journey."

"Wow. I used to think my mom was weird because she watched soap operas. The more people I meet, the more I think she was pretty normal."

Vanessa's smile was soft and sweet.

"Journey's full name is Journey Lyn. She tried really hard to go by Lyn, but she's got some shitty friends who wouldn't let that happen."

They shared a laugh, and then Parker stuck it to her again.

"So, why when you're in the middle of a...business meeting with me...would you need to text Journey?"

6

Vanessa wasn't a good liar. She was a terrible liar under pressure. And when Parker Moore was staring at her with those sexy blue eyes, she kind of felt compelled to strip away all the lies and bare herself to him. Or maybe those eyes just made her want to strip off her clothes and bare *that* part of herself to him.

"Because she knows what we're discussing, and she wanted to know what was going on, and I might have needed a little pep talk."

"You needed a pep talk?" He frowned. "Why?"

She shrugged and stood. If they were about to get into the nitty gritty of the getting pregnant stuff, she needed another beer. With the heat of Parker's stare on her back, she crossed the room to grab two more bottles from the refrigerator, considered grabbing her phone and looking to see if Journey had responded. But that would be rude. And what if he snatched her phone to look at the texts himself? She and Journey had started this afternoon with yet another debate over tonight's events, but they had quickly slid down the maturity ladder several rungs to debate how good Parker might be in bed.

Not really something she wanted him to see.

"I feel like you're gonna say no."

"Why?"

"I don't know!' She laughed as she handed a bottle over the table to him. "Do you always ask so many questions?"

"No, but we've already established that it's not every day that I get this sort of proposition."

"Right." She nodded as she took a long drink. "Okay, well, for the record, Journey doesn't approve of what I'm doing. She thinks—"

"Of me? Or the idea?"

"The idea." Vanessa settled back into her chair. "She thinks I should let things happen naturally."

"With me?"

"Not necessarily."

"Are there other men? Like, if I say no, will you cross my name off your list and move on to the next one?"

She dragged her eyes away from his, wondering how to answer him. She didn't have a list. But she didn't want to admit that to him. And if he said no, she *might* eventually try this scheme again. She would just have to start from scratch.

"No." She shook her head. "I don't have a list."

"But if I say no, will you…shop around? Find someone else?"

"I want a baby, Parker," she reminded him. "This isn't about finding the right guy. It's not about sex. I want a baby. Before…"

"Before what?"

"Before I'm too old," she confessed.

"And how old are you?" He tipped his head to study her.

"Thirty-three, and I know you're younger than me. I know you don't want to be tied down. I know this is a big thing. But I told you I would pay you."

He nodded. "I know."

"And I mean, I do like sex, and I don't want to be artificially inseminated, so I would rather do it the old-fashioned way."

Parker didn't answer her. But he kept his gaze fixed on her as he took another drink.

"I haven't been with anyone since Greg left, so…ten months…" She shrugged. "I'm clean. I see my doctor annually. I can give you proof."

"And how long? Do we do this? What if I can't get you pregnant?"

She hadn't considered that. How could she? Parker Moore was all delicious man and muscle. Granted, she'd never seen his package, and even if she could, she didn't know if he had swimmers or not. But still, not something she had considered.

"I don't know. Do you want a deadline?"

He sighed and let his eyes roam over the table.

"Not necessarily," he answered when he finally looked back at her. "But, maybe that's something to be decided later."

"Like if we're both enjoying ourselves, we can keep at it?"

He quirked an eyebrow at her.

"How much do you want?" she asked softly. She had searched average costs for sex acts. Nothing like falling down *that* rabbit hole on the Internet. That evening had left her feeling dirty, a little bit scarred. She had showered. Lingered in the shower. Used mouthwash after brushing her teeth. And still gone to bed feeling a little tainted.

"How much?" he repeated with a frown.

"Money."

"Oh." He shrugged and shook his head. "I don't...I don't know?"

"I researched." She cleared her throat when their eyes met again. "Um. What sex workers charge for different sex acts."

Parker groaned and rubbed his hand over his eyes. Scared she had just chased him away, she bit her lip and waited for him to look at her again. Finally, he huffed out a harsh breath and pushed his fingers back through his hair.

"Sex worker." He shook his head. "Please don't phrase it like that."

"I just wanna make sure I offer you a fair amount."

"Vanessa."

"I mean, AI isn't cheap. In vitro. Adoption. None of it's cheap. And the money? Here? This house? That was Greg. I do okay at the salon, but Greg's still making the house payments. Which I hate, by the way."

"I don't—" Parker squeezed his eyes closed and stopped talking.

"God, I'm sorry. You don't wanna know about my issues with Greg. I dunno, Parker. Do you want me to pay you per act? Per hour? Per time we're together?"

"The money—"

"And a cash bonus if I end up pregnant?"

"Doesn't matter to me," he finished.

"I'm paying you," she said firmly.

"Whatever." He shrugged. "I don't have any experience with sex workers, and I don't want to. So, whatever you think is fair."

"Are you saying you'll do this?"

He sighed and rubbed his eyes again.

"How...often? When? Where?"

His blue eyes pierced hers again. Vanessa felt her heart jump in her chest and then skid back down where it was supposed to be.

"Um." She swallowed hard. "I don't know. Once a week? Twice a week?"

Parker didn't have experience with sex workers, and she wasn't used to scheduling sex. Or talking about the particulars of having sex with a stranger. A good-looking stranger with sexy eyes.

He nodded, but he stared at her expectantly, and she remembered that he had asked more questions.

"Um. We can do it here." She licked her lips drawing his gaze to her mouth. She wasn't trying to be seductive. Not now. She was nervous. She hadn't worried this much about sex her first time back in high school. Rather than making this easier, talking it out and planning everything was making it that much worse.

Her belly clenched at the thought of Parker's hands on her. The thought of peeling his shirt off his body. Pressing herself to his warm skin.

"Anywhere else?" he asked. His clipped tone brought her back to reality. They weren't discussing sex for pleasure. They were discussing procreation.

"Um." She shook her head. "We don't have to. I mean, we have plenty of room here. Plenty of privacy."

"Okay."

"I—I've been charting my cycle. To find the times when I'm most fertile."

He stared at her blankly.

"You know. Like when a couple's doing fertility shots, and they have to record all of this, so they have sex at the right time of the month."

He nodded, but he looked pained. *Way to go, Vanessa. Kill his desire by reminding him of the other things your girl parts do. The things they have to do to make babies.*

"Are we following the chart? Or are we just gonna wing it for a while and see what happens?"

Winging it certainly sounded like more fun. Not that she was after fun, but it might be more exciting to Parker if they weren't pinned to a schedule.

"Um. We could wing it." She shrugged her eyebrows. "For a while."

"Okay." He sat back in his chair, beer in hand, and studied her. "Just...sex?"

"What?" she asked quickly. What the hell did that question mean? Was he worried she would want more from him? That she would get clingy and start stalking him? That she would expect him to support the baby?

"I'm gonna be honest with you." He tipped his head and raised his eyebrows as if in warning.

"Okay."

"If we're gonna do this." He dragged his eyes over her face and down over her breasts before looking her in the eyes again. "I don't wanna show up and mount you and get off and leave."

Her mind flashed back to his comparing what they were talking about to breeding horses.

"What do you want?" Her voice was thick with appre-hension. Maybe a little bit of longing.

"Everything," he answered simply. "If we're gonna get naked, Vanessa Mayne, I'm going to enjoy the fuck out of every last inch of your body and then some."

Stunned by the heat in his promise, Vanessa could only gape at him.

"And I deliver." He put the bottle down and stood slowly. Vanessa's heartrate climbed as he straightened. He stepped around the table to stand over her and reached for her. Vanessa wondered if he noticed her shiver as she took his hand. "I don't know if I can get you pregnant, because I've never tried it before. But I guarantee you'll enjoy the sex."

She considered reminding him again that it wasn't about the sex. Not for her, anyway. And it wasn't. But damned if his promises didn't make her toes curl with anticipation.

"Okay." She nodded, embarrassed to sound so breathless.

He kissed her mouth again. Just a slow, dry rub of his lips over hers, but Vanessa felt that touch everywhere on her body. She wanted more, but after preaching to him about wanting a baby and not desperately searching for sex, she decided she should be in control. Parker, on the other hand, seemed determined to prove her wrong. He cupped her face in his warm hands and angled his head to deepen the kiss. Vanessa kissed him back, sighing softly when he parted his lips over hers and flicked his tongue inside her mouth.

Knees weak and her heart in her throat, she reached up to cover his hands with hers. Kissed him back, their tongues sliding slowly together. She wanted to climb him. Wrap her legs around his waist. She wanted his hands under her dress, stroking her inner thighs.

"Vanessa?"

"Hmm?"

"What happens if you get pregnant? What then?"

"Um."

He couldn't have doused the flames any quicker if he had dumped his glass of water down the front of her dress. She groaned softly and shifted in his arms to rest her forehead on his chin.

"Nothing." She closed her eyes. While she would much prefer to have the whole package—the baby and the daddy—she wasn't naïve. It was bad enough to ask a relative stranger to father her child. Completely out of the question to ask that same man to stick around and play house. After all, her boyfriend hadn't wanted to stick around with her, and he had built a house to play in.

"Nothing?" His voice was gruff.

"No. I won't hold you accountable. I won't ask you to support me. Or the baby. I won't tell anyone you're the father, unless you want me to."

Under her hand, flattened against his chest, she felt something rumble. Like a soft growl. But he didn't speak right away. She should step back so he could leave. He might have other plans.

Plans. A woman. She had forgotten that whole part of the deal. She needed him to be exclusive. For one thing, she didn't want to imagine him having sex with other women when he was making routine trips to her bedroom to satisfy her. And another, even if he was using condoms with other women, he would presumably be ejaculating. She needed him to do that with her. And only her.

She wondered if that would be a deal breaker for him.

"Okay." He tipped her chin up and brushed another kiss over her lips. Vanessa watched him back up a step and pat his pockets down for his keys.

"Wait. You're leaving?"

"Thanks for dinner." He nodded.

"But. Just. You're just leaving?"

Well, duh, Vanessa, what the hell would you be doing next? Did you really think you guys would finish dinner and then scoot everything aside and climb on the table to get started making a baby?

"I would love to stay," he told her. "I would love to slide my hands under your dress right now. Palm your thighs."

She caught her breath. Had he read her mind a minute ago?

"You think I wasn't looking every time you shifted around on that chair and parted your legs for me?" His voice was low and tight with desire. This time, heat flooded her whole body, but she wasn't embarrassed. She was hot and bothered, and from the way Parker was looking at her, he could tell.

"If you want a baby, then we won't be using condoms." He tucked his hands in his pockets. "I'll go to the lab tomorrow for blood work."

Right. Because this was about making a baby. Not having sex for fun. Or out of sheer desperation.

"You're gonna do it?"

He winced and lowered his gaze. Vanessa felt a hollow spot inside, but she ignored it.

"I think so," he finally said. But he didn't sound certain. "I'll get the blood work done. You'll hear from me."

"Parker." She followed him to the door. He didn't look at her until he pulled it open. "I made dessert."

"Vanessa Mayne, when we have sex, that'll be all the dessert I need from you." He turned to her and flicked her hair off her shoulder.

Vanessa swallowed hard. Feeling a mix of longing for him and fear of how far he would push her in the bedroom, she hugged herself and drew his attention to her arms. To her breasts.

"You know what else I might like?" He stepped closer to her and lowered his mouth close to her ear. "Licking chocolate and whipped cream off your body."

7

So, apparently, he was doing this. Even though he felt off, as if he was walking around with one shoe on and one off, he was up and at the clinic at seven the next morning. Never the squeamish type, needles didn't bother him. Blood didn't bother him, but he still felt a little out of sorts as he teased the lab tech who tied a tourniquet around his arm and stuck him with a needle.

It wasn't like him to walk away from sex. Vanessa had been ready and willing last night. They could have practiced. Auditioned, maybe. Made sure they were compatible.

The thought brought a sharp laugh. The girl with the latex gloves on, holding the needle in his arm eyed him curiously, but he didn't share. Based on the kissing in Vanessa's kitchen, there was no question they were compatible and would burn up the sheets.

But still. He could have stayed with her last night.

They could have used a condom until all this formal, technical stuff was done. She wanted him just as much as he wanted her.

And yet, he'd left. He had gone straight home, turned the TV on, and crashed in his recliner. Naturally every damned prime time TV show he turned on had some kid or family story line. If he wanted some *awe shucks, family time*, he could have just gone by Nick's house. He had eventually grown tired of the channel surfing and turned the TV off. Picked up the latest book Mercedes had recommended, *Devil in the White City*, and stayed up way too damned late for having to drag himself out of bed so early.

"You okay there, cowboy?" The tech drew him out of his thoughts. She sounded amused, and when Parker stirred and looked up at her, she was wearing a smirk.

"I'm good."

He hadn't asked her. He didn't ask Vanessa if the whole skimpy bikini—*melon*, not orange—thing was a precursor to this proposition. If she set her sights on him to be her baby daddy and then set out to turn him on. And if that was the case, what the hell was it about him that prompted that decision? Sure, he was a good guy. He liked to think so, anyway. He had a degree. He had done well in school, and he was responsible with his business. His good work ethic kept his clients happy and continued to bring in new business for him. He could rock a business suit, and he worked denim like a male stripper—or so he'd been told.

He liked sex, but he liked women. Like Mercedes. He had known from day one they weren't going to be lovers, but he liked her. He loved that she loved his brother and the kids, but he loved that she was also his friend.

He was attracted to Vanessa. But.

Damn, Parker. Really. But? No need to make this complicated. A beautiful, alluring woman offered you no-strings-attached sex, not to mention cash, and you have to go and invent issues.

What if the whole bikini thing was just because she was attracted to him? Was it so wrong for him to want that? For him to wish she was into him as a guy and not just as a sperm donor? It wasn't her melon bikini or her curves in that bikini that kept him awake last night. It was the haunted look in her eyes when she spoke about Greg. The guy who had built a mausoleum for her to live in and then left her for an older woman. It was the sound of her laughter. Her tone when she defended her salon to him.

The fact that she'd been ballsy enough to put this crazy proposition on the table earlier in the day and then texted her girlfriend later in the day for a pep talk. Because she was nervous.

"All right." The lab tech yanked the end of the tourniquet to loosen it. Parker watched her press a cotton ball to the bead of blood on his arm and then grab a roll of tape to peel a piece off. "You're all set."

"Great." He flashed her a smile as he climbed to his feet. He had dated women who got woozy from the process. He wasn't woozy, but he was hungry, so he headed out to this truck and swallowed down all of his misgivings about what he was doing. Nick always had a stocked refrigerator. He could find something to eat there. If he was lucky, Mercedes would be fixing breakfast for the kids and offer to fix him something, too.

He just didn't want to walk in with his uncertainty painted on his face and arouse suspicion from his brother. Nick didn't approve of what Vanessa had asked of him, but Parker figured he didn't need to know what he decided to do. Then again, it might help to talk it through with his brother. Maybe if Nick understood the other stuff—the little things about Vanessa that drew Parker in —he would get why Parker couldn't just walk away.

Or maybe if he knew Parker had some feelings for the woman, Nick might tell him to get the hell out of dodge, ASAP.

The garage door was open; both Nick's SUV and Mercedes' Corolla were parked inside. Parker considered his own house. Too small for a family. One car garage behind the house. He kept his business equipment in the garage, though the overflow was now stowed in the little shed by the garage.

He opened the door and reveled in the pandemonium inside. Used to be, before Mercedes, Nick's house was dead silent and cold. It wasn't built for kids—no more than the mansion Vanessa lived in—and Nick was unhappy with his life, so he had punished himself and his kids, too, by never being around. The kids didn't know how to be normal kids. Instead, they had been quiet shadows who slipped in and out of the rooms like tricks of light.

Before that, when Nick was still married to Kiara? Parker made it a point to avoid the house completely. Which sucked, because one look at his niece as a newborn, and he had been head over heels in love.

Today, there was no TV, but there was music playing. Parker caught AC/DC singing as he closed the door and stepped into the kitchen. Mercedes gave him a sideways glance but turned her attention back to the bowl of batter in front of her. Pancakes? Waffles? Did it matter?

"AC/DC?" He looked around the kitchen, but Maisy and Eli were nowhere to be found. "Really?"

Mercedes laughed softly and wiped her hands on her apron. Rather than a cute saying about kissing the cook or even an ornery reference to cooking and smoke alarms, the black apron simply said *Good in the Kitchen*. Parker had laughed the first morning he had seen it, tried to keep his comments to himself, and lost the battle when Nick asked why he was propped against the counter eating his omelet. Parker had looked around the counters and then at the table and finally back at Mercedes.

"Trying to decide where in the kitchen," Parker had tossed out with a shrug.

"Dude. She makes pecan pie."

"Dude, I know. I also know you two have a problem keeping your hands to yourself, so I'll stand, thanks."

"Hungry?" she asked him now. He watched her squat and disappear from view only to reappear a moment later with the electric griddle in her hands.

"Yep."

She rolled her eyes, but she was smiling.

"Do I wanna know?" he asked, referencing the music again.

"Probably not, but I'll fill you in if you'd like."

"Kitchen again?" He groaned.

"Nope."

"Good." He eyed the coffee maker and reached for a mug from the cabinet.

"Not that one."

Parker looked over his shoulder when he heard Nick's voice behind him.

"Seriously?" He turned back to the blue mug and frowned. "Why not?"

"Because that's been Cedes' mug since she started here."

Parker stared at his brother, wide-eyed, and finally nodded. "Riiightt."

Nick was all smiles as he hip-checked Parker to move him out of the way and took two more mugs from the cabinet.

"So. Not in the kitchen and not in Nick's big boy bed," Parker mumbled and scratched his head. "Eww. The couch?"

"Nobody said she couldn't get in my big boy bed with me." Nick splashed coffee in the blue mug first. Parker shivered and took the mug to carry over to Mercedes. "Just that she can't sleep there with me until we're married."

"What if one of the kids walked in?"

Nick poured more coffee and aimed a frown at Parker.

"Well, my bedroom does have a door. And a lock," Nick reminded him. "And if they do, they do. We're getting married."

Parker nodded and sipped his coffee. He sighed contentedly and leaned his butt on the counter.

"Maybe you should move the date up a bit," he suggested. Mercedes, still wearing a smile, simply shook her head.

"The last I knew we didn't have a date." Nick, his own

mug in hand, moseyed over to Mercedes and kissed her cheek. "Just a vague spring or summer."

"I need some time." Mercedes poured batter on the griddle.

"To be sure?" Nick asked quietly.

She lifted her chin and tipped her head at him. Parker felt like a voyeur, like they were having mental sex and he was stuck here watching them.

"You have to ask me that? After last night?"

"Don't need to be married for that." Nick slipped his arm around her.

Parker cleared his throat. "Where're the kids?"

"Jealous?" Nick asked, but he winked.

"Kind of," Parker admitted. Not of the woman. But the love, the peace, Nick had with the woman.

Mercedes shot him a quick look and turned her attention back to the griddle.

"Mase!" Nick called. "Uncle Parker's here."

"Is she sick?"

"Reading to Eli and all of her stuffed animals," Mercedes answered him.

Parker felt that same pang of jealousy, but this time it nailed him in his gut and nearly knocked him off his feet. He wanted this. The house. A woman. The incredible sex, but also the intimate bond that came with it. The kids. The stuffed animals. Kids' rooms overflowing with toys and books.

He wanted Vanessa.

But what she had proposed was nothing like what Nick had.

"Uncle Parker!"

Parker set his mug down just in time to catch Maisy

when she rounded the counter in the kitchen and threw herself into his arms.

"Mase, you gotta quit doin' that," Nick scolded her. "You're getting too big for that."

Parker scooped her up and kissed the tip of her nose.

"Hey, Mase." He drew back and studied her face. "How's life?"

"I sat next to Lincoln at lunch yesterday."

Parker winced and shook his head. "You're my girl. You can't be sitting by cute kindergarten boys."

"Lincoln's my friend, Uncle Parker," she argued. "He has a trampoline."

"Oh." Parker shrugged. "Okay. Well, I guess you can be friends. But you still gotta love me, okay?"

Maisy grinned.

"You know what would be cool?" Nick's voice was muffled because his head was now in the refrigerator. Parker snagged his mug and carried Maisy to the table. "A December wedding."

"Really cool," Mercedes agreed. "Like cold."

"But imagine how pretty it would be." Nick set the butter on the counter and then went back for the syrup and jelly.

"Where's Eli?" Parker asked Maisy.

"Playing with trucks." She rolled her eyes. Parker glanced at the living room, but he didn't see Nick's son.

"Wedding pictures in the snow," Nick continued. "You would be gorgeous with snow-covered trees around you, Cedes."

Nonplussed, Mercedes flipped the pancakes and then peeked at him.

"Snow's great when it's falling. When it's fresh. But

then it's dirty and slushy, and it would ruin my dress, and also, I'm not wearing snow boots for my wedding."

Nick groaned.

"October would be a neat wedding month," Parker suggested.

"Not you, too!" Mercedes pointed at him with her spatula.

"I don't want to wait another six months, Cedes," Nick whined. "I wanna wake up with you here. In my arms."

Parker noticed Maisy paying close attention to her dad, so he tickled her ribs.

"Let's get pizza this weekend," he suggested to her.

"Daddy, too?"

"Nope. You and me and Eli."

"Really? Like a date?"

"Absolutely. You could wear a pretty dress. Eli could wear a tie."

Maisy giggled. "Eli can't tie a tie."

"But you can, Mase," Nick told her.

Mercedes carried a plate piled high with pancakes to the table.

"I'll get Eli." Nick disappeared through the living room.

"You have an ouchie."

Parker stopped in mid-reach for the pancakes. He looked from Maisy's finger on his taped cotton ball to Mercedes.

"Nope. It's fine."

"What's it from?" Maisy asked. "Do you need me to kiss it?"

"That would probably make me feel great." He nodded.

Maisy ducked her head to kiss his inner elbow. Parker locked gazes with Mercedes. "It's just from some tests today."

Maisy sat up and stared at him, eyes wide with fear.

"Testis? Like school testis?"

Mercedes wiggled her eyebrows and grinned. He watched her stab a pancake with her fork and put it on a plate to butter and jelly for Eli.

Parker fought a laugh and looked back at Maisy.

"Not a school test. I went to the doctor today. He had to draw some blood."

Parker felt Mercedes' eyes on him, but he kept his focus on Maisy.

"Why?" Maisy plopped her hands on Parker's cheeks and leaned into him. "Are you sick?"

"No." He tipped his forehead to hers and clucked her chin. "Just a checkup."

"Mase, you need to eat your breakfast," Mercedes reminded her now. Parker figured he was being stupid and sappy, but he loved the way Nick's girlfriend mothered Maisy and Eli.

"'kay." Maisy slipped off his lap and climbed into her own chair. Parker helped her butter her own pancake and then poured syrup on it for her.

"So." Mercedes finally sat down. She took a big drink from her mug and eyed Parker carefully. "You're doing this?"

"I dunno." He wasn't sure he wanted to talk about it, wasn't sure he wanted Nick to walk back into the conversation, but he did know they couldn't talk about it with the kids around.

Mercedes made a show of looking at the cotton taped to his elbow.

"Did you go to dinner last night?"

He nodded as he cut Maisy's pancakes into strips.

"You did? You went to her house?" Nick reappeared in the room with Eli thrown over a shoulder. Parker marveled at that; not long ago, Nick would have been too uptight about his shirt and tie to carry either kid like that once he was dressed for work.

"I did."

"And?" Nick put Eli on a chair and sat down.

"We had dinner. Talked for a while. I was home by nine."

Technically, he was home just after eight, but he didn't feel like going into why he left Vanessa's so early or why he hadn't come here or called Nick when he left.

"Is she nuts?" Nick sat back and studied Parker.

"No. She's fun."

Cute. Vulnerable. Sexy.

Parker could list a hundred things he liked about her after one evening together, but he kept his mouth shut.

"Did she serve dessert?"

"Nicholas," Mercedes groaned.

Parker rolled his eyes when Nick looked at her innocently. "He was here when I proposed to you."

"So were the kids," she reminded him.

"I didn't have dessert," Parker admitted.

"Really?" Nick sounded surprised. "Never known you to pass up dessert."

Parker shrugged and tended to his own pancake. Irritated with Nick, he stabbed another one and put it on his plate.

"You like her," Mercedes said softly. "Don't you?"

Parker, eyes on his plate, felt both of them watching him. If he had to swallow his doubts again this morning, there wouldn't be room for breakfast. He huffed out a sigh, shrugged, and offered them his usual grin.

"What's not to like?"

8

"So?" Journey tried again. Vanessa laughed softly and tossed her keys on the counter as she walked through the kitchen. She hurried through the cavernous first floor of the house to the staircase. "What's going on, Van? Have you seen him? Talked to him?"

"He was here for dinner the other night," Vanessa reminded her friend as she jogged up the steps. In the bedroom—same room she had shared with Greg, but she overhauled it and redecorated and made it her own before his feet hit the driveway—she stepped out of her sandals. Phone pinned in the hollow of her neck, she wiggled out of the capris she'd worn to the salon and found a pair of sporty shorts to step into.

"Yeah. When you discussed making a baby with him," Journey said in a hushed voice. Vanessa cringed. Journey was the manager of a parcel shipping company. She worked the store front on Saturdays; no telling who was overhearing her end of this phone conversation. "I mean since then. Has he gotten back to you?"

"He texted," Vanessa hedged. Parker had texted her the next afternoon to tell her he went to the clinic for blood work. He hadn't added anything personal, not that she expected him to. After all, she had stressed to him that this was just about making a baby. Most definitely not enjoying sex. Or each other.

Just knowing he had blood drawn made Vanessa fidgety. She wouldn't tell Journey that, though.

"And said?"

"He said he went to the lab."

"Honey, that was yesterday," Journey reminded her. "It's Saturday."

"Hang on a sec." Vanessa tossed her phone down and quickly slipped out of her blouse. She grabbed a clean sweatshirt from her drawer, pulled it on, and then grabbed her phone again. "Lab work takes time."

"Yeah." Journey's tone suggested she was about to add a *but*. "But."

Vanessa rolled her eyes. Stomach rumbling, she headed back downstairs.

"He could still text you. Or call you."

"And say what?" Vanessa argued. "This isn't a relationship. It's not about us. How many times do I have to tell you that?"

"You can really do this?" Journey asked quietly. "You're gonna be able to take your clothes off and get hot and heavy with a stranger?"

Vanessa's belly fluttered at the thought. Hell yes, she wanted to do just that. Parker Moore was smokin' hot, and now that he had kissed her, she was pretty sure sex with him would be earth-shattering.

"I just won't think about it," she mumbled. Her stomach rumbled again, so she headed straight to the refrigerator and yanked it open to scrounge for dinner items.

"You what?" Journey yelped. Vanessa shot a quick look at the microwave clock. Her friend still had another half hour on the clock. If she was currently at the counter, someone was overhearing this conversation. "You're gonna be able to lock that door and not think about what you're doing? I could do that, but that's not you, Van."

Vanessa rolled her eyes as she reached for a container full of spaghetti leftovers. No, it wasn't like her. She'd never been that girl; she had never been able to get into casual hook ups. She'd tried. Journey knew those stories all too well; Journey had been there most nights Vanessa had tried and failed to flirt and pick someone up. Well, no, the flirting part usually went well; it was just the actual pick up and leave-with-a-stranger-to-take-her-clothes-off thing that caused her to hesitate.

"This is different," she mumbled.

"How's it different? How're you gonna take your clothes off for that guy? You said you broke out in hives that first time you sat outside in your bikini for him."

"Are you at the counter?" Vanessa swung the fridge door closed and set the container on the counter. "Like, are people hearing you?"

"Nope." Journey laughed. "No one in here at the moment."

"Damn." Vanessa ducked her head and rubbed the back of her neck.

"I'm worried about you, Van." Journey's tone changed to one of sincere concern. "I know you want a baby. I just don't get what your hurry is."

"I'm thirty-three," Vanessa reminded her.

"So am I," Journey answered. "You don't see me shopping for sperm donors."

"If I do it in the socially acceptable order," Vanessa said as she started moving again, "I have to meet the right guy. I have to date him for an acceptable length of time. And then we would have to plan a wedding. And then get pregnant. Add in nine months of carrying a baby...I could be forty before any of this happens."

"Women have babies at forty all the time."

"My mom was thirty-nine when she had me." Vanessa pulled the lid off the container and took a plate from the cabinet.

"Your mom was great."

"Yes, she was." Vanessa ignored the stab of grief that always happened when she thought about her mom. "But there was such a big age difference. I mean, we didn't do a lot of stuff together. She was closer to my brother's wives than me. I remember asking her to go to lunch with me one day when I was like twenty. She couldn't, because she had plans to go to a card party with Dean's wife."

"I gotta go," Journey announced. "I have a customer. Just think about this, Vanessa. Maybe if you get to know him, you guys could—"

"No!" Vanessa interrupted her friend. "No. I'm not interested in Parker. I'm not interested in a relationship, Journey."

"Love you, Van."

The line went dead before Vanessa could respond. She

tossed her phone on the counter and turned her attention to the leftovers she intended to warm for dinner. Yes, Journey was only worried about her because she cared, but Vanessa was tired of the lectures. Yes, this was a totally unconventional way of doing things, but then, toeing the line and doing things the usual way hadn't worked out too well. Vanessa had dated a few guys back in her high school days, and she had been involved with someone when she was in college. That guy turned out to be overbearing and controlling. Starry-eyed over his good looks and too naïve to get that he wasn't good for her, she had dated him for just over a year. When he started nagging at her about her business degree, telling her she would be much better off just going to work as a stylist in someone else's salon, she had bristled. Eventually, he had pushed her too hard, told her she wasn't smart enough to own a business and that she should just stay home and let him take care of her.

She had ended that relationship, finished her Bachelors' Degree, and then started her classes in beauty school. With three brothers, she'd had plenty of practice cutting and styling hair. Their wives—for the most part—had always been happy to let her play with styles and cuts, and once she had nieces and nephews, she got to play with updos and cool cuts on them, also. Her family and friends kept her busy. And eventually, she did date again.

The microwave beeped and stirred her from her thoughts. She took the plate and carried it to the table where she and Parker had discussed how their arrangement would work. Tried to imagine having that conversation with any of the guys she had dated. She and Greg had obviously come closest to marriage and a family, but she hadn't lied to Parker. They had been okay together, but in hindsight, Vanessa couldn't say that she believed he was the love of her life. In fact, maybe she wasn't destined to have one great love in her life. Maybe all of her love and attention was supposed to be showered on a baby, her own baby.

Greg would think she had a screw loose if he knew that she had propositioned a stranger—*her lawn guy*—to get her pregnant. That right there made it seem like a pretty damned good idea to her. At least the part where she had hot and steamy sex with Parker Moore. Maybe she and Greg hadn't been head over heels in love, but that didn't mean it stung any less when he left her for an older woman. Granted, that woman was interesting and fun and sexy. Even Vanessa would admit that. Didn't mean she was happy to lose her live-in boyfriend to her.

She finished her dinner and then cleaned the small mess she made. Saturday nights used to be fun. Before Greg, she and Journey would go out on Saturdays for dinner or drinks. Sometimes, they went to the club and flirted with good-looking guys. Vanessa found herself making a face as she threw a load of towels in the washer. She didn't love Saturday nights at home alone, but she wasn't sure clubbing sounded like much fun. Maybe drinks with Journey? She could text her.

But she made no move to do that. As much as she loved Journey, she didn't want to sit through another night of lectures and chiding on the poor decision she was making. Maybe once she and Parker were doing this—if they did do it—maybe Journey would see that it was okay and lay off.

Tired of looking at the walls, Vanessa went outside to

wander the yard. The landscaping did need work. But she had no real desire to do it. She could hire Parker to do that, too, and she could have him bill Greg for his time and work. But truth be told, she wanted out of the house. Probably not a good time to think about selling the house and finding a new place to live. Not if she was ready to actively pursue having a baby. Still, this was Greg's house, and she hadn't loved it a whole lot when he lived here with her. She most definitely didn't love it now. She hadn't even mentioned this to Journey; her friend might have her locked up for a few days if she did. There was a cute little brick bungalow just a few blocks from her salon. Vanessa had eyed it often for the past few years when she happened to drive by. The pear tree in the front yard was gorgeous. The swing on the front porch stirred so much longing inside that now and then she found herself near tears thinking about living there. Raising her child there.

The house was for sale. She had noticed the sign two weeks ago. She desperately wanted to see it. Walk through it. She hadn't called yet. Her brother Dean would go with her if she asked him to. Well, they would all go with her, but Dean was a contractor and knew good bones and foundations. He would gladly do a walk through and tell her what he thought. The trouble with that was, he would tell her what he thought about everything else she was doing, too, if he knew about that.

Tired of her own house, of her yard, she took a short walk before going back inside. It was warm, but the humidity wasn't quite as high as it had been the past week. Vanessa waved at neighbors and flagged down a wild basketball to toss it back to the teenaged boys playing three on three down the street. One of them trotted out to take it from her. He thanked her politely, but she heard them mumbling about her as she continued on her walk.

Guys liked her honey-blond hair. Her big eyes. Thanks to her dad's paychecks, she'd had braces, so her smile was full of perfectly straight white teeth. She had good genes; her mom hadn't been an exercise fanatic, but she maintained a nice, slender figure through four pregnancies and middle age and a love for desserts. Vanessa wasn't exactly an exercise fanatic, but she enjoyed biking, and she hit the gym now and then, and she knew guys liked to look at her.

She'd banked on that with the bikini. She'd had the stupid thing for over a year, but she had only worn it once. Greg liked it, but they'd been together long enough when they went on that trip to the Bahamas that he had been more interested in drinking and sunbathing than playing with the strings or the tiny scraps of material or what was inside them. She had hoped that Parker would notice, that he would like what he saw.

Judging from the way he had kissed her Wednesday— more than once—he did. Then again, maybe just offering sex had turned him on. Vanessa hoped it wasn't just that, that he did find her attractive, but she had no right to demand it. Not when she had made it clear she wasn't interested in anything but making a baby.

The house felt even colder when she went back inside. Shivering in her sweatshirt and shorts, she grabbed her favorite fleece throw from the end of the sofa and curled up in the corner. She could watch a movie, but it was still early to hunker down for the night. With a groan, she leaned forward and scooped a magazine from the glass-topped coffee table. She wasn't much of a reader, but she did enjoy shorter pieces like magazine articles.

The doorbell rang when she was two pages into an article on the benefits of vitamin B. She climbed to her feet and tossed the magazine aside, figuring it was Journey at the door. Maybe they would go for a drink after all. She could steer the conversation away from her plan, away from Parker. She would have to run upstairs and change clothes, but that wasn't a big deal. She wouldn't fret over her hair in a messy twist at the nape of her neck, and she wouldn't even touch up her eyeliner.

"Hey."

Parker Moore's slow, playful grin did things to her body that Greg's fingers had never done. She laughed softly, a little bit surprised at the rush of heat in her skin. She hadn't been expecting him; after talking about him with Journey and then thinking about him, about wanting to entice him with the bikini, seeing him in the flesh made her uncomfortably warm.

"Hi." She tugged at her lower lip with her teeth and folded her arms over her chest.

"Busy?"

"No." She shrugged and looked over her shoulder at the couch and then back at him.

"Can I come in?"

"Um." She gulped nervously and then laughed and nodded. He stepped inside, all male and heat, making her retreat a step. "What's up?"

"I just had a date," he answered casually. Vanessa felt a pang of unwanted jealousy. She watched him tuck his hands in the hip pockets of his well-worn jeans. *A date?* He had a date? Why was he here if he had a date? "And I thought I would say hi."

"You had a date?" She cleared her throat. Parker moved to close the door. Vanessa breathed in his fresh scent and met his eyes when he looked back at her. "Why are you here? If you had a date?"

"Date's over," he said simply.

Vanessa looked at the sofa again, but her phone was much too far away—not to mention the screen was dark —to see the time.

"Who was your date with?"

"Are you going to invite me in?"

"Yeah." She tossed her hands up in surrender. "Do you want a beer?"

"I do." He nodded. Vanessa stared at him a moment longer, her chest uncomfortably tight. She watched curiously as he took her hand, irritated with her body for loving the sensation of his warm, dry skin on hers.

"So?" she asked. She turned to lead him to the kitchen, but he didn't let go of her hand. "Who were you with?"

"Are you jealous?"

She swung her gaze around to look at him when she heard the note of amusement in his voice.

"Well, no, but if you were on a date and the date's over, maybe…" She shrugged as she reached the fridge.

"Maybe what?"

She grabbed two bottles and handed one to him, careful to not meet his eyes.

"Did you have sex with her? And then come here?"

"We didn't talk about that, did we?" He let go of her hand to twist the top off his beer. "That whole are-we-seeing-other-people thing?"

"No." Still not looking at him, Vanessa opened her own beer and took a drink.

"I'm guessing you don't want me seeing other people—"

"It's not that." She shook her head. "But if you're with other women..."

"You need me to save it all up for you."

Heat in her cheeks, she skated her eyes over his and nodded.

"And what about you?" His voice—low and gruff— chased a shiver over her bare legs.

"What about me?" she asked quickly.

"Will you be seeing other people?" He tipped the bottle up for a long drink. "When I'm not servicing you, will you be spending time with other men?"

"Do you have to say it like that?" She squeezed her eyes closed and turned her back to him.

"Will you? Will you be dating? Getting cozy with someone else?"

"Why would I do that? Why would I ask you to do this if there was anyone else out there?"

When he didn't answer, Vanessa looked at him over her shoulder. Their eyes met; Parker arched his brows and tipped his head.

"Not sure how I'm supposed to take that question."

"Do you think it makes me feel good that I'm offering someone money to sleep with me?"

Parker took a deep breath and leaned on the counter.

"I find it hard to believe you don't have men knocking down your door to do what you're asking me to do."

"I don't want just anyone doing...this." She shrugged and nodded her head back and forth.

"Show me your house."

"What?"

"Show me around." He reached for her hand again.

"Parker."

"Look." He tugged her close enough that her sweat-shirt was touching his tee, but she couldn't feel his body beneath it. "If we're gonna take our clothes off and touch each other, then we need to be able to have a conversation."

Vanessa peered up at him, wishing she could read his mind.

"Most women need some foreplay," he continued, but his voice was softer, now. Warmer. "And for most women, talking and getting to know a lover is the first stage in foreplay."

"I told you I don't want a lover." Her whispered protest sounded weak to her own ears.

"I need you wet when I get between your legs. I need you ready, because I don't want to hurt you. I'm not suggesting that we actually *enjoy* talking to each other."

"Wow." She whooshed out a quick breath and dropped her head forward. "That's really sad, because that's the sexiest thing anyone's said to me in a long time."

Parker skimmed his fingers up over the back of her arm and then smoothed them over her shoulder to rest on the back of her neck.

"Show me your house."

"We can't have sex right now," she argued.

"I have condoms." He gripped her neck with a light pressure, drawing an appreciative moan from low in her belly.

"I'm not ready." She shook her head, but her traitorous

hand was on his arm, her fingers digging in deep to hold on as he rubbed her neck.

"How many rooms do you have? Did he build an audio-visual room?" Parker pushed his fingers into her messy hair.

"Yes."

"Can we do it there? With a movie playing?"

She laughed softly.

"Wait. Do you have a sauna?"

"No."

"Shoot."

Vanessa's knees went weak when he dipped his head and flicked the shell of her ear with his tongue.

"Will you model the melon bikini?"

"I have," she reminded him. "Day after day. Just for you."

"Mmm." His lips were soft and dry over her neck. "But will you put it on for me in the bedroom? And then take it off? Really slow?"

"Parker."

"Come on." He kissed the top of her head. "Show me the house."

9

She started with the main floor, because it was easiest. Going upstairs meant showing him her bedroom. Going to the basement meant showing him Greg's audio-visual room, and even though Vanessa was pretty sure Parker was teasing her, he asked if they could have sex there. So, she showed him the living room, which he had already seen. He wandered around, though, as if he hadn't. Vanessa watched him pick up pictures—colorful art prints and framed photos of her brothers and their families—and eye them curiously before replacing them. He trailed his fingers over the sofa and the throw she had covered herself with earlier. Vanessa wondered if he was thinking about sex there on the sofa. She wasn't against it, but for some crazy reason, she wanted things with Parker to be fun and dangerous and different than they had been with Greg. She and Greg had ended many Saturday evenings there on the couch.

"What else?" he asked as he turned back to her. Standing across the room, Vanessa took in his denim clad legs and the stretch of the gray tee over his wide, muscular chest. The unruly curls at the nape of his neck. The warm smile that felt vaguely sexy and a little bit predatory and very private. Which was stupid, considering he had come to her after a date with someone else. She wondered again if he had kissed her goodnight. Done other things with her before dumping her off and coming here.

"Um." She shrugged and led the way to the hall under the stairs. "Bathroom. Den."

"Den? What do you do in a den?" Parker leaned around her to peer into the small room. Greg had claimed it as his, although Vanessa wasn't sure what he did there. He had spent the majority of his free time downstairs, either watching movies or football on the giant screen or in his home gym. This room—the den—had never been used for much of anything.

"I suppose you could do anything you want in a den," she answered. "Greg used to watch football in here, I guess, but he spent more time in the basement."

Parker stepped into the room to study the framed prints on the walls. Vanessa watched him, wondering what he was thinking. The pictures were of exotic places —sunsets on beaches and sunrises over the ocean—that Greg wanted to see.

"Are these printed posters or photographs?" Parker asked without looking at her.

"Some of both." She propped her shoulder in the door frame and looked at the prints over his shoulder. "Greg liked to travel."

"Who wouldn't want to travel the world?" He sounded wistful. "Do you?"

He turned and pinned her in place with his direct gaze. Vanessa opened her mouth to answer him, but she couldn't find her voice. Finally, she nodded, though Parker looked unconvinced.

"What's your favorite place?" He broke the spell and looked away.

"Quebec City," she answered. "But I'd love to go to Ireland someday."

"Mmm." He nodded and hummed appreciatively. "Nice. Me, too."

"What about you? What's your favorite place?"

Parker turned away from Greg's pictures and moseyed back toward her. Rather than stand there and be frozen in his line of sight again, Vanessa led him back out of the room.

"Lake Tahoe," he said simply.

"Oh." She raised her eyebrows. "Because of the views? Nature?" She looked up at him as she stopped at the last door on the right side of the hall. "Or someone you were with?"

"Hey." He laughed. "That's not fair. I didn't ask you to clarify."

"Scared to answer me?" She wagged her brows.

"I went to Tahoe with friends," Parker answered.

"Friends."

"Yeah. Three guys and two girls."

"Were you involved with either of those girls?"

"No." He tipped his head. "We were all just friends."

"When was this?"

"About five years ago."

"Friends with benefits?"

"Nope. Just friends." He shrugged.

"Do you have friends with benefits?"

"I do." He nodded, a smirk playing at the corners of his mouth. "Do you?"

"No." She took a drink and turned her attention to the spare bedroom. "Sadly, I don't."

"Well, maybe you do now."

"I'm paying you, remember?"

"You don't have to."

"I am. Because I'm not looking for sex. This is about getting pregnant."

"Who sleeps in here?" Parker peeked into the room, decorated in shades of pale yellow and crème.

"Guests. His mom used to visit. She stayed in this room, because the steps were hard for her."

Parker looked back over his shoulder and pointed at the staircase.

"Those steps?"

Vanessa nodded.

"Where do they lead?"

"Up." She grinned.

"To the bedrooms? To the room where you sleep?"

"Yep."

"Can I see your room?"

A zap of electric excitement barreled through her as she nodded and headed back toward the staircase.

"What about you?"

"What about me?"

"The trip to Quebec City," he reminded her. "With Greg?"

"God, no." She frowned. "No. I was with my brother and his wife. I went along to watch their kids, but I loved it. We stayed in Montreal, but we visited Quebec City."

"Did you meet any French guys there?"

She snorted softly. "No. Did you hear me mention a brother? I have three of them. All older. All very protective of me."

"Now you tell me."

Halfway up the steps, she shot him a grin over her shoulder.

"Greg and I did the tropical scenes most often."

"Because he liked your melon bikini."

"Actually, he didn't seem to notice," she mumbled. "I enjoyed those trips. We had fun. I don't mean to sound like it was all a waste, but it's hard to remember the fun stuff. And wonder if it was fun for him or if he was bored with me and just biding his time to leave."

"Pretty sure he wasn't bored with you," Parker told her. His eyes roamed the long hallway, the white woodwork, and the hardwood floor. He glanced at her. "And if he was, it's his loss."

"You don't know that," she reminded him. "We haven't done it."

"So." He cleared his throat. "When you have this baby—"

"The one I'm not even pregnant with yet?"

He answered her grin with his own.

"Will you travel with him or her?"

"I don't know." She shrugged. "There are three bedrooms up here. Two are smaller. There's the main bathroom. And this is the master suite."

Vanessa watched Parker Moore meander through her bedroom. She assumed he would go straight to the bed and touch it. Maybe sit on it. Pat it for her to join him. Instead, he roamed along the walls, again studying the framed pictures. These were mostly art prints, though the framed pictures on the dresser were of her nieces and nephews.

"Do you want a boy or girl?" he asked from across the room. He stood at her dresser, fingers trailing over frames and her perfume bottles and a necklace she wore often.

She hadn't thought that far ahead. She didn't know what the hell she would do with either, but she wasn't going to tell him that. She had plenty of experience with babies, but suddenly the thought of raising her own—alone—was terrifying.

"I don't know."

He looked at her over his shoulder, but he said nothing. Vanessa wandered into the room, butterflies flapping their wings in her belly. She wanted him, but she was nervous. Anxious. She hardly knew him. She didn't know his middle name. Where he went to school. If he liked cold cereal for breakfast. If he was a sports fan.

If he would say sweet things to her or talk dirty when they had sex. Which she would prefer when they got down to business.

If she would satisfy him.

"Nieces and nephews?" He met her eyes in the mirror of her dresser. She nodded.

"Four nieces. Six nephews."

"Wow." He nodded. "How old are they?"

"The oldest is twenty-one. And the youngest is thirteen."

"Do you have names picked out?"

"What?"

"For the baby?"

Her mouth dry, Vanessa struggled to swallow. "Parker, I'm not even pregnant yet."

"But I'm guessing you've given this a lot of thought. A lot of daydream time."

Embarrassed that he was right, she ducked her head and nodded.

"Do your brothers know that you asked me to do this?"

Vanessa cut loose a startled laugh. "No. I'm an adult. I don't need their permission."

"True," he agreed as he turned to her. "I just don't want three big brothers coming after me for stealing their sister's virtue."

"My virtue?" she laughed softly.

"How old were you?"

"What?"

"Your first time." He moved to stand closer to her and reached for her bottle.

"We're talking about this?"

"We are." He nodded. Vanessa sucked in a sharp breath when he moved around her to set their beers on her nightstand. She felt a flicker of something weird, something wild and sweet when he made sure to put them on a magazine and not on the furniture.

"I was nineteen," she answered.

"*Good Housekeeping*?" He tipped his head at the magazine under the beer bottles. "Really?"

"There's an article about organizing your household in it."

"Do you look at dirty magazines?"

"Isn't that more of a guy thing?"

"Probably." He flashed her a little grin as he stepped

around her again. Vanessa watched him curiously as he moved around the end of the bed and looked out the window. She knew he was looking at her backyard. "But do you? Ever?"

"I have," she admitted. "But I don't make a habit of buying them."

"I knew this girl once," he told her, eyes still on the view out the window. "We were, like, fourteen. She and another friend had magazines. She was all weirded out because girls always look so good in the pictures. Like their boobs are always perfectly round—"

"And fake."

Parker glanced at Vanessa and nodded. "Right. But we didn't know that. Not at fourteen."

"Is there a point to this story?" She tipped her head. "Are you trying to get me to show you my boobs?"

"No, but I'm not gonna argue if you want to."

She smiled when their eyes met.

"Hallie—my friend—showed me hers. And asked if they looked like they do in the pictures."

"Oh." She nodded.

"They didn't, but to a fourteen-year-old kid they were pretty damned perfect."

"You were fourteen? Your first time?" Vanessa moved around the end of the bed. "Is that what you're leading up to?"

"No." He laughed softly. "But I had a boner for her for the rest of the year. She looked at me that day, too."

"At your boner?"

"Yep. I'm not sure, but I think she was a little bit traumatized, because it was throbbing and purple when she took it out."

"Wow." Vanessa grinned, but she couldn't hold the eye contact.

"She was my first," he added, "but it was the night before she turned sixteen."

"How was it?"

"Incredible," he answered, "but probably not for her."

"And you've improved your game since then?"

"I'd like to think so." He shrugged.

"I was dating the guy," Vanessa said simply. "Nothing too exciting. No fun stories."

"Did you mess around before that? Like in high school?"

"Of course, I did." She smiled at the memory. "Showed my boobs to Matthew Kessler when I was fifteen."

"Lucky Matthew Kessler." Parker reached for her hand. "Vanessa?"

Struck anew with anxiety, she couldn't speak over her heart in her throat. She looked at him silently.

"Can we sit down?"

"Yeah."

Rather than sit on the bed, Parker slowly lowered himself to sit on the floor. He tugged gently on her hand until she sat down near him. With the entire house empty except for them, Vanessa thought the floor on the wall side of her bed was an odd place to sit, but it felt kind of nice, a little bit cozy once they were sitting and facing each other.

"My date tonight."

She winced.

"It was my niece and nephew."

She wished she could hide her relief, but Parker was

watching her too closely. He had to see the way her shoulders sagged as she let go of a long sigh.

"How old are they?"

"Five and three."

Vanessa rolled her lips inward and nodded. "Where did you go?"

"I took them to Zaltan's," he answered. "We had cheese pizza."

Vanessa chuckled. "Are you still hungry?"

"Kind of, but I'm not in any hurry to move right now."

"Okay." She nodded and leaned back against the wall. Parker, propped the other way against her bed, eyed her intensely.

"I wanna talk about you showing your boobs to Matthew Kessler."

"There's not really anything to add to that."

"Did he touch them?"

"Did you touch your friend Hallie's?"

"That's what I figured." He winced. "Do you have any dirty magazines up here at all?"

"Why?"

"Does it put you in the mood?"

She laughed and rolled her eyes.

"C'mere." He leaned forward and cupped his hand around her inner thigh. Vanessa, sitting cross-legged, straightened her legs out and scooted forward a bit. She closed her eyes when he leaned in to kiss her. "I don't need anything to put me in the mood. Not sitting here in your bedroom with you. But I'm willing to look at stuff with you if it'll make you wanna mess around."

When she laughed again, he slipped his tongue inside her mouth to rub over hers.

"We are not having sex tonight."

"I think it would be good to break the ice."

At this, she pulled away from him to laugh.

"What ice?" She lifted her hands to cup his face and smoothed his hair back. "Parker, you're making me melt."

"And yet you're saying no."

"I'm not ready—"

"What do you mean? Are you afraid of me? Do you have to let someone know I'm here in case—"

"I need to shower. My hair's a mess. I didn't shave this morning."

Parker trailed his fingertips over her bare leg.

"You're telling me no because you didn't shave your legs?"

"Yes."

"I think you're beautiful," he said sincerely. "And I think messing around now will help ease…any awkward feelings when…it's time. To do it for making a baby."

"Yeah? And it's not just that you want sex?"

"I really, really do want sex right now with you," he admitted with a big grin. "I'm not gonna push you, but I've been hard for you since the first time I saw you in that bikini."

"Yeah?"

"Did you do that on purpose? Like, did you think you needed to show me some skin to talk me into this?"

"Greg didn't notice the bikini," she whispered, chin tipped down now. "I guess I wanted to know that I was worth a look."

"That tiny little strip of material?" Parker rested his hand on her thigh now, his thumb moving in a small circle over her skin. "Between your legs? It's like a neon arrow pointing at your hot spot."

Vanessa watched his thumb slide up her thigh until he stopped at the hem of her shorts. Without any urging from him, she opened her legs and held her breath. Parker pressed the pad of his thumb over her most sensitive area. Vanessa gasped and parted her legs further in askance.

"Just so you know." He kissed her forehead. "As long as we're doing this—as long as you want me...doing this to get you pregnant, I won't be with anyone else. Not for sex. No dates. Nothing."

She lifted her chin to meet his gaze.

"That's not me."

"Okay," she whispered, breathless with desire.

"Do you have plans for the night? Expecting anyone to come by?"

"No."

Parker pressed between her legs again and drew a quivering breath from her lips. His eyes bold and unapologetic on hers, he slipped his fingers inside her shorts and dragged his knuckles over her.

"Take your top off," he told her. "I want to look at you."

Vanessa was slow to move, caught up in the heat from his hand between her legs. She nodded, though, and finally tugged her sweatshirt off and tossed it aside. Parker's eyes roamed low over her shoulders and her breasts in her teal silk bra.

"This, too?" she asked softly.

"In a minute."

She swallowed hard when he eased his fingers around in the tight spot between her body and her panties. When he pushed the back of one knuckle the slightest bit inside her, heat flashed through her cheeks and she jerked her eyes up to look at him.

"I have the feeling you're gonna look so much better than any girl in a magazine."

"They're real," she said softly.

"C'mere." He leaned forward again to kiss her. Vanessa cried out in protest when he cut the kiss off, but she threw her head back when he dipped his head to paint her neck with his tongue and then bite the swell of her breast over the silk cup.

"Parker." She lifted her hips a bit to press into his hand. But he only smiled.

"Take it off."

Hands trembling with excitement, with need, Vanessa sat up and reached back to unhook her bra. Parker's eyes tracked her every move.

"Beautiful," he told her. "I'm gonna move my hand. Just for the time it takes to get these shorts out of the way. Okay? And then we're gonna go right back to sitting just like this."

She nodded, but she still moaned softly when he did as he said he was going to. He didn't touch her breasts, though. Didn't kiss her. Simply tugged at her shorts on her waist and eased them down. When he looked at her in askance, Vanessa stood gracefully and kicked out of her shorts and panties.

"So incredible." He breathed deeply and skimmed his fingers up the backs of her legs.

"You too?" She tipped her head and nudged his thigh with her toe.

"Not yet."

"I wanna see you," she whispered.

"Not yet." He shook his head. "Sit down."

She did as he asked, sitting somewhat closer to him, but Parker rearranged her so that she was sitting in front of him, knees bent, everything on display.

"Lean back," he told her. "Show me."

The last time she and Greg had had sex, it had been over in less time than this episode had taken. Vanessa's belly clenched so tightly now with need, she considered taking care of things herself. But the look on Parker's face was worth it. His eyes were intense and hot, the tip of his tongue visible between his parted lips, as if he wanted to taste her.

"I think about doing this," he told her. "At night. After I'm here, and you're outside in that bikini. I think about you propped up on that chair with your bikini on the ground."

"I wanted you to think about me," she confessed.

"I think about sitting on the end of the chair and putting my fingers inside you. Making you move with me, so your boobs bounce."

She laughed softly. "Not much bounce there."

"There is." He nodded. "Do you like this?"

"I feel a little exposed." She grinned, cheeks flushed under his heavy stare.

"You are, and that's exactly what I wanted."

"It feels good."

"This does?" He moved his fingers again.

"Yeah, but I meant…"

"You meant what?"

"You watching me. That you wanted to see me like this."

"I want a whole lot more, Vanessa," he promised her. "But I want this first."

Her mouth was bone dry again as he continued the gentle assault between her legs.

"Do you have sex toys?"

She nodded.

"Would you rather play with those?"

"No."

"Do you want me to touch you here, too?" He pressed his thumb over her most sensitive spot again, making her whimper.

"Yes."

"Watch me," he told her as he worked her body. She dipped her chin to watch his hand work magic. She realized suddenly he was watching her, when she saw that she was tilting her hips and lifting them from the floor to meet his thrusts. His eyes moved from his fingers to her breasts, indeed bouncing now with her movements.

"Parker," she whispered as a wave of heat rolled over her. "I'm gonna come."

"Come for me."

"This wasn't supposed to be about sex and orgasms," she insisted. "I just want—"

She seized against his hand, hips in the air, and her back arched, as if offering him more. Eyes locked with his, she chanted his name over and over as wave after wave of tingling heat and electricity rolled over her.

"I knew that would be the most erotic thing I've ever seen." Parker slid his free hand up her stomach, but he stopped just short of touching her breasts. "I'm gonna think about how you look at this moment for the rest of my life."

"Give me more," she whispered. "Please?"

He nodded, but he didn't move. Didn't draw his hand from her or skim his fingers over her breasts.

"Parker."

"Give me a sec." He gritted his teeth. "I'm gonna come just looking at you. Feeling you around my fingers."

Rather than be still and wait for him, Vanessa lowered her hips to the floor again and scooted closer to him. Parker's groan was all male need when she shifted to straddle him and pressed her naked body into his.

"How many condoms do you have?" she whispered into his hair. Parker clamped his hands around her hips to still her from grinding against him.

"Three or four."

She rested her forehead on his shoulder and reached to pull his wallet from his pocket.

"You want it here? Like this?" he asked when she opened it and plucked out a condom.

"Yes, now."

She shoved the condom into his hands and turned her attention to his zipper. His erection was impossible to miss, and she wanted to spend time looking at him naked —the same as he had just done to her. She had appreciated his lean, hard legs and his shoulders every day she lounged on the patio in the melon bikini, and she wanted to touch him. To mold her fingers over him and sink her teeth into him and drag her tongue down low over his belly.

Sitting in his lap, she lowered his zipper and pushed the denim and his briefs out of the way. His hard-on sprung up and thrust into her hand. Parker bit off a string of foul words that only turned her on more.

"Nessa, if you want me inside you, you need to stop touching me," he warned her. She let go reluctantly and rested her hands on his shoulders while he took care of the condom. "This is gonna be fast."

She met his eyes as she lowered herself to take him in.

10

How was he supposed to last two damned minutes with a naked, greedy Vanessa Mayne straddling his lap? Holy hell, she was hot and soft, and she wrapped her arms around his neck to hold on, dragging Parker under with her. He dug his fingers into her sweet little ass and held on, his own ass off the floor as he thrust up into her, desperate to satisfy her before he lost control. With her firm, loose breasts pressed to his chest and his face buried in her neck, Parker was dizzy with lust. She smelled so good he wanted to take a bite, but at the moment, every drop of blood in his body, every thought in his head was throbbing in his dick, buried deep inside Vanessa Mayne.

The tiny mewling sounds in her throat that vibrated against his lips did him in. She squeezed hard around him one last time, drawing a harsh, guttural shout that might have been her name and might have been *holy fucking heaven*. Poised above him, Vanessa drew back to look him in the eye as he erupted inside her. In a matter of days, he would come inside her like this without protection. The thought of plunging into her heat with no barriers made his whole body shake with pleasure. Anticipation.

There was plenty more of this beautiful woman in his life, and Parker's chest hurt with the sheer joy at the thought.

"Sorry." She cupped his chin in her hands and flicked her tongue over the center of his lips.

"Sorry?" He closed his eyes and dropped his head back to rest on the side of her bed. She was still squeezing him, and though she had already milked every last drop of that orgasm from him, he loved the heat, the sparks where their bodies were joined. The soft skin of her inner thighs over his hips was warm and inviting.

He remembered suddenly that she was naked and let go of her bottom to slide his fingers over her back.

"That was fast," she whispered. "I feel like I mauled you."

"You're kidding me, right?" Finally able to talk and breathe at the same time, the words still came out in a frenzied pant. "You're apologizing for mauling me?"

When she didn't answer him, he lifted his head to peek at her. She offered him a little grin when their eyes met.

"Okay, maybe I'm not *sorry*." She shrugged and tipped her head. "I just…kind of wanted…"

"What?" He dragged his fingers up to cup the back of her neck. "You wanted what?"

"More."

Parker blinked. "More—? Like, you didn't—? I thought you did. I'm sorry—"

"I did." She smoothed her fingers over his lips. Parker watched her look at him. The hungry roaming of her eyes over his lips made him hard again. "But I want to see you. To touch you."

"I have more condoms," he reminded her. "And I'll be back next week."

"You'll stay? Now?"

"I'd have to be pretty damned crazy to walk away from more of this." His voice was gruff with a truth he wasn't sure he was ready to spill.

"I'm a little…"

Parker eyed her curiously, watched her struggle to swallow. He had yet to touch her breasts, and he was dying to flip her over to lie on her back so he could look his fill. Touch her. Taste her. He waited, though, because she had that look again. The one where she might be wishing she had her phone, so she could text her bestie for a pep talk.

"A little what?" He moved his hand from the back of her neck to cup her chin and tilt her head up to look at him.

"Embarrassed." She met his eyes.

"Because?"

"I made such a big deal out of this being about me getting pregnant. Not enjoying sex. With you."

"You know what?" He traced her cheekbone with his fingertips and decided she was perfect. Flawless skin. A warm, beautiful smile. A body made for more of what they had only just started.

"Hmm?" She shook her head.

"If you want a baby so badly, I really hope I can give you that. But I told you the other night, if I'm in your bed, and I'm between your legs, we're both gonna have a damned good time."

Her cheeks flushed, but Parker noticed the heat in her eyes, too.

"That's nothing to be embarrassed about."

"When you came in tonight..." She cleared her throat and lowered her gaze to the floor. Parker might have thought she still had regrets, but he noticed the tilt of her lips and realized she was grinning.

"Yeah?"

"You eyed the couch, and I wondered if you were thinking about having sex there."

"Of course, I was," he answered with a one-shouldered shrug. "Guys think about sex all the time, and after seeing you in that tiny little bathing suit all summer, I was thinking about taking you against the kitchen wall the other day."

She met his eyes with a hesitant smirk.

"And that was before you propositioned me to be your baby daddy."

Naked and pliant and hot as she was, the laughter that rumbled up from her belly and crossed her lips was such a turn on he had to touch her. Now. She gasped softly when he explored her neck, dipped his fingers in the hollow at her throat, and then curved them around her breast to cup her in his palm.

"I didn't want to do it on the couch."

Parker, still holding her breast, rolled her nipple with his thumb, but he pulled his gaze from her to look her in the eye again.

"You made it clear you didn't wanna have sex tonight."

Vanessa reached to her hip for his other hand and placed it on her other breast.

"What? The couch isn't stain-resistant?" He tried

again.

She snorted and rolled her eyes.

"No. It's just boring."

"Translation. You and the compensating ex had sex on the couch. A lot."

She nodded.

"Uninspired," he decided. "Not that I wouldn't want it there. But I would make it fun."

"I'm sure you would."

"Do you wanna move to the bed?"

"No." She shifted in his lap, and Parker regretted the movement instantly. Her wet heat was gone from his body, but in the next instant, she slid her fingers in his hair and straightened over him to draw his face to her breasts. "I kind of like this."

Parker wasted no time. He sank his teeth into the curve of her left breast and then immediately sucked her skin into his mouth.

"I do, too."

"But I want you naked." She pressed her lips to the top of his head.

"Why me, Vanessa Mayne?"

When she backed up a bit and eyed him cautiously, Parker moved swiftly to yank his tee over his head.

"I'm not complaining," he promised her. "Just wondering how I got so lucky."

"I don't know." Her whisper was thick with longing as she turned her attention to the open fly of his jeans. "Something about you."

"I have no problem with playing around here on the floor of your bedroom, Nessa." He captured a loose curl and pushed it back behind her ear. "But next time, I'm gonna need to be on top, because I need more traction to get deeper."

She tipped her head a bit to look at him. "You can get deeper?"

"I'm damned sure gonna try," he promised. "I'm gonna tear you up and then kiss everything and make it better."

———

Parker strolled into Nick's house, singing an old KC and the Sunshine Band song, and set presents for the kids on the counter. He had lectured himself all morning—well, since leaving Vanessa's house—to get a grip and keep the damned just-got-laid grin off his face. Nothing like advertising to the world that he got some and that he had enjoyed every second of being buried balls deep in Vanessa Mayne's body. If he didn't get himself under control pretty damned quick, Nick would take one look and know.

And if Nick didn't, Parker figured Mercedes would. Damned if she didn't read him better than his own brother did. Then again, she was a woman, and didn't women just tend to be in tune with people they cared about?

Vanessa had sure been in tune with his body last night. He should have known after that first orgasm tore through her and left her quaking against his hand that she would be greedy for more. Not that he would ever complain. That first time, with her naked body straddling his almost fully-clothed-body, had been fast and phenomenal. But the second time, after Parker had indeed flipped her over to lie back on the floor and kicked out of his own jeans and got acquainted with every inch of her body—she had the sexiest ankles and her thighs tasted delicious, and one taste of her had probably ruined him for anyone else—he had driven her hard, and they made love at a frenzied pace, grasping and panting as if neither of them could get enough.

Drunk with satisfaction—drunk on Vanessa, herself—Parker had gathered her close and held her there on the bedroom floor. They stayed that way, dozing and sharing soft but lingering kisses and touches, until Parker's back reminded him he wasn't so young anymore. Vanessa had chuckled at him when he groaned about it as they climbed to their feet. But she learned fast that Parker recovered quickly when he chased her out of the bedroom and down the stairs to the kitchen. Completely nude. Laughing like a madman the whole way.

They snacked on cookies and drank another beer, naked on the kitchen floor. With only one condom left, they tried to find something else to talk about. Something other than how good it felt when he was inside her body. If she thought it was weird to discuss her landscaping project and the possibilities at such a time, she hadn't said so. Instead, once the cookies were put away and the bottles drained, Parker locked up the house and Vanessa turned the lights off, and then instead of going upstairs, she mauled him again.

Only this time, she pleasured him, and Parker found himself sprawled out on the couch they had discussed earlier with Vanessa Mayne working his dick and his hands in her hair, and when he orgasmed that time, he nearly wept with pleasure. From there, they returned to her bedroom where they curled up in her bed—she had assured him she had done everything short of an exorcism to rid the room of any Greg Mitchell vibes when he moved out—and made sweet, gentle love before going to sleep in a tangle of warm skin and twisted sheets.

"What're those?" Nick's sharp question was a swift kick in the ass out of memories of Vanessa's warm bed and back to his brother's kitchen. Parker looked at the toys on the counter and back at Nick, who was eyeing the Lite-Brite and the Lego set like they were ticking bombs rather than children's toys.

"Toys."

"For who?"

"For you and Cedes." Parker rolled his eyes. "Really, Nick?"

"Why are you bringing toys over on a random Sunday morning?"

"Where's Cedes?"

"What?"

"Saw her car in the garage. Where is she?"

"She's in my office."

Parker grinned and nodded. "Playing secretary and naughty boss?"

Nick groaned and moved to the refrigerator. "She's finishing up a blog post."

"Kids up?"

"Dude, it's noon. Of course, they're up. They're downstairs. What's with you?" Nick pulled the door open, but he was looking at Parker suspiciously. "You look like you need Ritalin."

"Nick, I can't find my bra—"

Mercedes stopped talking as she entered the kitchen and realized Parker was watching her.

"You *were* playing secretary and naughty boss." Parker nodded his approval at Nick. "Good for you. But you can't have your secretary walking around half dressed. That's a pretty risqué crew-neck T-shirt."

"Stop looking at her breasts," Nick growled as he turned back to the fridge.

"Who says I was the secretary?" Mercedes quirked an eyebrow at Parker. "And we can't have my bra vanishing in the house with two little kids."

"Not until you marry me, apparently," Nick grumbled. Mercedes gave Parker a deadpan look that drew a big laugh.

"About that." Parker leaned on the counter. "Anything? Date picked out? I might be free next weekend."

"Wedding takes me and Mercedes," Nick reminded him. "Not you."

"You need a best man, bro." Parker shrugged.

"What're these?" Mercedes inched into the room to stand at the counter near Parker. She reached for the Lite-Brite.

"Don't stand so close to him," Nick told her. "When you're not…" He straightened and waved his hand in a circle at his chest.

"Nick, c'mon." Parker sighed. "I'm not looking at her." He dipped his chin to look Mercedes in the eyes. "They're for the kids."

"Obviously." She nodded.

"And this is for you." Parker pulled a gift card from his back pocket and slid it over the counter toward her.

"Why are you giving my fiancé gifts?" Nick stepped closer to the counter and strained to see the gift card.

"It's a gift card for Dewie's," Parker told him. "It's for

both of you."

"Why are you giving us gifts?" Nick frowned. "What are you? Santa Claus?"

"Nope. I want you guys to go out and have a nice dinner. And I want to watch the kids."

"Parker." Mercedes leaned into him to bump his arm with hers. "That's so sweet of you. I'd hug you, but your brother might go homicidal since..." She rolled her eyes and waved her hand at her own chest. Parker snickered, but he bit his lip to keep a straight face when he saw Nick's glowering face lean in closer.

"Dewie's? Really?" He slapped his hand on the card and pulled it closer to look at it. "Thanks, Parker. That's cool."

Parker shrugged, uncomfortable with Nick's sincerity.

"Babe, was I wearing a bra when I came over?"

"Yep." Nick turned away from her and went back to lunch preparations. "You're thinking of the time you came over in nothing but sweats."

"No!" Mercedes argued. "Am I? That was pretty fun, huh?"

"Oh my God," Parker groaned. "Enough!"

"You kissed her first, man," Nick mumbled. Parker watched him dump a package of raw burger into a skillet. "Not my fault you don't know your way around a woman's body."

"What does that mean?" Parker tipped his head at Nick, but he flicked his gaze to Mercedes. "I get that it wasn't like a smokin' hot thing. But did you tell him I don't even have moves?"

Mercedes snorted.

"I watched you, man. She had a handful of dishes. You leaned over the table to kiss her."

"And what?" Parker shook his head. "I was supposed to swipe the table clean and throw her down there?"

"Well." Nick took a spatula to the meat.

"You didn't. She said you didn't even give her tongue when you kissed her the first time."

This time Nick shot Mercedes a look of shock.

"I also told him it was perfect," Mercedes reminded both of them. "Stop it. This is stupid. Thank you for the gift card, Parker."

"Yeah." Nick shrugged, back to them again. "Thanks. But you don't have to send us out on a date to be with the kids."

"I know." Parker nodded enthusiastically. "Please get married. Soon."

"Why the hurry?" Mercedes asked him.

"Hurry? Are you kidding me?" Nick dropped the spatula in his haste to turn and look at her. "We're adults sneaking around in our house so we can be together without our kids seeing us."

Parker winced, unsure how Mercedes would feel about Nick referring to the house as theirs, let alone the kids. But Mercedes' smile lit up the room. She laughed softly and then ducked her head to cover her eyes.

"They're Kiara's kids, Nick," she whispered.

"They are," he agreed. Parker stepped away as Nick moved closer to take Mercedes in his arms. "But they're yours, too. They are so crazy in love with you, Cedes, and I'm so in love with you, and Kiara's given us her blessing —not that we need it."

"Mm." Parker tssked as he picked up the spatula Nick had dropped on the counter and continued chopping at the raw burger. "Shoulda stopped at blessing."

"Why are you here?" Nick rested his chin on top of Mercedes' head. "I feel like you're always here. Always involved in my business."

"Just got your back, man," Parker mumbled. "And maybe if you would hurry up and get married, you would get bored with each other at least enough to keep it in the bedroom."

When they didn't answer him, Parker sneaked another peek at them over his shoulder, not surprised to see them kissing.

"Nope. You have no idea how much fun Sunday morning kitchen sex can be."

"Um." Parker dropped his head back and closed his eyes.

"What're you doing? Do not picture that!" Mercedes laughed.

"Trying to remember what time it was when I was sitting buck naked on a kitchen floor eating cookies and drinking beer. That would count in my book for fun Sunday morning kitchen sex. But might have been before midnight."

"I don't want to know about you sitting on your kitchen floor naked and eating cookies."

"Who said it was my floor?" Parker shrugged. "*I* didn't say that."

"Nick?" Mercedes asked quietly.

"Hmm?"

"Do you want a big wedding?"

Parker turned the burner down and hitched his hip on the stove. Mercedes sounded serious after all the teasing going on.

"The only thing I have to have out of our wedding is

you being my wife." Nick, arms draped over Mercedes' shoulders, kissed her forehead. Parker felt a pang of jealousy, though not for Mercedes. He and Vanessa had played in her kitchen; of course, they had. Wasn't like they sat on the floor, completely nude, and ate cookies like prim, well-behaved kindergarten children. Last night had been perfect.

Incredible.

The only thing that might make the sex even better? No condoms. Parker shifted now, his dick poking around with interest and straining at the fly of his shorts.

Bareback sex.

Yep, that and those sweet, tender moments. Jeez, his brother was the master of sweet, tender moments. And he had found his person. While Parker loved the game-plan set out before him and Vanessa, he wished there could be more.

"Do you want a church?"

"What do you want, Cedes?"

Mercedes swallowed hard and shrugged. "It's just that spring is a long time from now."

"It is." Nick nodded. "And fall is the perfect time for a wedding."

"Fall?" Mercedes yelped. "You were talking about winter just the other day."

"Winter's perfect." Nick's voice was warm and happy, and though Parker had walked in earlier feeling higher than a kite after spending the night with Vanessa, he was reminded now that all he and Vanessa would ever have was sex.

Fan-fucking-tastic sex.

And maybe a kid.

11

Parker grilled a few pork chops and downed a couple of beers. His backyard was nothing like Vanessa's, but he liked being outside, and the evening hours weren't bad. The back of his house was in the shade after noon, and the humidity wasn't near as bad as it had been last week. So, he took the meat from the grill, kicked a lawn chair around to face the yard rather than the house, and ate with his plate in his lap. Enjoyed the quiet, the occasional sound of a car driving by out front, and the call of kids on the block, playing something, somewhere.

He and Nick were outdoors all the time when they were kids. They played in pickup football and baseball games. Rode their bikes everywhere. Before Mercedes, when Nick had been married to Kiara and even after the divorce, it bothered Parker that Maisy and Eli were rarely outside. Hell, Kiara had them on such a bizarre schedule with sitting quietly in their rooms for long stretches at a time to playing the grand piano—Parker could still hear his niece's horrid plunking on the keys—and picking up toys and making their beds, he thought the woman had a few screws too fricking tight in her head.

What still surprised him was that Nick had let Kiara run the show. Not the marriage; the details of his brother's marriage were none of his business. But he still didn't get how Nick had rolled over and let Kiara steamroll him into submission with the kids. How had Nick gone from his brother—a kid who rushed for twenty touchdowns one summer in just a handful of pickup games—to a man who enforced rules like quiet time or thirty minutes of meditation for a three-year-old and a one-year-old? Sure, when Parker questioned Nick on that one, Nick had rolled his eyes and said the meditation was for Maisy. It was just naptime for Eli. As if a *three-year-old* needed meditation.

Did other people parent their kids that way? Had life changed that much since he and Nick had been kids living at home? Parker hoped not; he hoped that Kiara just didn't get it. The woman hadn't wanted kids, and again, he wasn't going to touch that fact or the fights Nick and Kiara had with a pole that spanned the universe. He was thrilled that Nick and Kiara had finally divorced, but even after Kiara was gone, Nick still acted like he had a stick up his butt as far as the kids were concerned.

Parker got it. Parenthood couldn't be easy. And he should be the last to judge his brother or anyone parenting kids. But he wanted to believe he would do better. Nick was awesome now with the kids, and though Mercedes had been the magic to pull his brother's family together, Parker wanted to believe that if things hadn't worked out as they had between Nick and Mercedes,

Nick would still have come around to being the father—the daddy—he is now.

Parker wanted to be a daddy. Not a father.

Not a sperm donor.

Not that he could walk away from Vanessa Mayne now if he tried.

After spending far too long outside, thinking about his childhood, his relationship with his father, about the time he spent with Nick's kids, Parker went inside to tidy up his little galley kitchen. He passed on his book and turned the TV on, intending to find an action movie to kill some time. And instead, he got hung up on a channel that showed old reruns and got sucked into *The Brady Bunch*.

Probably, he stopped because of Greg. Because he and Vanessa had talked about Greg Brady when she told him about her ex, Greg Mitchell. And maybe he watched the first few minutes just because he liked the family feeling and for the first time in his life, Parker desperately wanted his own family. But he got stuck on the channel because he had to watch the antics play out again and again. He wanted to watch Jan and Tiger and the episode when Mr. and Mrs. Brady thought Jan was allergic to the dog. He was drawn to Alice, her constant, nurturing presence. She sort of reminded Parker of Mercedes, though Parker figured if he said so to Nick, his brother might throttle him. The character Alice was great, but Mercedes was a breath of fresh air with those green eyes and her big smile.

He went to bed that night wondering what Vanessa would say if she knew he had binge watched several episodes of the old show. At least when he climbed between his cool sheets and turned the lamp off, his brain was done with TV. The trouble was Vanessa. Thoughts of her naked between his sheets. Straddling him. Riding him reverse cowboy. She hadn't yet, but he decided it was a pretty good thought to close his eyes to.

Mid-morning on Tuesday, he noticed a voicemail on his phone when he was between jobs. Assuming it was about a job—either a cancellation or maybe a request to do some added work for someone, maybe the Pattinsons —he played the message on speaker as he started his truck. The call was from his physician's office, asking him to call back. With what felt like a buzzsaw eating away at his stomach, he returned the call and spoke with his doctor's nurse. His lab results looked good, though his doctor did suggest cutting back a bit on red meat. His good cholesterol was a little bit low, his bad a little bit high, but mostly Parker kept hearing the word healthy. No evidence of sexually transmitted diseases. The nurse told him they had mailed his results, and his dick rejoiced at that with a party in his shorts, not quite as wet and uncomfortable today since the humidity wasn't terrible.

But then, he didn't particularly want to drive around with his dick at full salute, either. He wasn't opposed to jacking off, but he wasn't the guy who took time out of his workday to handle that, either. Instead, he drove to his next client's house with his thoughts on his finances. He did okay. He wasn't rolling in big money, wasn't really rolling in any money, but he had low overhead, too. His house was tiny and less than fancy. And paid for. His truck was older, but reliable and paid for. He didn't love malls, and he owned enough clothes for a lifetime as far as he was concerned. He had few bills to worry about.

But with winter coming, he had fewer clients, too. He

moved snow for a few businesses in town. Had some residential customers, too. But those clients didn't do much for him if there wasn't enough snow to worry about. He had considered finding something else. Something to complement what he was already doing. Adding a landscaping arm to his yard business seemed like a good idea, but it would mean investing more money. He would have to get a loan. Parker had no worries that he couldn't get a loan; he just wasn't sure if he wanted to dive in like that.

His dick got the message, anyway. The A-okay from his doctor didn't mean he was going to point the truck in the direction of her house. They weren't going to get naked and play immediately. He had work to do. By the time he pulled his truck to the curb at his next job, he didn't worry that the neighbors who were home might think he was a perv, walking around with a hard-on while pushing a mower. He would just wait until he had the actual letter in hand to see Vanessa and share his results with her.

———

"How many do you want?" Mercedes asked him. Parker, hunched over the island counter in his brother's kitchen, wished for a second that she was talking about kids. That he and Vanessa were in a relationship and that it would be normal for his almost sister-in-law to ask a question like that. True, it might be more likely she would ask Vanessa—seemed like that was more of a woman-to-woman conversation. But even that thought warmed him from the inside out. True, he and Vanessa barely knew each other, but he would like to have a relationship with her where he could bring her here to meet Nick and Cedes.

If Mercedes were asking about kids, Parker decided he might say four. Maybe six.

"Parker?" Mercedes nudged him with her elbow as she moved past him to carry a plate of biscuits to the table.

"None, thank you." He stood up straight and looked into his coffee mug. He hadn't talked to Vanessa since he left her house Sunday. Seemed wrong to him to walk out after mind-blowing sex and not call her. He might not be Mr. Commitment, but he wasn't a jerk, either. When he was involved with a woman, even just for a few weeks at a time, he called and texted and took her out for fun dinner and movie dates. He liked to dance. He loved going to baseball games—local high school and collegiate games as well as the big leagues. He had done a paint and sip night with a woman he dated last year.

But this no contact thing, this let's-just-have-sex-to-make-a-baby rule was already making him nuts. And they hadn't started trying yet.

"You don't want any bacon or eggs on your biscuit?" Mercedes sounded incredulous.

"No biscuit, either," he mumbled absently. "My cholesterol's high."

"What?"

He looked at her finally and gave her a quick grin.

"Well, my HDL—my good cholesterol—"

"I know." Mercedes rolled her eyes.

"It's low. My LDL is a little high." He shrugged. "My doctor recommended I start eating more veggies. Less bacon and eggs and butter."

"Wow. You sound like an old man." She arched her eyebrows as she turned back to the stove.

"I ate some cereal this morning."

"Right." Mercedes, still with her back to him, nodded. "You'll be hungry by the time you walk out of here to go to the first job site."

He didn't doubt it, but he wasn't up for the verbal debate today. He had done Vanessa's yard yesterday. All the night before, he had looked forward to seeing her. He hadn't gone so far as to assume he would get a quickie in the kitchen, but he had looked forward to seeing her, maybe seeing her in the melon bikini. She'd been there, but she hadn't come outside in the bikini. She appeared to be in a rush. Stepped outside dressed in work attire, he supposed, and offered him a big smile and a cold bottle of water and told him she had to run.

All fine, probably totally legitimate. She ran her own business. She might have had a client scheduled at that time. She might have had an appointment of her own to keep. But the whole situation had Parker tied in knots. And he wasn't that guy. He wasn't used to feeling like this. Had no idea what to do with it.

"So." Mercedes looked at him over her shoulder as she turned a piece of bacon in the skillet. "C'mere."

"Why?" he asked, but he moved closer to her.

"Nick's not here," she told him.

He gave her an overly dramatic quirk of his eyebrow. "I'm not that kind of brother—"

"You had lab work done last week. I know you did; we discussed it. Remember?"

"Yep." He nodded. "Maisy asked about my testes."

Mercedes snorted. "She did not. She asked about your tests."

"Yes, Cedes, I remember."

"And now you're telling me you got your results back."

"I did."

"So? When do you start?"

Parker barked a laugh. He skated his eyes over Mercedes, but suddenly a little hesitant to get into it with her, he looked away quickly.

"Don't put it that way."

"Wow. Mr. Sensitive." She frowned. "Seriously, though. I assume if you're this far into this, you've agreed to it. To sleeping with her to get her pregnant."

Parker shrugged uncomfortably.

"Look, Parker, Nick's just concerned about you."

"I was with her last weekend."

"Before you both had your results?"

"We used condoms."

"Oh." Mercedes nodded. Parker noticed a tiny bit of pink flush her cheeks. "So. You weren't kidding about cookies on the kitchen floor."

"No." He sighed and cleared his throat. "We took a break for snacks."

"And?"

"Nope." He shook his head. "Not doing this."

"Not asking for details." Mercedes glanced at him and rolled her eyes. "But. Parker, c'mon. I know it's more than this. For you. You've had eyes for her all summer."

"You would too, if you saw her in that bikini."

"Well, maybe I'd think she was sexy, but I'm kinda into Nick."

"Don't I know it." His turn to roll his eyes.

"Can I meet her?"

"What?" Parker shook his head. He swallowed the last of his now lukewarm coffee and set the mug in the sink. "No, you can't meet her. We're not dating, Cedes. She's paying me money to have sex with her."

"And you're okay with that?"

"What's not to be okay with? She's sexy. She's good in bed. I'm making money."

Mercedes turned the burner off and scooted the skillet off to the side on the cooktop. She turned to study Parker's face and finally nodded.

"Okay."

"What?" Parker yelped and moved with her when she moved to the cabinet to get plates for the kids. "Not okay. What? What're you thinking?"

"You just don't seem very happy. For a young, good-looking guy. Who's about to get paid to have sex with a woman he's crushed on all summer. Bareback sex, no less."

"You think I'm good-looking?" He grinned.

"Parker." She groaned out loud.

"Sorry." He squeezed his eyes closed and then scrubbed his fingers over his head. "I don't think I can stand here and talk to you about having sex with her and not using a condom. I've never..." Frustrated with himself for being embarrassed, for getting a little choked up over something that to other people might seem stupid, Parker shook his head and turned away from her. "I can't."

"I'm not judging you, Parker," she said quietly. "And we don't need to discuss condoms and sex. All I'm sayin' is I know you like her. Nick's concerned about the legal ramifications. Whose name she's gonna put on the birth certificate when that baby comes along."

"She might not even get pregnant," Parker reminded Mercedes.

"I'm concerned about you," Mercedes ignored him. She patted his chest as she lifted her face to his, her eyes warm and filled with worry. "I don't wanna see you get hurt."

12

"Sorry, we're closed!" Vanessa called from the back room when she heard the front door of her salon open. She flinched as she folded the last towel in the bottom of the basket and then stretched to put the freshly laundered towels on the shelf. She did a good business, but she was always happy to find new clients. Hollering from somewhere out of sight that she was closed wasn't good for customer relations. The girls who leased space from her would sure be frowning right now if they had heard her.

"Nice try."

Journey Ryan appeared in the doorway. She tucked her hands in the hip pockets of her uniform khakis and tipped her head at Vanessa. The look on her face made Vanessa stand up straighter and taller. She ignored the jolt of nerves that socked her in the belly and pulled in a deep breath.

The woman was her best friend. Had been for years. And she could read her mind like the billboard at the café two doors down. Vanessa had been avoiding Journey since the weekend.

Because she hadn't told her yet about Parker. About the steamy night they'd shared. Truth be told, she hadn't even thought about Journey the rest of Sunday. She'd lounged the morning away; well, correction. She'd spent the morning in bed, but not necessarily lounging. No, if anything, Parker had given her body one hell of a workout.

When he left, she dragged herself out of bed, show-ered, and made coffee. She did laundry. Cleaned her already clean house—only so much one person could get dirty in a big house like that. She rounded Sunday evening out with a trip to the grocery store and a few episodes of her latest TV obsession—*Dead to Me*.

Monday, she considered calling Journey, but she told herself to give it some time. There was no need to call and gush to her best friend about the incredible sex. Especially not since she had been so adamant from the beginning that what she was doing with Parker wasn't about sex or emotions. It was biology. With a purpose, an end game. Journey wouldn't go so far as to judge her, but still, Vanessa knew her friend worried about her.

All day Monday, she worked with a smoldering heat radiating from the center of her body. She had almost checked her temperature, but she knew in her heart it was Parker. She wanted Parker with a fierceness she'd never experienced before. She would have considered her sex life good before that night with him. But the man had blown her mind.

By Tuesday, Vanessa could at least admit to herself that she didn't *want* to call Journey. Not because she wasn't dying to share the sexy details about her night with Parker. But because she was.

She couldn't tell Journey that, either.

Because she'd made such a big deal out of the business side of what she wanted with him. Because she had sworn to Journey—yes, on two bibles stacked together, one a little paperback version Journey had used in a religion class back in college and the other a bigger, fancy gold hardback book that had belonged to Journey's grandma—that all she wanted from Parker was a baby.

Now here she was with shame in her cheeks—had she seriously sworn on a stack of bibles that all she wanted from sex with him was a baby, that her sole purpose in her latest endeavor was to procreate??—because she was lying to herself and to her best friend and trying to avoid said best friend on top of it.

"Hi." Vanessa grinned, all too aware of the guilt plastered on her face at the moment.

"Hi, I'm Journey." Her friend stepped into the room. "I'd like to make an appointment."

Vanessa winced as she folded her arms over her chest.

"Finally here for that color we talked about?" Vanessa tipped her head. "Blue, right?"

"Mm-hmm." Journey nodded. She reached for Vanessa and plucked her wrist away from her chest. "Come with me."

"Where?" Vanessa was tempted to plant her feet and stand still, but she allowed Journey to drag her out to the front of her shop. On the counter behind her chair, she spotted a bouquet of flowers. Heart in her throat, she dragged her eyes from the flowers to her friend and finally to the bottle of cheap wine on the reception counter. "What—?"

Journey arched her eyebrows at her in a you-tell-me look, but she turned to the front door and flipped the closed sign.

"Gimme your keys," she commanded quietly. Without hesitation, Vanessa crossed the room to the counter and grabbed the keys from the top drawer. She tossed them to Journey and then turned to inspect the wine. Two clear plastic cups hung from the top of the screw top bottle. Most definitely a gift from Journey.

But the flowers?

"These are stunning," Journey announced as she moved to Vanessa's station. She set the keys on the counter and leaned over to smell the bouquet.

"They are," Vanessa agreed. "Why would you bring me cheap wine and flowers like this?"

"Heard you would put out if I did." Journey didn't miss a beat with her sarcastic response. Vanessa joined her by the flowers, heart in her throat as she got closer to the mix of orange and yellow roses and daisies.

"Wow."

"I brought the wine." Journey moved back over to the reception counter to grab the wine. Vanessa glanced at her, but she tore her eyes away from Journey's hands on the bottle to look at the flowers again. "Because I miss you. And I knew if I called you for a catch-up session, you would blow me off. Again. So here I am. We're going to sit down right here, have some wine, and talk."

"Journey." Vanessa closed her eyes. "I wouldn't—"

"You would. You have." Journey shrugged. "I get it. I'm

not mad. But I am gonna be selfish and demand that you sit down now and talk to me."

Vanessa sighed and nodded. She turned her attention back to the flowers and gently moved them aside to find a card in them.

"The first thing you can tell me," Journey eyed the glasses closely as she filled them, "is a little something about those flowers."

Vanessa swallowed hard as she slipped the card from the plastic prongs.

"They're roses. Daisies—"

"Who're they from?" Journey handed her a glass and sat down in the chair to the right of Vanessa's station. Cheeks on fire—with hope? fear?—Vanessa tipped her chin down to look at the card.

Feeling sorry for Matthew Kessler today.

Vanessa snorted before she could stop herself.

"Van?"

"Oh my God." Vanessa laughed softly. She plopped in her chair and turned it to face Journey.

"What's the card say?" Journey leaned forward and reached for it.

"You wouldn't get it." Vanessa shook her head and rolled her eyes. But she laughed again as she took a healthy drink of the wine.

"You're keeping secrets already?"

"No secrets." Vanessa shrugged and leaned forward to hand the card to Journey.

"I don't get it." Journey shook her head. "Tell me."

"You remember Matthew Kessler?"

Journey nodded. "Yep. Spelling bee champion in seventh

grade. Highest scoring point guard in school history. And his mom got pregnant when he was eighteen and leaving for college. He was mortified. But his dad was pretty hot."

"Scandalous," Vanessa nodded, "yes, but there was more."

Journey lifted her own cup for a gulp, but she kept her eyes on the card in her other hand. She studied it, turning it over and over—Vanessa almost snatched it away from her, because it was from Parker. Which made her want to save it. Which probably made her sound like a stupid kid crushing on a guy.

Which was totally how she felt since last weekend.

Well, no. That wasn't entirely true. She had her eyes on Parker all summer but had only recently found the courage to proposition him.

Journey, still studying the card, repeated *Matthew Kessler* over and over.

"Was he your first kiss?"

Vanessa waited for Journey to look up at her before rolling her eyes.

"No."

"Oh my God!" Journey's whole body shook with her enthusiastic nod. "I remember. You let him touch your boobs."

Vanessa blinked at Journey but said nothing.

"Right? He was the first guy you took your shirt off for? You let him touch you?"

"Yep."

"And so…the sender of the flowers…which are so gorgeous and definitely not cheap…feels sorry for Matthew."

Vanessa nibbled on her lower lip.

"Because he had to look at your boobs?"

"Can we stop naming particular body parts?" Vanessa cringed. "My boobs have been a hot topic lately."

Journey laughed softly and shrugged. "They're pretty hot, but I've got some, so no thanks. The flowers are from Parker Moore."

"The flowers are from Parker," Vanessa confirmed quietly. She met Journey's eyes boldly, ready to field a hundred questions.

"You slept with him already?"

"Last weekend."

"Wow." Journey gulped more wine. "Why didn't you tell me?"

"Because it's just," Vanessa took a quick breath and reminded herself that Journey was looking for signs that she would get in too deep and get her heart broken, "business, Journey. Just sex."

"Is it?" Journey fluttered her eyelashes and raised her brows. "Those flowers don't look like just business."

They didn't.

The flowers looked like an emotional train wreck waiting to happen. Like romance and fun and flirting and passion and—

Not sure what to say, Vanessa took a drink and smoothed her other hand over her navy pants. She was nervous. About reporting to Journey, sure, but also about Parker. And what he might be thinking. What had possessed him to send such an extravagant arrangement?

"He showed up Saturday night after he took his niece and nephew out for pizza. We hung out for a while. Talked some. And messed around."

"Messed around," Journey repeated.

"Greg's been gone almost a year," Vanessa mumbled. "He didn't touch me like that for six months before. Maybe a year."

"Van." Journey sighed.

"Maybe ever, Journey," Vanessa whispered.

"Did you use protection? Until you know he's clean—"

"Yes, he had condoms with him." Vanessa huffed out a sigh. "I was nervous. But he thought it might be better to do it like that first. To break the ice."

"Of course he would say that." Journey rolled her eyes. "He wanted sex, Van."

"It was…" She almost said perfect, but somehow she knew it would come out soft, on a dreamy sounding sigh, and make her sound smitten. "Pretty incredible," she finished. "God, that body."

"Yeah?" Journey eyed her suspiciously and then glanced at the flowers. "Still. Those are *love* kind of flowers. Not thanks-for-incredible-sex flowers."

"You don't know Parker well enough to say that."

"Neither do you," Journey reminded her. "I mean, at least tell me you gave him a blowjob. That those flowers are a thanks-for-sucking-me-off and not an I'm-a-crazy-stalker, you'll-never-be-free-of-me-bouquet."

"I had my mouth on every inch of his body, and I did blow him, and judging from the way his hips shot off the couch—"

"Okay." Journey nodded. "I'm convinced."

"That this is a good idea? Because I was thinking last night about taking my child to Europe one day. Like when he or she's ten? Twelve?"

"I'm convinced for now that he's not a stalker, but no, I'm not convinced that this is a good idea, Van."

"Journey, it'll be okay. He's a good guy."

"How good of a guy can he be if he accepted your crazy-ass proposition? He's going to take money from you to do you, Van. He's getting your money and your body."

"He doesn't want the money."

"So he says." Journey shrugged. "And that worries me more. What if you do get pregnant, and he demands parental rights? What then?"

Vanessa swallowed hard. She hadn't considered that Parker would want parental rights. Didn't most guys just want no-strings-attached sex? Here she was, reasonably attractive, offering a good-looking guy who was known to be a heartbreaker free, no-strings-attached sex and a paycheck.

"He won't," Vanessa said softly. "You're kidding, right? Guys do anything to get out of this situation. He's a player. He likes women. He likes sex. I'm not gonna turn his head. I'm not gonna change the way he feels about that."

"I hope you're right, Van," Journey mumbled. She sighed and lifted her cup in a toast. "To incredible sex and blowjobs and—did he return that favor?"

Vanessa grinned as she held her cup up in answer. "Cheers."

"Now I'm jealous."

Vanessa glanced at the flowers again. She wanted to see him. Now. He had been at her house two days ago to work in her yard. Unfortunately, she had a new client scheduled during that time and didn't want to change the appointment to get her fix, even if it was just to lounge around in the bikini Parker had confessed to liking.

"I want to meet him."

"You can't meet him," Vanessa argued.

"Why not?"

"Because we're not a thing. We're not a couple. We're just doing biology stuff. We're mating. I can't introduce you to him."

"What if you think he's incredible when this is over, and I decide I want a baby? I should meet him now, so he and I can have a little chemistry in case I want him to be a baby daddy for me."

The sharp knife of jealousy poked Vanessa just under her heart. Slipped right through her ribs and stole her breath.

"You would do that?" she whispered. "You would have sex with the same guy I did? Just for a baby?"

"Of course not!" Journey groaned. "But someone else out there is gonna sleep with him when you get done with him, Van. Think about that. If he got someone else pregnant, too, your child would have a sibling out there he or she wouldn't even know."

"I'm not even pregnant yet. I don't even know if I can get pregnant."

"Well, why wouldn't you be able—"

Journey's pocket rang like an old-fashioned telephone. She sucked in a breath of irritation as she lifted her butt from the chair to lift her leg straight out and dig in her pocket.

"I gotta go," Journey groaned. "Lenore's having a heart attack over this damned party she's having for my dad."

"Can I help?"

Journey climbed from the chair and waved her phone at Vanessa.

"I'll let you know," she told her, still ignoring the phone. "Van, be careful. Please."

"I will," Vanessa promised. She watched Journey set her nearly empty cup on the counter and dig her keys from her other hip pocket. When she was gone, Vanessa eyed the flowers again, wondering what the hell kind of message Parker was sending. She sighed as she scooted off her chair and then snatched the card from the counter where Journey had left it. She read the words again, this time letting her mind wander back to the weekend and the way Parker had watched her undress and then staged her body so she was on display for his eyes only.

No man had ever looked at her that way.

She wasn't sure if she was thrilled with that knowledge or disappointed that those looks, the sex, the time she had with Parker was limited.

13

Maisy leaned over his shoulder and pressed her cheek to his head.

"Wow, Mase." Parker studied the paper she brought home from school. "That's excellent!"

"Do you know what else starts with the letter C, Uncle Parker?" She crunched a bite of carrot right next to his ear.

"Carrot?" He turned his head to find himself nose to nose with his niece. Maisy laughed as she swallowed that mouthful, but she shook her head and pointed around his shoulder to the paper again.

"Candy."

"Oh, yeah. Okay." He skimmed his fingertips over the drawing again. There was a big car in the center of the paper, a bright yellow Camaro cut from a magazine ad if he had to guess. Parker wondered where Maisy had found a magazine since they hadn't had any for the letters A and B as recently as last week. There were several small drawings at the bottom of the page. One looked like a cat now that he thought about it, and one was apparently candy. He wasn't sure about the third one, so he decided to play it safe and see what Maisy said about it first.

"Parker, your phone is blowing up over here," Mercedes announced.

"Cell phone?" he mumbled, eyes still on the picture.

"See? It's candy carns." Maisy tapped the picture. "And this is a cat. I asked Daddy for a cat. We could name it Captain."

"Captain Ain't Gonna Happen," Nick told her as he stepped back inside the kitchen. "The chicken's ready."

"Chicken?" Parker looked at Maisy hopefully.

"No."

"But it does start with the letter C."

"Nuh-uh." Maisy frowned at him and shook her head. "Then you would say kicken."

Parker swallowed hard and bit his lip before he could argue with her.

"They haven't studied digraphs, yet, bro," Nick reminded him. "With it being a month into kindergarten and all."

Parker eyed Nick and resisted the urge to flip him off.

"Parker?" Mercedes called.

"What?" He turned to look at her.

"It's a cow!" Maisy punched him in the shoulder.

"You're right." He nodded at her, but he reached for his phone as Mercedes handed it to him. He left it on the counter when he came inside earlier. Partly because he wanted some quality time with Mase and Eli and partly because he didn't particularly want to hear from Vanessa.

Did he?

He had sent flowers. In a moment of utter weakness?

Insanity? Whatever the hell it was, he had sent flowers. And he wasn't sure what she would think about that. Of the fact that he sent them. And then there was the whole sex thing.

He was *clear*. Healthy. *Clean. There's a C word for ya, Mase. Clean.* Good to have unprotected sex with his summer *crush*. Ready to stick his naked *cock* as far inside Vanessa Mayne as deep it would go, so they would both *come*.

As much as he wanted to do exactly that, the thought also scared the absolute hell out of him. Because in doing so, they could *create* a *child*.

So, instead of rushing home after work to shower and show up at her place with his lab results in hand, he had come to Nick and Mercedes' to hang out. Or hide. He looked at the phone now. Mercedes was right; he had a few missed calls from buddies, two texts from an old girl-friend who he supposed was more of a friend with bene-fits now, and two texts from Vanessa.

Those from Vanessa were the ones that mattered to him, but before he could open them, his phone buzzed again with a phone call.

"Shit." He gritted his teeth together.

"Uncle Parker said shit," Eli announced from his spot on the kitchen floor. Parker flinched and squeezed his eyes closed. Three-year-old Eli had only recently started talking, so Parker doubted anyone cared that the kid had just repeated the slang. But he still felt guilty for saying it front of the kids.

"Answer it." Nick nudged him as he walked by the table, stepped over Eli, and carried a plate of grilled chicken to the counter.

"Hey." Parker put the phone to his ear. Maisy, who had been standing on the back of the same chair he was perched on, jumped to the floor and dropped there to play cars with Eli. Parker felt Mercedes' eyes on him as he slipped out the sliding doors to the deck where he could talk privately with Vanessa.

"Hey, yourself." Vanessa sounded normal. Happy, he guessed. "Where are you?"

Parker felt a spike of heat in his chest. He stood silently for a second as it radiated through his arms and legs. Hell yes, he wanted this woman, but for so much more than a quick, steamy affair.

"At my brother's house." He took a deep breath, but he was careful to exhale slowly and quietly, so she wouldn't hear him.

"Oh." She sort of hummed and then the line was quiet.

"Am I on the job tonight?"

She laughed softly, but he thought he heard a touch of uncertainty.

"Um." She cleared her throat and then laughed again. "Of course not. I mean, we can do that when it's convenient for you. Did you hear from the clinic—"

"Vanessa—"

He stopped talking when he heard the sliding door behind him.

"Park?"

"What?" Phone still at his ear, Parker turned to look at Nick leaning out the door, an urgent look on his face.

"Dinner's ready."

"Okay."

"Is that Vanessa?"

Parker wouldn't swear to it, but it sure seemed like

Nick spoke those words just a bit louder, as if he wanted her to hear him.

"Is that your brother?" Vanessa asked in his ear.

"Yes," he answered Vanessa, but he saw Nick nod.

"Invite her over."

"What?"

"For dinner," Nick told him. "Invite the woman here for dinner."

"It's Friday night, Nick," Parker argued. "She probably has plans."

"Ask." Nick propped his shoulder on the doorframe now, apparently enjoying himself.

"You're being a dick."

"Do you not want me to meet them?"

Vanessa's words were a sucker punch in his gut. He gritted his teeth and turned his back to Nick. Yes, he wanted Vanessa to meet his family. Well, he wanted her to meet Cedes and the kids. Jury was still out about Nick. He figured Nick was going to screw with him for a while since he had kissed Mercedes before Nick did. Even though it was just a test kiss.

"Do you want to meet them?" He tipped his head curiously, even though Vanessa couldn't see him.

Vanessa's answer was so long in coming, he wondered if she had ended the call.

"Kind of."

Her words shocked him. She was adamant that they were only having sex to make a baby, so he had assumed she wouldn't want anything to do with his family. Or him, once she was pregnant or they gave up trying to get pregnant.

"Then come over," he suggested.

"I don't want to impose," she argued. "I'm sorry. Just feeling a little bit weird right now."

Weird because she suddenly decided she wanted to meet his family? Or weird because he had sent her flowers?

"It's not an imposition," he promised her. "I can't promise you that my brother will behave, but you would love Cedes and the kids."

"Why did you send me flowers?" she whispered.

Parker almost doubled over with pain at the sadness in her voice. He wasn't sure what he was supposed to say. Most women liked flowers; it was the first time he ever felt guilty for sending them, that was for sure.

"Because I was thinking about you," he answered truthfully. He almost added that he had spent the entire week thinking about her, but he bit his tongue. He'd said enough. More would only scare her away.

"You could just come by later," she suggested.

"I will," he told her, "if that's what you want. But honestly, Vanessa, I would kind of like it if you stopped by."

"Do they know? What we're doing?"

"For the love," Nick said loudly from behind him again. "We're sitting down in five."

"Nicholas!" Mercedes's voice was heavy with frustration. "Leave them alone!"

"Like he left us alone? Are you kidding me?" Nick grumbled.

Parker glanced over his shoulder. He didn't want to admit to her that his brother and his brother's fiancé knew their story, but he couldn't lie to her, either.

"Yeah."

"Oh, God." She sighed. "They probably think I'm a monster, don't they?"

"Vanessa." He scrubbed his hand over the top of his head and closed his eyes. "Are you okay?"

"I'm good," she answered immediately. "What's the address there?"

"You're coming?"

Her deep, throaty chuckle sparked a fire in his groin.

"I sure hope so."

Parker gave her Nick's address and then stood on the deck for a minute even after they ended the call. He needed a few minutes alone—to talk his dick down, yeah, but just to think about that phone call. At first, he had assumed she was calling to get the ball rolling. If she'd had any lab work done, odds were hers was ready, so she would assume his was, too. She had been a hungry, eager participant in the intimate things they had done last weekend, so if she was anything like him, she wanted more. Now.

But after talking to her, he had to wonder if sending her flowers was a bad idea. If he had upset her. What if those were the same kinds of flowers Greg used to send her? Or what if the guy had never done little things like that for her?

"Hey." Mercedes stepped out on the deck with him. Parker turned to her as she rolled the door closed. "Nick's gonna be a pain in the ass about all of it. You know that, right? No matter if it's Vanessa or the girl after her or the one after her. If you find Mrs. Right, Nick's gonna be in your face about it."

Parker grinned. "First of all, she's not Mrs. Right, so please, do not say anything to that effect when she's here.

Please. And please make sure Nick knows that. That's not what we're about."

Mercedes arched her eyebrows and opened her mouth to respond. Parker watched with interest as she took a deep breath and then shook her head.

"But she's coming here? Tonight? For dinner?"

"Yeah." Parker lifted one shoulder in a lazy, hesitant shrug. "I thought she would say no."

Mercedes studied his face for a second.

"Did you want her to say no?"

"Really?" Parker rolled his eyes, but he refused to meet Mercedes' gaze. "What I really wish is that she would be so damned charmed by you and those adorable kids that she would want to be around me more."

"You're pretty charming yourself, Parker Moore."

He shook his head and straightened from the deck railing. "Can I ask you something?"

"As long as it doesn't involve condoms or the lack of said condoms during sex."

"Would you talk to me about sex if Nick was out here, too?"

Mercedes narrowed her eyes at him and tipped her head. "Is this really about sex? Your question?"

"No." He grinned. "But I'm curious."

"My boyfriend might kick your ass, Parker," she warned him.

Parker chuckled, but the laugh fizzled out quickly. He sighed and tucked his hands in his pockets.

"If Nick had sent you flowers," he shrugged, shooting for nonchalance, "after the first time you guys messed around—" Here, he stopped and looked Mercedes in the eyes. "No details. Just go with me. If you hadn't exactly professed undying love for each other, but you had done some stuff, would you be mad?"

"Would I have been mad at Nick if he had sent me flowers after groping me in his kitchen?"

Parker ducked his chin and shook his head. "Did you hear that part where I said no details?"

"No," Mercedes said softly. "I wouldn't have been mad."

Relieved, but still confused, he sighed and nodded.

"But I would have been really confused with how that worked in with everything else going on with me and Nick."

14

Vanessa almost turned around halfway to the address Parker had given her. What in the world did she think she was doing? What good could come of going to see Parker at his brother's house? For one thing, the only reason she and Parker were spending time together was for sex. Sex to get pregnant. That didn't need to involve meeting his family, did it?

Well, maybe. Maybe it was a good idea to meet his brother, to see how Parker interacted with him and the guy's kids. Not because Parker would be interacting with her child if she were to get pregnant, but she could see for herself if he was responsible and courteous—both qualities she would want in a child when he or she grew into an adult.

Then again, seeing as how she'd already propositioned Parker and they'd already had a night of ice-breaking activities, it was a little late to observe him in his everyday life. And still, she kept her foot on the gas and the front of her car aimed in the direction of his brother's house.

She lost her nerve again as she pulled to the curb in front of the house. They knew. Parker's brother and his fianceé knew what she and Parker were doing. If they knew that, they had to know she had propositioned Parker, that the whole scheme was her idea. Vanessa took a deep breath and put the car in park. Could she really walk inside and face two total strangers who knew she had asked Parker to get her pregnant?

"Why not, Vanessa?" she mumbled. What was wrong with wanting a baby? Just because she wanted to get her baby the old-fashioned way didn't mean anything. Well, mostly old-fashioned. Ideally, she would be in a happy, committed relationship with the love of her life, and they would create a baby together and then raise the child together. Too bad she had given up on part of that equation. She was over Greg enough to know that he wasn't the love of her life, but she had been hurt often enough that she wondered if she *had* a great love of her life. And she had decided that she was going to have a child, with or without that love.

With that thought, she nodded to herself, grabbed her purse and keys, and climbed out of the car. The evening sun stretched lazily over the neighborhood, bouncing off windows and cars and painting deep shadows around the houses and trees. Vanessa heard kids' voices from up the street. A country music voice drifted to her from somewhere nearby. Sounded like Kenny Chesney, but she wasn't sure.

The neighborhood reminded her a lot of her own. She might not love the house Greg had built and left to her, but it was a beautiful area. Might be the perfect home for someone. Like the one Parker's brother lived in. She eyed the stately home, the brick, the pot of mums on the porch, as she reached for the doorbell.

She had a moment to realize that if Parker's brother knew she had asked Parker to get her pregnant, he and his fiancé might also know that she and Parker had burned up the sheets last weekend. Some guys talked just as much as girls did; would Parker have told Nick about last weekend? If he did tell him, did he give him details?

Before she could decide if she was okay with being here, with meeting Nick and his family, someone yanked the door open from inside. Vanessa felt the heat in her cheeks as she met the guy's eyes. She swallowed hard and forced herself to hold the eye contact, even though that night with Parker was front and center in her head right now. The memory had her a little bit breathless, and the worry that this guy at the door could read her mind had her ready to turn and run to her car.

"Hey." The guy flashed a friendly smile at her. He looked a little bit like Parker. Blue eyes. Dark hair, just a bit unruly around his ears and his collar. His dark T-shirt emphasized wide shoulders; the pushed-up sleeves revealed wiry, muscular forearms. And his bare legs beneath the perfectly acceptable length gray athletic shorts were nice to look at.

But he wasn't Parker. Not quite.

"Um." She grinned and then cleared her throat.

"The doorbell doesn't work," he announced. "And yes, I could get it fixed, but there's a little story behind that doorbell and a certain woman just walking in one day and turning the house upside down, so I'd rather not."

Vanessa stared at him, mouth hanging open, uncertain what to say in response.

"I'm Nick." He nodded for her to come inside. "My daughter saw you pull up."

"Hi, Nick," she said softly as she took a hesitant step inside. "I'm Vanessa."

"It's nice to meet you." He sounded sincere, but then, maybe he was just polite. Parker certainly seemed polite. He might have seduced her last weekend with the charming smile and the magic hands, but then, she'd been the one to start that ball rolling, hadn't she? And he had sent her flowers after the fact.

Nick met her eyes again, and the rest of the world dropped away. He grinned at her and tipped his head. Vanessa held her breath for a second.

"What?" she finally gave in and stumbled over the word, embarrassed by his attention and desperate to breathe.

"Just happy to meet the woman to bring my brother to his knees." He shrugged.

"Nessa." Parker appeared behind Nick. Vanessa flitted her eyes to Parker over Nick's shoulder. Nick's words still rang in her head. Bring his brother to his knees? What did that mean?

"Hi." She smiled uncertainly.

"You've met Nick?" Parker stepped around Nick and reached for her hand. "Please don't judge me based on anything that comes out of his mouth."

Nick laughed. "Come in. We're just sitting down for dinner."

"I don't mean to impose," Vanessa argued.

"You have to meet Cedes." Parker took her hand and tugged her through the living area. Vanessa marveled at the snowy white room, curious how it looked so clean if the guy had two kids. A deep green throw was tossed over the center back of the sofa, and there were a couple of books tossed haphazardly near the arm. Vanessa could make out a cover that looked familiar, but before she could really process it or anything else in the room—a grand piano? Did Nick play?—Parker dragged her into the kitchen.

A petite blonde stood at the counter with her back to the living area. She appeared to be stirring a glass of chocolate milk.

"Cedes." Parker nudged her.

"Can you grab the ketchup for Eli?" she asked as she looked up. "Oh." She flashed a grin at Parker and then twisted around further to look at Vanessa. "Oh. Hey. Hi. I'm Mercedes."

"Cedes, this is Vanessa Mayne."

Vanessa half expected him to slide his arm around her shoulders or her waist. Busy trying to process how she would feel about it if he did, she almost missed the brush of his fingers down the back of her arm.

"It's so nice to meet you," Mercedes said softly. No question she was sincere, but the thought made Vanessa feel guilty. She really didn't have reason to doubt Nick's sincerity, did she? Only her own self-consciousness over what had already transpired between her and Parker.

"You, too," Vanessa answered, relieved that her voice sounded normal.

"Are you Uncle Parker's girlfriend?"

Vanessa looked down as warm, soft little fingers closed around her other hand. Mercedes let go of her and turned to grab the chocolate milk.

Her heart hitched at the sight of the little girl standing by her side. Soulful brown eyes stared up at her. The girl's eyebrows were drawn in a suspicious frown.

"Vanessa is Uncle Parker's friend, Mase," Nick answered before Vanessa could find her voice. "Don't be rude."

"You're Bandessa?" The knowledge lit the kid's face up with a smile. Vanessa wasn't sure how she felt about that. Surely Parker hadn't discussed their situation in front of the kids?

"Vanessa," she answered. "But you can call me Van."

"You're a van?" The little girl screwed her face into a dramatic frown.

"You know how you call me Cedes?" Mercedes scooped the girl up for a quick hug. "And we call you Mase?"

"Nicknames." The little girl nodded.

"Yep. So, Vanessa's nickname must be Van."

"Oh." Maisy nodded. "I'm Maisy." Still in Mercedes arms, legs wrapped tightly around her waist, the girl ducked her head into the safety of Mercedes' chest. "Nick is my daddy."

Vanessa hesitated but before overthinking it, she lifted her hand and stroked a fingertip over Maisy's cheek. "I can tell. You look like your daddy."

"I do?" Maisy lifted her head and swung around to look at Nick. "But he's a boy."

"I know. You're much prettier," Vanessa agreed, "but I see him in your smile."

"Have a seat, Vanessa," Mercedes told her. Vanessa started to argue again that she didn't want to impose on their family time, but Parker took her hand and pulled her to the table. She didn't want to be rude, so she simply sat in the empty seat Parker indicated for her.

"Whatcha need, buddy?" Mercedes asked a small boy in a booster seat at the other end of the table. Vanessa watched as he looked up at Mercedes and flashed her a huge, sloppy grin. Mercedes ruffled his hair and then leaned over to drop a kiss on the top of his head.

"Ketchup."

Vanessa was surprised at the deep timbre of the little boy's voice.

"Oh, sorry, Eli." Parker crossed the kitchen to get the ketchup from the fridge.

"Do I get one of those kisses?" Nick asked Mercedes.

"Please, no," Parker mumbled. He glanced at Vanessa and shivered. "They get all kissy and gross if we're not careful."

Mercedes laughed. "We do not."

Parker's brows shot up in disbelief. He handed the ketchup to Mercedes and then looked back at Vanessa as he sat down by her. She laughed softly when he mouthed the words *yes, they do.*

"Eli, Van is Uncle Parker's friend," Maisy announced. Eli watched Mercedes squirt ketchup on his plate and sneaked a peek at Vanessa. "Eli is my little brother."

Vanessa nodded at Maisy, but she turned back to Eli.

"Hi, Eli."

The boy ducked his head, but not before she saw his cheeks turn pink and his lips tip up in a small smile. She loved that Maisy was unabashedly outgoing and talkative and Eli was apparently shy.

"I go to kindergarten," Maisy told her. "My teacher is Mrs. Moany."

Vanessa pressed her lips together and cut her eyes to Parker.

"Mrs. Mahoney, Mase," Nick corrected her.

"That's what I said." Maisy sounded frustrated.

"So, Parker said you own a salon." Mercedes glanced at her as she pulled a small piece of chicken apart for Eli.

"I do." Vanessa nodded. Parker must have realized she wasn't going to reach for a platter to serve herself, because he held the plate of chicken up for her in askance. Again, more to be polite than because she was hungry, she picked up the fork at her spot—they had set a place for her at the table!—and selected a small piece.

Parker eyed her with a small smile as he put the plate back on the table. He nodded to a serving bowl filled with what looked like potato salad. She wondered if Mercedes had fixed the dinner. If she cooked all the time.

"Cedes is an excellent cook," Parker told her. Vanessa nodded and reached for the serving spoon. Maisy addressed her father this time to tell him something about a boy named Jefferson. Parker leaned closer to her and brushed his lips over her cheekbone. "You're gonna need some energy to keep up with me tonight," he whispered.

Vanessa laughed softly, but she turned toward him to hide her blush from Nick and Mercedes.

"Do you do guy hair, too?" Mercedes asked her now. Vanessa flicked her eyes up to meet Parker's before she turned to look at Mercedes.

"I do." Vanessa nodded. "And I have a couple of girls who lease from me who style guys."

Mercedes studied Nick for a moment. Vanessa laughed softly when she pursed her lips and Nick groaned out loud.

"What?" He finally tossed his hands up.

"You need a haircut," she told him.

"I do not," he argued.

"Yep. You need a trim."

"You said you liked—"

"If we're getting married, you need a trim."

"Pretty sure I've got time to get a trim." Nick shrugged.

"You just said the other day you want a fall wedding."

Nick dropped his fork and stared at Mercedes, clearly surprised.

"I thought you said it was too fast." He tipped his head. "That you wouldn't have time to pull everything together."

"I don't," she answered simply. "But if I start harping on you now, maybe you'll get it trimmed so we can have a winter wedding."

"Oh, that would be beautiful," Vanessa agreed. "My oldest brother and his wife got married in December. We wore emerald green dresses. It snowed two days before the wedding, so the pictures at the park were stunning."

"Mmm." Mercedes smiled wistfully. "It sounds perfect. How do I order up fresh snow?"

Vanessa laughed. She took a small bite of the potato salad and decided Parker was right. Mercedes knew what she was doing in the kitchen.

"I'd be happy to cut your hair, Nick," Vanessa offered. "Whenever you guys are ready."

"If we don't get married until December, I could get my hair cut five more times before that."

"That'd be a little much," Mercedes argued quietly. "I like it a little bit long."

"She's a little bit bossy," Nick told Parker.

"Just what you need."

"How about updos?"

"Of course," Vanessa answered. "Anything you want."

"Would you do an updo for a winter wedding, though?" Mercedes frowned.

"Would you make me pretty for Daddy and Cedes' wedding?" Maisy piped up beside her.

"You're already a very pretty girl," Vanessa told her. "But yes, I would make you look like a princess for a day."

"She's already Uncle Parker's princess, aren't you, Mase?" Parker winked at Maisy.

"I am, but I wanna wear a princess dress and curly hair and carry flowers."

"Do you have a date set?" Vanessa looked from Maisy to Mercedes.

Nick snorted. "No. She insists she needs until spring to pull it together."

"Hey." Mercedes narrowed her eyes at Nick. "We're talking about a winter wedding. That's less than four months away."

"Four more months of not sleep—"

"Cedes can't sleep in Daddy's big boy bed until they get hitched," Maisy announced. Vanessa coughed slightly and nodded. She had nieces and nephews, so she shouldn't be surprised by what could and did come out of a child's mouth. On the other hand, her nieces and nephews were quite a bit older, so she hadn't been around a kid who called it as she saw it in a long time.

"I would be happy to help you with anything I can," Vanessa told Mercedes.

Mercedes opened her mouth immediately, maybe to politely reject Vanessa's offer, but she seemed to think better of it. She stared at Vanessa silently for a second and finally nodded.

"Really?" She sounded hopeful. "Because I've never done this before. And I'm a little overwhelmed."

"Absolutely." Vanessa sipped from the glass of tea Parker had poured for her. "Three brothers. I'm practically a professional bridesmaid."

Mercedes sighed and let her shoulders sag with relief. Vanessa felt Parker's eyes on her, and it hit her that she had just committed herself to something involving his family. What if they didn't hit it off after a few times in the sack? What if they did, and she was lucky enough to get pregnant right away? What then? Would his family still be comfortable around her? Would he?

"Where are you going?" Mercedes asked when Nick pushed his chair back to stand up.

"Getting my phone, so we can look at a calendar and pick a date."

Mercedes watched him, clearly amused. Vanessa liked that one of them—or both of them, who knew?—had made the rule that Mercedes wouldn't sleep in his bed with him until they were married. Not that that would stop them from—

"Nick, we have to call people. We have to make sure there's a church with our date open—"

"I know." He nodded, eyes still on the phone in his

hand. "But I'm ready to do this, Cedes. I hate that you have to leave here every night after you're with us all day and evening. Let's pick a date and get it going."

Mercedes nodded when Nick looked up at her. The smile on her face made Vanessa shiver with longing. She glanced at Parker to find him watching her with dark, brooding eyes.

15

Feeling restless, Parker stacked Vanessa's plate on his and carried them to the counter. The girls were relaxed at the table, talking about weddings, of all things. Nick was doing man-of-the house kitchen things. Parker watched him wash a serving bowl, and then he glanced across the room. Eli was in Mercedes' lap now. Maisy wasn't quite in Vanessa's lap, but she was perched on the edge of her seat, leaning into Vanessa.

His heart hurt a little bit watching Vanessa smooth her fingers through Maisy's hair and then down over her back. Over and over again, obviously without thought, but just as obviously, a tender gesture. It struck him how hungry his niece was for female attention. She had fallen head over heels for Mercedes, so crazy about her nanny that she had decided to ask Santa to make Mercedes her and Eli's new mommy. Thankfully, Mercedes had proven worthy of that love.

Now it looked like Maisy had her heart set on winning Vanessa over. And for all appearances, Vanessa seemed perfectly at ease with his niece and soon to be sister-in-law. Maybe this was a bad idea. Yes, he wanted Vanessa to be comfortable here. He wanted her to like his family, he wanted her to fit into his life somehow. Definitely as more than a woman he provided stud services for.

But if she had no interest in a relationship with him, Maisy and Eli could end up getting hurt. Parker eyed the plate in his hand. He yanked the dishwasher door open and nearly slammed it into the bottom rack.

"Hey." Nick shot him a look over his shoulder. "Jesus. That's not plasticware."

"Sorry." He huffed out a quick breath and shook his head.

"You alright?" Nick asked quietly, but Parker could only nod. His chest was a little tight, wasn't sure he could breathe, let alone speak.

Nick dried his hands as Parker set the second plate in the dishwasher and straightened. He peeked at the table again, noticed the look of genuine happiness on Vanessa's face as she laughed at something Mercedes said.

"Hey." Nick stepped around him. "Let's shoot some hoops."

Parker watched him snag a couple of longnecks from the refrigerator. He glanced at the table, ready to say no. He had told Vanessa he was free tonight. When he had said so, he had been excited at the thought. Now, though, rather than looking forward to making love to her, he felt like he was gearing up for a performance.

"C'mon. They're talking. You know how women are." Nick shoved a bottle at him until Parker had no choice but to take it. Part of him wanted to smack his brother in the back of the head as he followed him out through the garage. The wave of envy passed before Parker could make an ass of himself. Yes, Nick had everything Parker hadn't known for sure he was ready for, but he had fought to get here. His marriage to Kiara had been a fiasco, except it was Kiara who had given him the most precious part of his life.

Nick sure as hell deserved a woman like Mercedes to love him and his children. Parker would never wish her away.

He just wished he had the same sort of shot at this life thing with Vanessa.

"What's eating you?" Nick took a long swig of his beer. Parker watched him dig one handed through a toy box for the basketball.

"Noth—"

"Don't tell me nothin.'" Nick shook his head. "You look constipated."

"What?" Parker drew back like Nick had punched him. Nick found the ball and trapped it against his side to walk out to the driveway.

"You have this mean look on your face. Like you wanna grunt and moan about something, but you can't. Say it." Nick shrugged.

Parker took a drink and set his bottle in the corner of the drive. Pissed at Nick's less than attractive observation, he held his hands up for a pass. Nick sent the ball at him in a crisp, one-handed chest pass and then set his own bottle aside.

"A December wedding's gonna make you all crazy," Parker mumbled as he took a shot. The ball banged the backboard, hit the rim, and bounced off to Nick. "You know that, right?"

They had decided on the Saturday after Christmas. Even though Nick was the father—even though he and Mercedes were the parents—of two young kids who still believed in Santa Claus. Nick insisted on referring to the kids as Mercedes' kids, which Parker loved. The first time Nick had done so, Parker was worried about how Mercedes and Kiara would deal with it. But both women seemed okay, more than okay, with his brother's syntax.

"I would marry that woman on Christmas day. On Halloween. On any random Tuesday night after pizza and chocolate milk. I would marry her in sweats, with her hair pulled up in those cute, sexy buns she does. I would marry her and drive her into the next county and call it a honeymoon. I would fly her to Paris for the wedding of her dreams, Parker." Nick's voice was small and tight. "You get what I'm saying? I will do anything to make that woman my wife."

Parker nodded, but he looked away from Nick's intense stare.

"Anything to get her into your big boy bed," Parker said in a soft, singsong voice.

Nick barked a begrudging laugh, but he shook his head.

"She completes this family. She completes me." Nick propped his hands on his hips. "I hate every minute that we could be together and we're not."

"I know." Parker nodded. "I get it."

Nick's intense stare hung on Parker's face and probed deeper, as if he was trying to read his mind. He was; Parker knew damned well Nick was trying to read his mind. Worse yet, he knew Nick saw far too much in the firm set of his jaw and the frown over his eyes.

"I know you do," Nick mumbled as he finally turned away and reached over to scoop up the ball that had rolled to a stop near his foot. Parker watched Nick execute a perfect jump shot, shocked by Nick's comment, wondering if his big brother was going to add anything. But Nick only rebounded the ball as it bounced back to him after swishing through the net. He flipped the ball to Parker without looking at him. Parker dribbled further out on the driveway and put the ball up for a long shot. The ball sailed just short of the rim and bounced into the garage. Parker muttered with frustration as it bounced up and hit the bumper of Cedes' car.

"Too much," Nick told him.

"What?" Parker shot him a look telling him he thought he was nuts. He'd just put up an airball, missed the rim and backboard and everything, and Nick was telling him too much?

"You're taking on too much at a time." Nick still didn't look at him. Parker retrieved the ball from where it had stopped, wedged against Cedes' back tire. From the corner of his eye, he saw Nick reach down for his beer and take a long swallow. No desire to hear Nick explain his comment, Parker put another shot up. This one banged the backboard and bounced wild to the right.

"Dammit." Parker huffed out a sigh and tipped his chin to his chest. He propped his hands on his hips as Nick set his bottle down and spun around to look at him again.

"Start smaller and go big."

"What the hell are you talking about, Nick?"

"You don't walk onto the wood and shoot your first shot from half-court."

Parker arched his eyebrows, but Nick ignored him and

grabbed the ball from the yard. He dribbled once. Twice. Finally turned to look at Parker.

"Thanks for the advice, Coach." Parker's voice was cool, coated with sarcasm.

"Seriously, Parker." Nick shook his head and shrugged his shoulders. "What the hell are you doing?"

"I can sink twice as many shots as you, and I don't need your—"

"I'm not talking about shooting baskets." Nick dropped his head back to look at the sky and cut loose with a frustrated groan. "What're you doing with her?"

"Stay out of it, Nick," Parker muttered. "I didn't ask for your opinion."

"Except you kinda did, though, Parker," Nick reminded him. "Remember? And I told you I didn't think it was a good idea?"

"Well, it's not your business now." Parker cringed inwardly when he heard the petulance in his voice. He had come to Nick and Mercedes before making a decision, and they talked about it, and yep, Nick had been super negative about it. But Parker had already made up his mind the night he had come here looking for *support*. Not *advice*. He had wanted Mercedes at least to be his champion.

And she kind of had been, hadn't she?

"Why not start at the beginning with her? Why not—?"

"She wants a baby, Nick!" Parker snapped as he stepped toward his brother and swatted the ball away from him. He put it down in a dribble and then aimed it at the basket. The ball swished through the net and bounced back to him. "She wants a baby. I spent my entire summer watching her and wanting her, and she hit me up to father a child."

"Yeah, okay, but do it right, man."

"What does that mean?" Parker shook his head. "What does that mean, Nick? I'm dying to know what you would do in my shoes. You handled things with Mercedes so well."

Nick grunted. "Low blow."

"What would you have done? If Mercedes was hanging around and watching your kids, and she asked you to get her pregnant?"

"I would have said no," Nick answered simply. "I have kids. I know the responsibility—"

"I call bullshit." Parker shrugged. "If Mercedes had come to you and propositioned you to father a child for her, you would have been all in. You wanted her."

"I wanted all of her. I wasn't just—"

"I know that, Nick. Why do you automatically assume it's different for me? That I'm in this with for Vanessa for an easy lay? Or do you think I'm after her money?"

"I don't assume that, and that's the point I'm trying to make. You're being too damned thickheaded to hear what I'm saying."

Parker's face flushed with heat. He took a deep breath and reminded himself he was considering punching his brother. And more than that, if he punched his brother, he would be putting on a show for Vanessa and disappointing Mercedes, to say nothing of scaring Maisy and Eli.

"What?" Nick stepped closer to him. "You gonna hit me? Go ahead. Take a swing."

"Dick."

"Even I see the way you're mooning over her." Nick threw his hands up in frustration. "Mercedes is inside right now planning our wedding with a woman who's just a business deal for you? Mase is in there hanging on Vanessa's every word, and you're still gonna tell me you're the hired help? That once you make a baby with her, you're gonna be able to walk away and forget her or a child you create together?"

Parker snapped his mouth shut and grinded his back teeth in anger.

"Is that what you really think of me?" His voice was deadly quiet. "That I'm the guy who wants to be in a woman's pants so badly he's gonna jump and take money—"

"Dammit, no!" Nick shouted. Parker heard the back door open, but he was too furious with Nick to look away from his brother at the moment. "You're a standup guy, Parker. That's what I'm saying, dammit! You played the field, sure, but you're not this guy. So why the hell are you doing this? What the hell's wrong with you?"

Both of them glanced toward the garage when they heard a loud cough. Mercedes and Vanessa stood between the vehicles; Vanessa was carrying Eli and looking down at Maisy, listening to the kid tell some whopping story. Mercedes, however, stood with her arms crossed over her chest, her head tipped, and a mask of horror on her face.

"Really?" she said quietly.

"Hey, babe." Nick cleared his throat and stepped away from Parker.

"What're you guys doing?" Cedes lowered her arms and stuck her hands in her pockets as she moseyed on out to the driveway.

"Just shootin' some hoops."

Parker thought the little dribble move Nick did was overselling his casual response, but he kept his mouth shut.

"Were you arguing?" Mercedes snatched the ball away from Nick mid-dribble and held it against her hip.

"Nope." Nick sounded like a kid caught arguing with his little brother by a parent. Cedes turned her eyes to Parker and leveled him with a cool stare.

"Just trash talkin'," he finally mumbled, because God no, they couldn't have this conversation right now with Vanessa, of all people, standing right behind Cedes. Not to mention the kids. Good grief, the way Maisy latched onto things? She might tell Mrs. Moaney that her uncle's job was making babies.

Cedes studied Parker's face for a few seconds and then dragged her gaze back to Nick. Parker saw the look between them, the way Cedes seemed to be warning Nick with her eyes. He was tempted to razz Nick about being pussy-whipped, but right now, he needed his brother to be pussy-whipped, because Mercedes was trying to support Parker.

Although it seemed that maybe Nick was trying to say the same thing. Just in a dicky big brother sneery way. Parker moved to grab his beer. He was exhausted. The last ten minutes with Nick had worn him out. And he had to follow Vanessa home and give her a follow up to last weekend. Since when did sex with a gorgeous woman like Vanessa Mayne feel like work?

"I should get going," Vanessa announced as she joined the three of them on the driveway. She seemed oblivious to the tension between Parker and Nick and Cedes, but

Parker figured she'd heard everything and was well aware that he and Nick had been arguing. She probably knew they had been arguing about her; she was just doing an admirable job of hiding her reaction. "Thank you so much for dinner."

"You're welcome, of course." Mercedes turned to her with that smile that made Parker feel at home with her, like they'd known each other all their lives instead of only just this past summer. "Please come back again. It's hard work being the only adult female around these two brutes."

Vanessa laughed, but Maisy tugged at Mercedes' hand. "What is a brute?"

Mercedes tilted her head to look down at Maisy. "Your daddy and your uncle. Sometimes, I like to hang out with pretty girls and talk about girl stuff."

"Like me and Band—Van? To talk about updos and baby's breasts?"

Nick barked a loud cough and smacked his chest painfully hard. "What?"

"Yes, Mase." Cedes snickered. "To talk about pretty hair styles and baby's breath."

"What is that?" Maisy screwed her face into a frown of confusion.

"It's a plant," Cedes told her. "With little blooms that look like clouds. People put baby's breath in flower arrangements."

"Cloud flowers?" Maisy mumbled doubtfully. Cedes snorted and nodded, but Maisy turned to look at Nick. "Daddy? Can I play with you?"

Cedes and Vanessa laughed softly. The whole episode made Parker's heart hurt. What if he and Vanessa made a child? So, they would have some incredible sex, make a baby, and Vanessa would hand him a check, and she would have a lifetime of moments like this with their child.

The thought of missing out on being a daddy stole his breath away for a moment.

"It was nice to meet you, Nick."

If Parker wasn't sure before that Vanessa knew he and Nick had been arguing about her, he was damned sure now from her reserved demeanor. That made him feel just as empty as thinking of Vanessa raising his child without him.

"Hey." Nick reached for Vanessa's hand and pulled her in for a quick, brotherly hug. Parker wondered if Nick felt guilty because it was obvious the tension between them made Vanessa uncomfortable or if he was aiming to steal a kiss to pay Parker back for his test kiss with Mercedes. Only knowing that Nick would never do that to Cedes made Parker feel better. "Thanks for coming by, Vanessa. It was really good to meet you."

"Do you hafta leave?" Maisy held the basketball now. Parker gave her hair a gentle tug and then leaned over to kiss the top of her head.

"We do," he told her. "But I'll be back."

"But what about Van?"

Parker winced and patted his hand over his heart. "Holy cow. I bring my friend over one time and already you're willing to throw Uncle Parker aside for her?"

Maisy smiled, but she ducked behind Nick's leg when she realized all of the adults were staring at her.

"I would love it if Vanessa wanted to come back with me to see you guys." Maybe he felt like going for broke, or maybe he felt like saying so because he was talking to Maisy. Whatever the case, he meant it, and that brought him straight back to the argument he and Nick were waging only a few moments ago.

Maisy took his word for gospel, as if by his saying so, Vanessa would surely be back again soon. She ran to Vanessa, dropped the ball, and hugged her legs.

"Goodbye, Van."

Vanessa's face lit up when she tipped her head to look at Maisy.

"Goodbye, Maisy. And Eli. I'm so glad I got to meet you guys."

Parker slipped his arm around her waist, called good-night to his brother's family, and walked to the end of the drive with Vanessa.

"I'll follow you home."

Vanessa drew in a deep breath. Parker watched her look around at Nick's neighbors' houses and the few cars parked in the streets, and then down at her feet, and finally, she met his eyes.

"You don't have to."

He didn't exactly want to go home with her and have sex. Good God, what was wrong with him? He almost touched his forehead to see if he was feverish. No, he didn't particularly want sex with her right now. But he did want to be with her, and he did want to follow her home.

"I want to," he said simply. She nodded. Parker wanted to kiss her, but she stepped away from him and walked to her car. He offered her a wave when she started the engine and then pulled away from the curb. Of course, he couldn't just kiss her goodbye like a guy kisses his girl goodbye. Vanessa wasn't his girl; she didn't want to be his girl or anything else special. She wanted his dick and his sperm. Best he remember that, or he would lose his heart, too, and not because she had it, but because she didn't want it.

16

Vanessa wasn't sure what to make of Parker's family. On the one hand, she loved hanging out with Mercedes and the kids. Mercedes was pretty and down-to-earth and happy. She'd talked a bit about how she had met Nick, how she'd shown up to interview for a nanny position and met Parker first. She chattered nonstop about love at first sight and how she fell for Nick, and she had tended to Maisy and Eli like they were her kids, even as she told Vanessa the bare bones facts about Nick's ex-wife.

The thing about love at first sight piqued Vanessa's interest. Of course it did. In fact, she was tempted to call Journey on the drive home and tell her about the conversation. Maybe if one Moore brother could fall in love that fast, the other could, too. Vanessa had watched Parker from afar all summer. She hadn't just pulled this baby idea from thin air; she wanted a child. She had wanted a child for a long time. But that didn't mean she couldn't be attracted to Parker as a man. Not just as a sperm donor.

She didn't call Journey, though, because her friend was already dead certain Vanessa was in over her head and just asking to have her heart broken. And also, because Parker was following her home, and as much as she liked Mercedes and felt that they could be fast friends, she was equally as sure that Parker's brother didn't like her and didn't approve of her plan.

Her stomach was in knots when she pulled her car into the garage. She was thankful now that she had only nibbled on her dinner, careful to finish the small portions on her plate. What if Nick had talked Parker out of it? What if he had reminded Parker of all the things that could go wrong with the plan?

What could go wrong with the plan? Vanessa wondered as she climbed out of her car. Parker swung his truck door closed and in a few big strides joined her in the garage. Well, they could work each other's bodies down to the bone and not get pregnant. How long would they try? Wouldn't things end up tense if that happened? Would Parker get bored with her and resent her for keeping him from other women? Would she resent him for not wanting to be with her? And okay, if she did get pregnant, Parker might worry that she would sink her claws into him the first time she might need money for the baby. Or heaven forbid, what if their baby had health issues? What then?

"Hey." Parker cupped her chin in his hand. "You okay?"

Vanessa blinked away the emotion gathering in her eyes and nodded.

"Yeah." She gave him a quick smile. "I'm good."

He was slow to loosen his gentle grip on her chin. "You sure?"

"Yes." She turned away from him so he wouldn't see any doubt on her face. Because she wasn't sure if she was okay or not. Was she being selfish? Asking a man to commit himself to sex with her *and only her* until she was pregnant? And then asking him to walk away?

Truth be told, she wasn't sure she wanted him to walk away. Especially after meeting his family tonight. Well, except his brother. Nick Moore probably thought she was a flake. Or a conniver. She doubted he looked at her and saw mother material.

Once inside the house, the knots in Vanessa's stomach pulled tighter. She tried to take a deep breath, but that made her feel worse. Tossing her keys and purse on the counter, she turned to Parker ready to call it a night. Maybe if she slept on it, if she had time to digest the evening, maybe those knots would go away. Or maybe distance from the evening with Mercedes and Nick and the kids would make the shiny halos on them fade a bit, and then she would remember she wanted a baby. Not a boyfriend. Not Parker. Not in-laws. Not another risk of a failed relationship and a broken heart.

But Parker was there when she turned to him, and his eyes were dark and hot, rather than brooding. He reached for her, and Vanessa breathed in his scent that was already familiar to her. Surprised, she gasped softly when he slipped his arms around her and sank his fingers into her butt to haul her closer. The knots in her stomach were still there, but there was heat now, too—a slow burn in her thighs and her core that needed tending.

But his kiss was tender. His lips caressed hers softly, almost gently, and his tongue slid over hers cautiously. Open mouth over hers, he waited for her to kiss him back, and when she did—How the hell could she not kiss that hot, sweet mouth back?—he slid his hands up her back and into her hair.

"I've been dying to kiss you since the second you walked into Nick's house." He kissed her again, a quick peck on her lips, and then stepped back from her.

Vanessa stared at him silently; Parker stared back. His eyes stayed locked with hers even when she licked her lips.

"No, that's not true," he said quietly. He shook his head. "I've been dying to kiss you since last Sunday around noon."

"That's when you left the house," she reminded him.

"I know." He nodded.

"You don't have to do this. Stay here tonight. I mean, you could have just stayed at Nick's. I don't expect—"

"Are you angry with me?" He tipped his head and eyed her with an intensity that made her feel naked.

"What?" She drew back, surprised by his question. "No. No, I'm not angry with you. Why would you ask that?"

"I dunno." He shrugged and turned to pace away from her. Vanessa watched without a word as he propped his hands on his hips and then turned back to look at her again. "The flowers. Are you angry with me for sending them?"

Vanessa whooshed out a sigh at the mention of the flowers. She wasn't angry. Confused, maybe. And her mistake, yes, but going to Parker's brother's house tonight had only added to that confusion.

"No." She pressed her lips together and shook her head. "No. They're beautiful, Parker."

He stared at her silently for a second and finally gave her a curt nod.

"It's just." He frowned and lifted a hand to rub the bridge of his nose. "Maybe I'm not Mr. Commitment. But I'm not—I don't—" He groaned, clearly frustrated.

"This is a first," she said softly.

"What is? You getting flowers?"

"No." She offered him a small smile. "A guy apologizing to me, making excuses for sending me flowers."

Parker grinned and tossed his hands up in defeat.

"I know you don't want this to get personal, Nessa," he mumbled. "But it's hard for me to be *that* casual about sex."

"Also, a first," she told him around a bigger smile. "I'm really not angry. They were a lovely surprise."

He nodded, but he didn't appear to be in any hurry to kiss her again or touch her. Or undress her.

"You don't wanna do this, do you?"

"Do what?"

"Did your brother talk you out of it?"

"Vanessa—"

"I'm not stupid, Parker. I know he doesn't approve of what I've asked of you. I know he didn't like me. And I know you guys were about five seconds from throwing punches about it on the driveway."

Parker licked his lips and laughed softly.

"Nick doesn't make my decisions for me," he promised her. "And he did like you."

"Mm-hmm." She nodded. "Still." Unwilling to whine to Parker about what his brother might think of her, Vanessa folded her arms over her chest and lifted her chin to stare at Parker boldly. "I don't want this to seem like…" She stopped herself before she could finish her thought. She had been about to say she didn't want it to seem like a job, like something he had to do. And yet, she had offered to pay him, hadn't she? So, by insisting that she wanted Parker only for his sperm, she was making sex with her his job. Something he had to do, rather than something he might enjoy.

Maybe this *was* a bad idea. She turned her back to him and made her way across the kitchen to grab a glass from the cabinet. She wasn't thirsty, but she couldn't just stand there and look at him anymore. She wanted him to take her upstairs and make that same kind of crazy love to her he had last weekend. But something felt off now, and she felt funny asking him for it.

"What if—" Parker started and stopped so suddenly she had to look back at him over her shoulder.

"What?"

At the counter, she turned sideways to prop her hip and looked at him expectantly.

"Well, I was gonna say what if tonight we just hung out? Like friends. Because I think we're both a little tense about the situation now." He arched his eyebrows for a second and then looked away with a shrug. "Like, now, it's not just sex. There're expectations. Now there's a purpose."

Vanessa nibbled on her lip and wondered if Parker felt as funny about being with her now as she did about being with him. Was he nervous?

"But I guess you made it clear you don't want to be friends," he finished his thought without looking at her again.

She did want to be friends. Dammit to hell, she wanted

a hell of a lot more than that after the short amount of time they'd already spent together. After meeting his family. After watching Parker interact with his family. She wanted to be friends. She wanted to know every damned thing about him. And God, yes, she wanted his mouth on hers and his hands laying claim to every inch of her body and soul.

Journey would kill her.

"Are you nervous about this?" she asked quietly.

Parker snapped his gaze back to hers and stared at her sullenly for a moment. She wished she could read his mind, because she had the feeling he wouldn't share what he was thinking.

"No." He shook his head, a frown creasing his forehead. "No. I'm not nervous. But like I said...I've never been the guy to stick in a relationship, but I've never been a guy who uses women for sex and walks away, either."

"Okay." She nodded, but she still had no clue where to go next. What to say, what to do. Should she ask him just to go for the night? Should she do a strip tease and see if she could interest him in making use of that kitchen wall space he had mentioned last weekend? Dig out family picture albums to share her life story?

"What if we sat on the patio for a while?"

His suggestion both surprised and comforted her.

"Sure." She shrugged and set her glass on the counter.

"Change your mind?"

When she met his eyes again, he nodded his head toward the glass. His lips tipped up in a small smile, putting her more at ease. She nodded but said nothing, taking his hand when he reached for her. Vanessa let him lead her to the sliding door and followed him outside. The sun was a fiery orange glow in the western sky, melting deep pink and purple across the horizon. Vanessa shivered at the chill in the air.

Parker sat on the lounge chair she used whenever he was working in her yard. Vanessa moved to sit at the table, but he reached for her hand and tugged her toward him.

"Really?"

He parted his legs so she could sit there between them, and when she did ease down to sit in front of him, Parker gently eased her back to lean on him.

"I've missed you." He kissed her hair and slid one arm around her. His words threw her belly for a flip-flop and her heart into her throat, and for a moment, Vanessa felt ten again, riding the crazy Rocket ride at the county fair— the one that completely flipped you upside down and left you deliciously wrecked and breathless and needing that same rush again.

That's what Parker had done to her last weekend.

She wanted more.

Just exactly what Journey had warned her about. Dammit.

"Can I ask you something?" He spoke so softly his words chased a chill over her skin. Heart stuck in her throat now—what would he ask her?—she nodded.

"What's your favorite book ever?"

"What?"

Certain he was going to ask her something incredibly personal and embarrassing, his simple question caught her off-guard. She turned her head slightly to try and look at him.

"Do you like to read?" he asked. Before she could

answer, Parker nuzzled her neck and caught her earlobe in his teeth. The sensation racked her body with a hard shiver.

"Now and then. Mostly magazines."

"Okay. What's your favorite book?"

"*Water for Elephants.*" Her eyelids fluttered closed as he rubbed his lips over the spot just below her ear.

"Would I like it?"

"I don't know." She sighed with pleasure when he nibbled down the length of her neck. "Do you like to read?"

"Mercedes got me started on books," he explained. "She's been loaning me all kinds of books."

"What're you reading right now?"

"*All Quiet on the Western Front.*"

"Did she give you that one?"

"No. It's a library book."

"Why are we talking about books?"

"Because I wanted to feel you relax on me, Nessa. You were stiff as a board."

"So." She cleared her throat. "Mercedes is a reader?"

"She's a book blogger," he told her. "She totally turned Nick's kids into bookworms."

Vanessa rested her head on Parker's shoulder. "Those kids are adorable."

"They are," he agreed. "I love the hell out of them." He kissed her cheek and then added, "All of them."

"Does Nick's ex-wife ever see them?"

Parker's chest heaved under her with a deep breath. When he spoke again, his voice sounded a bit harsh.

"She does more now than before Mercedes was in the picture."

Vanessa was dying for the whole story—everything from the beginning of Nick and Kiara to how it ended up Mercedes and Nick and how they all seemed made for each other. But she felt nosy asking him about something that technically wasn't her business and never would be.

She locked her gaze on Parker's arm around her waist and before she could stop herself, she brushed her fingertips over the back of his hand. Vanessa wondered if Kiara was jealous of the woman Nick was in love with or the woman her babies loved so fiercely.

"Like she wants back in the picture because she's jealous?" She hated herself for asking, but she supposed somehow, if she had to—if Parker called her out on the questions—she could loosely work her desire to get pregnant into a discussion about kids, Nick's kids.

Okay, probably not. She sighed, ready to apologize for asking, but Parker slipped his other arm around her and drew circles over the back of her hand.

"No, actually. Kiara left Nick. And I don't know. I guess she tried with the kids, but she didn't want to be a mother. She's very career-oriented. Very independent. She was okay with Mase when she was little, but the older Mase got…"

Vanessa felt him shrug.

"And then when she got pregnant with Eli." He shuddered behind her. "I don't know. Now, it's like she knows Nick has someone who loves the kids like she should. So, she's come around more…like she can just check in and see that they're okay and not feel responsible for them."

"Wow." Vanessa shivered. "That sounds kind of terrible for the kids."

"Kind of. And it was kind of rough when she first met

Mercedes. Insisted she wasn't the right fit for them. Kiara's kind of a snob with some stuff, and it bothered her that Cedes dropped out of college."

"Mmm." Vanessa took a deep breath, eyes on Parker's fingers drawing over her arm. "Guess she wouldn't think too much of me then."

"Why do you say that?"

"Well, I went to beauty school."

"But you own your own business," he reminded her.

Vanessa shrugged. "I do. And I have a business degree. But, I didn't like school."

"Nessa?"

She loved that he called her that. No one ever had. She had always either been Vanessa or Van. Even with Greg. That Parker had given her a new nickname that only he called her by made her feel special.

"Hmm?"

"Who cares what Kiara thinks of you?" His voice was a bit gruff, and for a second, Vanessa thought he was reminding her that they weren't a thing, anyway, and most likely, she would never meet Nick's ex-wife. "There's nothing wrong with enjoying beauty school more than getting your business degree. Nothing wrong with Cedes dropping out after a couple of semesters. That's Kiara's issue, not yours."

Her throat tight, she could only nod in response.

"You seem very fond of Mercedes."

"I am." He leaned his cheek on her head now. "She's perfect for Nick. They tiptoed around it for a while before finally giving in. And she's so damned good with the kids. That makes me so happy."

"I liked her," she said softly. She didn't add that she

would love to get to know her better. That definitely went beyond the scope of her and Parker's relationship.

"By the way." Parker stroked his hands up over her arms. The gesture made her shiver again. "Don't be surprised if you're ever around Nick again if he lays one on you."

"What?" She snorted and sat forward so she could twist around to look Parker in the eyes.

"Before they were together," Parker hesitated. "Well, Mercedes and I became friends before they did, before they ever admitted to each other how they felt. And I talked to her about things. I needed to know if there was chemistry between us, because I was sort of attracted to someone else."

Vanessa nodded and waited for him to continue.

"She's cute. We hit it off immediately. Had to know for sure."

"And what? God, please don't tell me you slept with her."

"No!" Parker yelped. "God, no. I kissed her. Like a test kiss. To see if sparks flew."

"And?"

"No sparks. She was already head over heels for Nick."

"So, what do I take from that? You're secretly pining away for your future sister-in-law?"

"No. As much as I like Mercedes, I was too attracted to another woman to even think about pursuing her, even if she wasn't into Nick."

"And what? That's already over?"

"It's you, Vanessa. You had me tied up in knots every damned day you were out here in that doll-sized bikini."

"Me?"

"And what I'm saying is that Nick is still a little sore over the whole test-kiss thing, and I wouldn't put it past him to lay one on you to get back at me."

Vanessa snorted and rolled her eyes.

"Wow. That's—" She shook her head. "I don't think Nick's gonna touch me with a ten-foot pole, Parker, I'm like a jezebel trying to deflower his brother."

"Nessa."

"No, no, worse. I'm a crazy stranger who asked his little brother to get me pregnant. He probably thinks I'm scheming to drain your bank accounts."

"No." Parker leaned into her and pulled her close. "Nope. Actually, I think money is the last thing Nick's worried about right now."

17

Since Parker had avoided Nick's house since the night Vanessa had come for dinner, he wasn't surprised to find Mercedes at his door halfway through the next week. Didn't mean he was excited about finding her there or that he knew what to say to her.

That night—dinner at Nick's house—had been both good and bad. Fun and scary as hell. Parker had been thrilled to have Vanessa there with him. He loved introducing her to Mercedes and the kids and, sort of Nick, though his older brother was definitely part of the scary as hell factor there. Parker loved seeing his niece and nephew baptize Vanessa into the family. Watching the kids climb over her lap and relax into her the same as they did with Mercedes had made him happy.

Happy in a way Parker had never known. Happy in a way Parker didn't know he needed to be happy.

Scary. As. Hell.

Because while for seconds at a time, he could forget the true basis of his relationship with Vanessa and pretend that they were a thing, and that he could invite her over for anything and everything and then take her to his home and crawl into bed with her and love her all night, the truth would come crashing back at him like a shovel right between the eyes. She didn't want that sort of relationship with him.

He had followed her home that night because, well, he thought he was supposed to. He and Vanessa had both been given the all-clear, so he assumed the sex fest would begin immediately. While he couldn't wait to taste her, couldn't wait to press his lips to hers and remember her sweet scent and the soft sounds she made in her throat when he touched just the right spot, he wasn't ready to start. The job. The sex fest sounded like every single guy's wet dream. Who the hell wouldn't want a woman like Vanessa Mayne willingly naked beneath him every damned night?

But. Sex. Without a condom. Impersonal, business-like sex. Even if it was incredibly hot, he had never been a wham-bam-thank-you-ma'am kind of guy.

And the money. That thought actually made him sick to his stomach.

They had snuggled together on the lounge chair. Talked about books and movies. It was the best non-date night he spent in ages. But he didn't tell her that.

He went back two nights later. Found Vanessa on a ladder washing windows. Hair twisted up in a messy bun, long legs bare under soft shorts, and face without a lick of makeup. Vanessa hadn't said anything, but he noticed the way she pushed the escaped strands of hair back from her face and kept her arms folded over her faded old T-shirt.

She had been embarrassed for him to catch her looking like that.

Parker helped her finish the last of the first-floor windows. She offered him frozen pizza. They ate in the living room on the couch where she apparently had uninspired sex with Greg and had more recently given Parker a top-notch blow job. TV turned to *Wheel of Fortune*, they played along as they ate, and once the pizza and Pat Sajak and Vanna White were gone, they engaged in a hot and heavy make out session on the couch.

He still hadn't gotten the whole situation right in his head, so he still wasn't ready to start operation-baby. But remembering how Vanessa had referred to sex on the couch with Greg as boring, he took his time undressing her and he worshipped every inch of her body as if she was the last woman on earth.

"You gonna invite me in?" Mercedes asked him now. "Or you wanna hang out on the porch?"

"Where's Nick?"

"He's having some daddy time with the kids," she answered. "They went to see your dad."

"Tab and Andrea?" He sounded hopeful, and he hated that Mercedes caught it, too. She quirked an eyebrow at the mention of her best friend's and her wife's names.

"If I didn't know any better, I'd think you were trying to get rid of me, Parker Moore."

"I am." He nodded.

"Remember that night you showed up at Tab's? They catered to you. Tab made you drinks, and Andrea fed you spaghetti until you couldn't move?"

"Um. As I remember it, Tabitha was mixing your

drinks, and you're such a lightweight that I had to drive you home."

"Details," she mumbled and shook her head. "Let me in."

Parker sighed and stepped back to let his brother's woman in. Did it make him a pussy that he wanted them to get married? No, nothing to do with frilly dresses and weird hairdos. He just wanted Nick and Cedes married, sharing a home, and maybe giving him another niece or nephew someday.

"I get why you would avoid Nick," she announced as she moved past him to go to the kitchen. Parker laughed softly as he closed the door and followed her. "But why are you avoiding me?"

"Just busy," he mumbled. He turned his back to her and dipped his hands into the sink full of dishwater. He had grilled polish sausage earlier tonight. That and a skillet full of fried potatoes had been dinner. Unfortunately, he was still cleaning up, and the leftover sausage was still on the counter, and Cedes would bust his ass about it.

"Right."

Even without looking at her, he knew she just rolled her eyes at him.

"What in the heck is this?"

Parker glanced at her over his shoulder to see her frowning at the sausage.

"Polish sausage."

"Well, I know what it is, but I thought you were watching what you were eating now. Pretty sure this isn't healthy. Looks like a heart attack waiting to happen."

"Done with the lecture?"

"Damn, Parker." She groaned. "This is bad, huh?"

"Nick's at Dad's house?"

"Yeah. Kiara was over earlier."

Parker flinched as he dried his hands.

"Everything okay?"

"Yeah, but she wanted to know if the kids wanted to go see a movie with her this weekend. And Nick was planning to see your dad this weekend. So. He went tonight. Mase is stoked about the movie."

"Kiara invited the kids to go to a movie?"

"She's trying, Parker."

"To be a friend, not their mom."

Mercedes sighed and raised her eyebrows. "It's better than it was."

Parker nodded his agreement.

"Give me a beer."

"Yes, boss." He turned to the fridge and grabbed two bottles. "Seriously. How are Tab and Andrea doing?"

"They're good." Mercedes nodded. She thanked him when he handed her a bottle. "Andrea's supposed to go in next month." She shrugged and twisted the bottle cap off. "You know. To be—"

"Yeah, got it." Parker cleared his throat. He didn't want to talk about Vanessa, but he didn't want to talk about Cedes' best friend and her wife going through artificial insemination to get pregnant, either.

"So." Mercedes took a long drink of her beer, lowered the bottle, and wiped the back of her hand over her mouth. Parker almost laughed. Yes, he had kissed her. Yes, she was pretty. But they were friends. Hanging out with Cedes was comfortable like motor oil, ballcaps on lazy days, and armchair quarterbacking. She was like one of the guys, except maybe just a bit more sensitive. At least more sensitive than his brother.

Parker chugged a long swallow, anticipating what would come next.

"I loved her."

"What?"

"Vanessa. She's perfect, Parker. Oh my God, she's perfect for you."

"She's not."

"She is. She's pretty, and she's sweet and fun. She's a natural with kids—"

"Mercedes, she's looking for a baby. Not a family."

"She likes you."

"Well, yeah, we have chemistry. We could have burned the paint off her walls last weekend, but that doesn't mean anything."

Mercedes leaned on the counter and studied him. Thankfully, she didn't seem to have more to say.

"Nick likes her, too," she finally mumbled. "Just so you know."

"Nick thinks I'm making a big mistake."

Mercedes looked away, but not before Parker saw her wince.

"I think at first Nick was worried about the legal ramifications. And the logistics." Mercedes licked her lips. "Now, if anything, he's worried about you, Parker."

"Well, you can both relax," Parker said pointedly. "I'm an adult. I don't need either of you to worry about me."

"Have you done it yet?" she asked boldly.

"Jesus, Cedes." Parker groaned.

"I mean, I know you had that kitchen thing last weekend." She waved her hand to dismiss the image. "But have you done it without protection?"

"Why are we talking about this?"

"You wanna talk to Nick about it?"

"No." Parker nearly slammed the bottle on the counter. He dipped his head and thrust his fingers back through his hair. "No, I don't. But it's not super comfortable talking to you about bareback sex."

"You had your tongue in my mouth, Parker," she reminded him. "And I'm gonna marry your brother. I think we've bonded."

Parker looked at her with a smirk.

"Sounds like the stuff of talk shows."

Mercedes laughed.

"We haven't," he admitted, but he refused to look at her.

"Cold feet?" She slid her foot a few inches to nudge the toe of his tennis shoe with hers.

"I don't know. It's," this time he dropped his head back to stare at the ceiling "it's a big step."

"Yeah, it is," she agreed. "You're talking about a baby, Parker. A little human life. You're talking about giving her someone incredible like Mase or Eli and walking away, never to know anything at all about your child."

"I know." He ground the words out through clenched teeth.

"That's not you." She touched his arm, but she was quick to drop her hand away from him. "You can't tell me you want to do that. You're crazy about Maisy and Eli. You really think you can service her, cash her checks, and walk away when she sees two pink lines? You're gonna miss out on a kid rolling over and a baby's first tooth and tucking a kid in at night and hearing him or her call you daddy?"

"Cedes."

"And what if she finds someone else? What if she gets married, and her husband adopts your child? What then?"

Parker's nostrils flared as he pulled in a deep breath.

"Isn't that the process women go through when they're pregnant? When they don't want children? When they're not ready? Don't women have to examine their conscience before giving a baby up for adoption?"

"Yes, of course, Parker. But—"

Mercedes was right. Her pleas for him to rethink his decision were like a hammer, whacking away at his last nerve, but he wasn't ready to admit that to her.

"What about guys who donate to sperm banks?" He shrugged. "How is this different?"

"Parker." Mercedes rolled her eyes.

"At least I'm getting incredibly hot sex from the deal, too."

Mercedes took another drink and set her bottle down next to his.

"Look. I am crazy about Nick. You know that. I would do anything for him." She tipped her head as she stared up at Parker. "But I care about you, too, Parker. And yeah, okay, some mad money, some crazy monkey sex with a woman who looks like a centerfold. Great."

"Exactly."

"She's gonna hurt you, Parker. You know how I know?"

"I thought you liked her."

"I do." She nodded. "But I wasn't just watching her the

other night. I was watching you, too. And you look at her the way you look at the rest of us."

"What does that mean?"

"You love her."

"I don't," he argued. "I'm not interested in love. In settling down."

"That's what you think. But you feel something for her. You start mixing that something with crazy, monkey sex, and you're a goner."

"Can you stop saying crazy monkey sex?" He arched an eyebrow. "It's not a good visual coming from my future sister-in-law's mouth."

Mercedes snorted. "Get your ass over to our house tomorrow. Have dinner with us. If she's not important to you, don't let this put a wedge between you and Nick."

"Your house," Parker repeated. Easier to rib her about the wedding than admit that Vanessa was important to him. "Really?"

"Shut up, Parker," she said with a laugh. "See you tomorrow."

Parker stood still when she pressed a kiss to his cheek. He watched her walk back through the small house and wondered how it would fit Vanessa.

Too small, probably. Too tight. Maybe too old. Too simple.

If she didn't stay in the house Greg built, she might eventually marry someone else and move into some other mansion on a hill.

And she just might do that with Parker's kid.

18

J ourney set a box of gourmet cupcakes on Vanessa's table and then turned to look at her. Vanessa had moped all week after Parker went home the other night. Without touching her. She wouldn't admit it to Journey, but she loved the snuggling with him on the lounge chair, and she loved talking to him about everything. She had been especially interested in learning more about his family.

Still, even after he told her he had kissed Mercedes to see if sparks flew in some bizarre test for chemistry level with her and then admitting to Vanessa he had been attracted to her that long ago, he had gone home without making love to her. Without touching those parts of her body that craved him. A sweet, soft kiss at the door. Nothing more.

The mope fest lasted for two days. Fretting over what was happening, over what he might be thinking, she had dug out a ladder and a bucket and started washing windows, of all things. Times like those, she hated Greg.

Nice of him to build her a castle and then run off with an older woman and leave Vanessa there to tend to the house and not him. She would sell the damned thing in a heartbeat if she had the energy to find something new and box her stuff up and move.

If she could find the courage. She still eyed that little brick bungalow. It was still for sale.

Naturally, Parker had shown up while she was in window cleaning fashion. Just what she wanted him to see if he was doubting his attraction to her now. Maybe they had had one hell of a one-night thing, and after sampling her goods, he just wasn't that interested in her or the deal he had agreed to. They hadn't signed any paperwork; she wouldn't hold him to it.

But the moping. Well, she missed him. Everything about him.

And then he had shown up and helped her with the windows. He didn't seem put off by her grungy attire or lack of makeup. He had hung around for frozen pizza and *Wheel of Fortune*, and he had proved himself insightful with his guesses. She supposed she should be ashamed to have assumed he wasn't a cerebral, word smart kind of guy.

Or the kind of guy who could do a woman and get her pregnant and walk away.

He had stripped her of every stitch of clothing that night, but he hadn't even taken his shoes off. With the TV droning in the background, he had kissed her everywhere, lingering each time he chased a soft moan from her lips. He had kissed her lips and her neck and her collarbone. He'd nibbled on her shoulders and her upper arms. Flicked his tongue over her inner elbows and wrists. The backs of her knees and her ankles. The most sensitive skin at her core. He had left that for last, teasing her for what felt like an eternity, and finally, Parker had given her wings and taken her to flight as a delightful orgasm climbed her body from her toes to the roots of her hair. When he kissed her goodbye that night, she had tasted herself and hope on his lips, but then he disappeared again, and the moping started all over again.

Vanessa didn't want to explain any of that to her friend, so she plastered on a fake smile and whirled around to fetch wine from the kitchen.

"I have a perfect cab for those chocolate caramel cupcakes."

"Should you be drinking?" Journey frowned and let her gaze lower to Vanessa's belly.

"Not funny." Vanessa groaned as she grabbed glasses. "Are these from Confections?"

"You know they are." Journey pulled a chair out and sat down. Still in her work khakis, she looked crisp and cute and a little bit tired. Dark hair pulled up in a pony-tail, her eyeliner smudged a tiny bit under her eyes, she looked ready to kick back and relax. Or maybe kick back and grill Vanessa about Parker.

"I love cupcakes from Confections." Vanessa sighed wistfully as she joined Journey at the table. "You came over here to interrogate me, didn't you?"

"Yep." Journey swatted Vanessa's hand away from the pink and brown box. Vanessa laughed and turned her attention to the wine.

"How's the party going? Lenore doing okay?"

"Yeah. She is. I think she's about got it wrapped up."

"So, what is it? A backyard barbeque thing? Cooler of beer and a Bags tournament?"

"Don't I wish." Journey rolled her eyes as she slipped her finger under the dark pink sticker to break the seal on the box. "Oh, no. Lenore went all out. This will be a fancy-ass shin dig. Three course dinner at Signature Estates. A dance. Like I want to work all damned week and then stuff my ass into a cocktail dress and shake it on a dance floor in a room full of my parents' friends."

Vanessa snorted and then coughed and covered her mouth to hide it.

"Laugh all you want, Van. Your ass will be doing exactly the same thing as mine."

"Joy." She pulled the cork from the bottle and poured them both a healthy amount.

"How's Operation Preggers?"

"Oh, man, don't." Vanessa squirmed in her seat. "That sounds like some cheesy sitcom plot."

"Sorry." Journey sounded anything but sorry. "How's Parker?"

"Fine."

"Not pregnant yet, though?"

"You know, not all women get pregnant the first time they have unprotected sex."

"Yeah, well, Lenore did," Journey mumbled. "And she proceeded to horrify me with those details every year starting with my twelfth birthday."

Vanessa pursed her lips. "To be fair, Gia Bartell got caught giving Shelby Morton a blowjob when she was twelve."

"Do you think she still had baby teeth—"

"Try the wine," Vanessa insisted.

"Seriously. I mean." Journey sipped her wine and nodded appreciatively. "Are you charting when you're ovulating? So you have a particular time to do the nasty with him?"

"I am, but no. We decided not to use it." Vanessa relaxed back in her chair, glass in hand. "And there's nothing nasty about it."

"Make me jealous," Journey whispered and squeezed her eyes closed.

"Honestly, Journey, we haven't had unprotected sex yet." Vanessa kept her eyes on the cupcake box. "Please, may I have a cupcake now?"

"Why haven't you?"

"I don't know." Vanessa shrugged dramatically. "He's been over a few times. I had dinner with his brother's family—"

"Is that wise? Fraternizing with his family?"

"I dunno." Vanessa's mouth watered when Journey opened the box and lifted a cupcake from it. "But his soon to be sister-in-law sort of asked me to do her hair for her wedding. And Nick's little girl's hair. And maybe even Nick's."

Journey simply stared at her.

"And I might have volunteered to help Mercedes with anything she might need for the wedding."

"Have a cupcake." Journey pushed it at her. "Are you insane?"

"I liked her. You would like her. She's fun. The kids are adorable, J."

"You asked Parker to have sex with you because you want a baby. The next thing you know, he comes over with condoms to have practice sex to quote *break the ice*.

And you tell me it's mind-blowing. You gave him a blowjob so memorable he sent you a gorgeous bouquet of flowers. And now you tell me you're gonna help Mercedes with her wedding stuff?"

Vanessa peeled the paper cup from the cupcake and nodded. She stuffed the chocolate and caramel concoction into her mouth for a bite and moaned at the delectable flavor.

"He was here a couple of nights ago," she said with a mouthful.

"But you didn't have sex?"

"No, but he performed for me. Good grief, that man knows what he's doing with oral sex."

"I hate you." Journey narrowed her eyes at Vanessa.

"Sorry."

"Does he have any single friends?"

"I can ask." Vanessa winked.

"What you're doing with him isn't business, Vanessa."

"What's so wrong with me liking to be around him? Does it have to be sterile and scientific? Should we only shove our pants out of the way and grope around in the dark? How's that different from just going to a sperm bank?" Vanessa jumped when her doorbell rang.

"Expecting someone?" Journey asked her.

"No."

"Is it him?"

"Probably."

Journey's grin put the fear of God in Vanessa. She stood slowly.

"What you're doing is dangerous," Journey said quietly. "You're falling for him when you've told him you only want a temporary sexual relationship. He might be lining up women to take your place the second—"

The doorbell rang again.

"Behave. Do you hear me? Be. Have. Your. Self."

At least this time, she was dressed better. Dark skinny jeans and a navy blouse. Bare feet. Her hair was tucked up in a messy bun again, but she had on makeup, even lip gloss. Although she might have licked it off a minute ago when she took a bite of that cupcake.

"Hi." Shoulders hunched and hands in his pockets, Parker looked more like a high school kid with a brand-new driver's license there to pick her up for a first date than the man who had completely wrecked her the other night with his mouth.

"Hi."

She opened the door wider and welcomed him inside. As she moved to close the door, Parker cupped her face in his hands and kissed her. The long, slow, wet kiss caught her by surprise, and for just a second, she forgot Journey was in her kitchen. Or more likely, standing somewhere just behind them watching.

"You had," Parker drew back and flicked the tip of his tongue over the center of her upper lip, "a bit of frosting right there."

Vanessa grinned and ducked her chin.

"And that kiss tasted like chocolate and caramel, and either you're gonna have to kiss me again or please, God, tell me you have more of that delicious whatever in the kitchen."

"More in the kitchen."

Before she could slip away from him, he snatched her

wrist and pulled her back. A heavy shiver raced up her spine when he leaned in to whisper in her ear.

"Better yet, let's go upstairs and play with that frosting. I know just where I want it."

Vanessa felt her knees go weak and heat flood her face and fingertips and the exact spot where Parker wanted the frosting.

"Come and meet my friend."

"Really?" He grinned and tipped his head. "I get to meet one of your friends?"

"Yep, and if you're lucky, she'll give you a cupcake."

Parker followed her, fingers still linked with hers.

"Let's not tell her what I just said I wanted to do with those cupcakes," he said quietly, so only Vanessa heard him. Vanessa laughed, even though his words reddened her cheeks. Journey was still at the table, head bent over her phone, when Vanessa led him into the kitchen.

"Journey." Vanessa hoped she sounded nonchalant, like Parker was just another guy she knew and not the man who had been holding her heart in his hands for a couple of weeks now. "This is my friend, Parker. Parker, this is my friend, Journey."

"Hey." Parker oozed charm as he reached to shake Journey's hand. Vanessa eyed him curiously for a moment, wondering if he simply wanted to impress her because she was Vanessa's friend or if he oozed charm and sex appeal all over every female he met. Hadn't he admitted to kissing his brother's fiancé before she was serious with Nick?

"Hi, Parker." Journey offered him a reserved smile. She flicked her gaze to Vanessa's, maybe as if to make a point that she was behaving. "It's nice to meet you."

"You too." He sat down at the table, eyes on Vanessa now. "I've heard a lot about you."

"Well, that's terrifying," Journey mumbled. "Whatever it was, I've changed."

Vanessa snorted. "Parker, would you like some wine?"

"Um." He looked at the cupcakes and then at their glasses. "I would love some, but not if I'm interrupting a girls' night. I should have called."

"No girls' night," Journey answered. "More like a truth-seeking mission."

"Journey." Vanessa shot her a look to shut her up before going to retrieve a glass for Parker.

"A truth-seeking mission," Parker repeated.

"Have a cupcake." Journey pushed the box toward him.

"You sure?"

"Yeah. They served their purpose."

Vanessa kneed Journey's thigh when she returned to the table. She poured wine for Parker as Journey drank the last of hers.

"More?" Vanessa offered.

"I'm good." Journey stood up. "Thank you."

"Don't run off on my account," Parker argued. "Seriously."

"You know I know the deal here. Right?" Journey tipped her head at him and sat down again.

"Mm-hmm." He nodded.

"And doesn't that seem a little weird for you? Sitting at this table with a woman who wants to pay you for stud services? With her best friend?"

Vanessa felt her stomach flip a bit when Parker cringed and looked away.

"I suppose it's a bit weird," he finally agreed. "But we're all adults. And Vanessa wants a child."

Journey studied him for a moment. "What about you?"

"What about me?"

"Don't you want kids?"

"Maybe someday."

"And someday when you meet Mrs. Right, and you have a family with her, and Parker or Vanessa Junior comes knocking on your door to claim you? What then?"

"Journey, what part of *behave yourself* do you not understand?" Vanessa groaned as she dropped into her seat again.

"I'm just concerned for you, Van."

"I get it, Journey." Parker nodded. "I get your concern. The last thing I want is for anyone to get hurt. Not Vanessa. Not a child. Not anyone in my future. But I don't see the harm in a woman wanting a child. She's not interested in a relationship, but she wants children. That should be okay."

"It is okay," Journey agreed. "That's why there are clinics—"

"Journey, please?" Vanessa said softly.

"You're right." Journey nodded. "Not my business. Of course, I want this all to go however you both want it to go."

Vanessa watched Journey climb to her feet again.

"Let's do have a girls' night this weekend," Journey suggested. "You and me and Kate and LeeAnn."

"Kate's in Mexico, and LeeAnn's pregnant."

"She can still go out and have dinner with us," Journey argued. "Don't tell me pregnant women can't go out with their friends, or I'll chase him away with a baseball bat."

Vanessa glanced at Parker with wide eyes when he snorted.

"You should totally do a girls' weekend." He licked his lips, the cupcake almost halfway gone already. "This is so delicious. I could eat a dozen. Mercedes and her friends go out now and then. She loves it."

"Who's Mercedes?" Journey asked him.

"My brother's fiancé," he answered. "You would love her. Because everyone does."

"We should invite her." Vanessa heard the words roll out of her mouth and cringed, waiting for Journey to tear into her for it.

Journey mumbled something about business, but Vanessa didn't hear her clearly. She didn't want Parker to hear her, so she didn't ask Journey to repeat herself.

"Find a date for Lenore's party."

Vanessa stood.

"A date?" she whined. "Why do I need a date?"

"Who else are you gonna dance with?"

"You?"

"I asked Bryant Abbott to go with me." Journey shook her head. "Find a date. Call me."

19

P arker had to bite his tongue to stop himself from offering to be Vanessa's date. He had no idea what sort of party the girls were talking about. Didn't particularly care. He would willingly go to a square dance or a history symposium as Vanessa Mayne's date.

But he wouldn't invite himself.

Damned if he would even suggest it. She didn't want to *date* him. She wanted to use him. And even now, certain parts of his body were hard as steel, thinking about what they had done together. What they were planning to do together.

But part of him wanted to *date* her. To walk around the whole damned world with a beautiful woman like Vanessa on his arm, as his date. To spend that time with her. To see movies and share cocktails and dinners and laughter. He would love to get up early and go for a hike with her at the state park just under an hour's drive away. He would love to go fishing with her. Dammit to hell, he wanted to hold her in his arms and dance with her.

And he sure as hell couldn't handle the thought of some other guy getting to do any of the above with her. Especially holding her in his arms and dancing with her. Naturally, his mind decided now would be a good time to throw Mercedes' questions up for consideration. Like what if Vanessa got married? Because if she got married, odds were, she had found a man to love her and satisfy her every need. The thought of another man putting his hands or mouth on her made him see red.

And if she got married, that same man would probably adopt Parker's child and then that guy would be his child's father in all the ways that count. Because Vanessa sure wasn't going to tell their child when he or she reached a certain age that she had paid for him or her.

Vanessa appeared in the kitchen again. She hovered behind the chair Journey had vacated, a small smile on her face.

"What's wrong?" she asked him.

"Nothing. Why?"

"You kinda look like you want to kill someone."

Again, he bit his tongue. Couldn't very well admit he wanted to kill her future date. Dates. Yep, plural. Lovers. Husband.

"I'm fine." He shook his head.

"I'm sorry." Vanessa picked up the paper cups from the table and wadded them in her hand.

"For what?"

"Journey." She carried the muffin cups and Journey's glass to the other side of the kitchen. "She's just concerned."

"It's okay." He shrugged. "What kind of party was she

talking about?" Parker hated himself for asking, but maybe if he brought it up, she would ask him to go with her.

"Oh." Vanessa shook her head as she returned to the table. "Just a party for her dad."

"Mmm." Disappointed, he relaxed back in his chair. Vanessa studied him for a second and then apparently made a decision. Parker lifted his hands, surprised when she moved to straddle him at the table. She was feisty once they got started, but she hadn't made this sort of bold move since the night she had freed his dick from his pants and climbed on for a ride.

Her heated eyes roamed over his face as she cupped her soft, warm hands around his mouth. Parker's dick popped a tent in his jeans as she leaned into him and kissed him. The sweet chocolate and salty caramel taste on her lips was intoxicating. She delved her tongue deep into his mouth and swirled it over his teeth and his tongue. He wondered if she tasted the chocolate and caramel on him, too.

She kissed him for long minutes, barely pausing to breathe. Her hands smoothed alternately over his cheeks and up into his hair. Her fingernails over his scalp made him shiver with desire.

"You're gonna make me come," he told her.

"Kissing you."

"Kissing me." He nodded. "You have no idea what sort of dirty thoughts I have in my head."

She pulled away, but rather than climb from his lap, she moved her hands to unbuckle his belt and open his jeans.

"Vanessa."

"What about some frosting or...better yet...caramel filling..." She cupped his length and raised her eyes to meet his gaze. "Right here?"

His hips shot off the chair as he grinded into her hand.

"I love caramel," she told him.

"Love it best on your mouth."

"I don't know why we're playing with oral sex instead of making love. But I need you, so..."

Parker groaned when she freed him from his briefs. She circled his shaft with her fingers and looked over her shoulder at the cupcakes.

"There's three left."

"I can think of three perfect spots for all of that sweetness."

She smiled, but her eyes were hooded and hot, and her hand continued to squeeze him gently.

"Parker, I want this. Either here." She licked his lips. "Or here," she added as she leaned in to grind her center against him.

Undone, Parker reached for her blouse. He made quick work of her buttons, parted the material, and pushed it open. Vanessa shrugged it away and reached back to unhook her bra before he could blink. The scrap of silk tossed to the floor, Parker cupped her breasts.

Vanessa moaned softly, but she wasn't content with that touch. Parker watched her open her own jeans and then she stood to wiggle out of them. Parker watched her, his heart racing with growing lust and horror. She was getting naked. Vanessa Mayne was taking her clothes off with the intent to straddle him again and take him—bare-back—inside her body.

He adjusted his dick, a little bit worried that he would come just anticipating how good it would feel. And a little bit worried that he would come inside her, and in two minutes it would be over, she would be pregnant, and he would be kicked to the curb. While she met someone else. Who didn't know just how to play her body and make her fly apart in ecstasy. She could marry that dickless wonder—

"Vanessa." He slid his palms up over her bare thighs when she straddled him again.

She hissed with frustration and dropped her head to rest on his shoulder.

"Why?"

"What?"

"You've obviously changed your mind. Why?" She lifted her head to look him in the eyes. "Something your brother said? Journey? What?"

Parker sighed. He hated that he had upset her. But.

Yeah.

He couldn't do this the way they had originally agreed to do this.

"Nessa—"

"Or is it just that we had a crazy incredible night, and now you're ready to move on? My loss?" She climbed off of him again and snatched for her panties on the floor by her feet. Parker felt his heartbeat slow as she stepped into the blue silk.

"Do you not want me now? It was good but not good enough? Or is it just that you have too many women, too little time?"

"Damn, Vanessa. That's not fair!" He stood up so quickly, he nearly knocked his chair over.

"But something's changed."

"Maybe." He shrugged.

"Someone else?" She reached for her blouse and slipped it on. Parker wished she would button it, because the way it covered her breasts but not the skin between them was more enticing than an ice cream sundae with cherries on top.

"No. No, Vanessa, it's nothing like that."

"But?" She ducked her chin to her chest and rubbed the back of her neck. "Just say it, Parker. God, I'm humiliated enough as it is. At this point, it might be easier never to see you—"

"Do you really doubt how much I want you?" He threw his hands up in frustration. "Look at my dick, Nessa."

Both of them looked down as Parker moved to tuck his straining purple dick back inside his pants.

"Okay, I've been with a few women. But I have never loved being buried inside a woman the way I was with you that night. And one other thing, Vanessa Mayne. I don't lie."

"Then what's the problem? Don't tell me Journey scared you with the baseball bat comment."

The smirk on her face was ornery. Parker cupped his package and cringed.

"That's not even funny." He shook his head.

"Tell me," she whispered.

"I can't take your money."

"Because she called you my stud services." Vanessa turned her back to him and paced into the living room.

"No," he insisted. "No. This isn't just tonight. I didn't just decide this."

"Yeah." She nodded as she lowered herself to perch on the edge of the couch. "I noticed. You haven't wanted to touch me since we both got the okay."

"You wanna rethink that comment?" he suggested, eyes roaming over her and the sofa. Reminded of the orgasm he had given her the other night, Vanessa's cheeks flushed red.

"So, it's something Nick said."

"I don't—I can't do this. For money." He lifted his hands to cup the back of his neck and paced away from her. "I can't walk away from you if you get pregnant and think you'll never speak to me again, because what we had was a business deal."

"What're you saying? Like you would fight me for custody?" She tipped her head and narrowed her eyes at him.

"God, no!" He rubbed the heels of his hands into his eyes and gave himself a mental shake. "No. I'm not in the market for a baby."

Damn. He had just lied to Vanessa Mayne.

Little white lie, but still.

"I just—" He drew a deep breath. "Can we be friends, Nessa? Can we make love and make a baby and part as friends?"

"What do you get out of that?"

"Well, I still get to make love to you, and Sweetheart, that is incredible. I get to talk to you after you get pregnant. I get to wave at you, and you acknowledge me if we see each other at a movie. Or at the store."

Vanessa swallowed hard. "And the baby?"

"Maybe I could at least see him or her now and then?"

"As my friend."

"I'm not asking you to tell our child how he or she was conceived."

Vanessa licked her lips.

"Why do you want to be friends?"

"Because I like you," he said simply. "And I don't want to have to stop liking you or thinking of you fondly when we're done. You with a baby, and me with some bank. That's not—that's not who I am."

Face giving away nothing, Vanessa eyed him without comment.

"I know you're not that guy," she finally mumbled as she turned away from him again. "That's what drew me to you in the first place."

Parker managed to keep his mouth shut, because he was pretty sure anything he said right now would be stupid. Like if he were to admit to her that he hadn't felt like this before. With any other woman. That she was special. That he had watched his brother and Mercedes fall in love and maybe watching them fall, watching them interact with Nick's kids, had started a yearning inside him he didn't even know was there.

And then spending the summer with blue balls because Vanessa repeatedly put herself on display when he was around. Those little scraps of melon-colored bikini and all that luscious skin and the soft, sweet curves —any wonder that he was in over his head now that Vanessa had asked him to father a child for her?

Well, but, she hadn't asked that, had she? She wanted his sperm. No more. She didn't need him around to help with changing diapers or 2:00 a.m. feedings. She didn't want him to cart their daughter around on his shoulders or teach their son how to shoot a jump shot.

So, yeah, definitely too soon to say any of that. Maybe there just wouldn't be a good time to say any of that to her, because she was adamant that this wasn't personal.

"Is it gonna make this weird?"

Parker looked up, shocked by her question, and watched her fiddle with the buttons on her blouse. He considered going to her to stop her. He didn't want her to button her blouse and get dressed. Hell yes, he wanted to go back to that moment on the kitchen chair, her bare thighs over his, his dick sliding inside her as she lowered herself over him. He just needed to clear this part up first.

"What?"

"Being friends." She cleared her throat. "Is being friends? Gonna make what we're doing weird?"

"I'm not complaining at all, but everything about this situation is a bit—" He swallowed the word *weird*. Probably not a good idea to say that to her. "Unorthodox." Vanessa took a deep breath and considered what he said. Parker tipped his head to watch her think it through. "Do you have sex with friends?"

Vanessa's eyebrows shot up to her hairline. "Um. Right now, I have about three friends. And they're all girls, so no."

"It doesn't have to be weird."

"Does it bother you that I told Mercedes I would help with wedding stuff?"

"No." He shook his head. "That's why I wanted you to come over there. To meet them."

"Okay." She huffed out another deep breath and nodded.

"Okay?"

"I would love to be friends, Parker." She spoke so softly, he could hardly hear her. "Just so you know, Journey's going to be even more suspicious about this now."

"Because I wanna be friends with you? Rather than bilk you for money?"

"Not sure it's my bank account she's worried about."

"This is," Parker hesitated. "This is the first time in my life I've done this without protection."

Vanessa worked her mouth to answer him, but no words came out. She aimed a curious frown at him; Parker took the look as an invite to come closer. He stood in front of her and reached to unbutton her blouse again.

"This?" Chin tipped to her chest, she watched his steady hands on her blouse.

"I have never had sex without a condom," he told her. "Ever. I've never been in a relationship with a woman long enough to...not need it."

"Is that why you're freaking out about this?"

"Well, I mean, it's kind of a big deal." He shrugged. "I'm assuming you've been on the pill, so when you were having boring couch sex with Greg, he didn't bother wrapping it up. This is a big deal to me. And also, stud services." He shook his head and frowned. "It doesn't feel right to me."

Vanessa lifted her hands to rest them on his chest.

"So, are we doing this? Or not?" The tip of her tongue slid over her upper lip and drew Parker's eyes from hers. "I get it if you want—"

"I would very much love to be the man to get my friend Vanessa Mayne pregnant." He tipped his head. "The only payment I need for that is to know she will always be a friend."

Vanessa smoothed her hand up over his shoulder and then pressed her thumb to his lips.

"Parker, can we have boring couch sex now?"

"Oh, no. Sex between you and me will never be boring, Nessa. I promise you that."

Vanessa still wasn't sure about the whole friendship thing. Even after spending another night with Parker. Oh, she *wanted* friendship with him. She was drawn to *everything* about him, including his eyes and smile and easy-going charm. She had seen enough of him with his family in just one night to know he was a good guy, which since she had asked him to father her child should make her feel good.

But the whole thing kind of gave her butterflies now. Because first of all, after seeing Parker with his family, she was second guessing the wisdom of her proposition. She had wanted a decent guy to sleep with her and get her pregnant and then take money from her and walk away. What *decent* guy would do that?

She had asked herself that a good ten times since Parker had left her bed early the morning after their second night together. Parker might not be ready to settle into fatherhood and provide for a family now, but he was clearly that kind of guy. He had been raised to respect women, even if he did move too fast right now to catch feelings and end up in a relationship. He had grown up with parents who spent time with him; that much was obvious just from observing him and his brother with his brother's kids.

It should make her feel better about the situation, knowing she had found a good, solid man to father a child. But it didn't. For one thing, she felt guilty. Her proposition had been incredibly selfish and even a little self-centered, assuming Parker was a playboy who would jump at the chance for no-strings-attached sex. What if they did make a baby together, and Parker fell in love with someone else and flash forward fifteen or twenty years and that baby approached him? What would his wife say to that?

And worse than all of that—and this is where Journey would kill her—Vanessa didn't just want friendship and a baby from Parker. Somewhere in the past couple of weeks, she had started falling and though it was too soon, she was still zooming headfirst into feelings she didn't want. Feelings Parker didn't want. Feelings he wouldn't return. And no matter how things ended up now, Vanessa was going to have a broken heart.

She would do her best to hide that from Journey, of course, but her friend knew her too well to believe her lies. God forbid Journey got a glimpse of Vanessa's true feelings. She might go after Parker with a baseball bat, after all. Vanessa didn't want to see his eyes blackened, his nose broken, or his family jewels injured.

Besides, even though he was going to break her heart, it wasn't his fault. They had been open from the beginning. Vanessa had insisted there was nothing personal between them, and Parker had called her on that. Parker wanted some form of relationship with her, even if it was only friendship. If she fell in love with him, that was on her, not him.

Journey wouldn't see it that way.

"Hey."

Vanessa looked up from the magazine spread open on the reception desk as Mercedes pulled the salon door open and stepped inside.

"Hey!" Vanessa felt a flood of warmth that had everything and nothing to do with Parker. She liked Mercedes; she already thought of her in vague terms as a friend. Journey would like her. No matter that Parker had introduced her to Mercedes, no matter how things ended with Parker, Vanessa hoped she would get to see more of Mercedes.

"Are you busy?" Mercedes' gaze skated over the walls and then down to the phone in her hand. "I wasn't sure what time you closed."

"Technically, the door's unlocked." Vanessa grinned. "But I don't have any more appointments in the book until tomorrow."

"Yeah?" Mercedes arched her eyebrows. Her small smile was a little bit shy and a little bit hopeful.

"Do you need a cut? Color?"

"Oh, no!" Mercedes shook her head quickly. "I actually thought maybe we could get a drink. And talk about wedding stuff."

"Wedding stuff," Vanessa repeated. "And a drink. I mean, how does a girl say no to that?"

"Nick and Parker took the kids to the park. They

packed whiffle ball stuff and the wagon. They might be gone for a while."

"You didn't want to go?"

"Eli and I took three walks today." Mercedes moved further into the salon. "Two of which involved me pulling him in the wagon. And then we played tag outside. I love those kids, but I am beat!"

"One of my nephews loved playing tag when he was about Eli's age. Except it was more like Aunt Van chases Alexander everywhere all day."

Mercedes laughed softly. "Exactly. Anyway. I thought it was a good thing for Nick and Parker to hang out for a while. And maybe a good time for you and me to hang out."

"Perfect," Vanessa agreed. "Let me lock up."

"Are you sure? I know I just barged in unannounced—"

"Yep. It's all good. Lanie left over an hour ago, and Cherlyn's been gone almost as long. I get easily distracted." Vanessa picked up the magazine and waved it at Mercedes. Mercedes' eyes widened when she saw that it was a hair style magazine.

"Do you have anything for brides?"

"Of course!" Vanessa scrambled to grab the newest couple of style magazines for brides and tucked them in her oversized purse. She tossed her phone in, too and then grabbed her keys. "So, there's a cute little wine bar a couple of blocks east of here. Wanna go there?"

"That sounds perfect."

"We could walk."

"Yep." Mercedes hovered on the sidewalk outside as

Vanessa flipped the *Closed* sign and then locked the door. They headed east toward Sips, a trendy wine bar Vanessa and Journey had stumbled upon accidentally last winter. The neighborhood was a mix of residential and small businesses, which is why Vanessa loved it. She had a bit of walk-in traffic at the salon, but there was never enough commotion outside to make her nervous when she was there alone at night.

"I love fall." She tipped her chin back as she walked to study the tree branches that stretched in canopies above the sidewalk.

"Me, too." Mercedes nodded. "But I hate that Mase is in school now."

"Yeah?" Vanessa looked at her with a smile.

"I mean, Eli and I have a great time, but I miss having her home with us."

"I love that you're so into them."

"I'm not into them," Mercedes said softly. "I love those kids like they're mine."

Vanessa nodded.

"But." Mercedes laughed. "Mase has to go to school. And within a couple of years, Eli will be in kindergarten."

"Do you want more?"

Mercedes eyed Vanessa silently, long enough that Vanessa decided it was a rude question and she should take it back. "Sorry."

Mercedes dragged her teeth over her lower lip. "I do. Yes. Nick and I have talked about it. I love that you didn't say do you want children of your own. That you asked if I want more."

"I don't think you have to have a blood relation to be a parent." Vanessa shrugged. They crossed a quiet street;

Vanessa nodded ahead down the sidewalk. "Sips is just down one more block."

"Thank you for saying that."

Vanessa felt her phone vibrate in her bag against her side. She wondered if it was Parker. He called her yesterday. Texted a few times earlier today. Never anything serious or gushy. Just fun, silly things that mostly seemed to say he was thinking about her.

Nice. Because if they were lucky enough to get pregnant, she would like to think their child would have that innate sense of kindness and compassion that Parker did. But also, the fact that he might be thinking that much about her was confusing.

"My friend Tabitha was so depressed when she learned she couldn't have children," Mercedes explained. "I can't imagine how that would feel. She has severe endometriosis. So, she and her wife finally started talking about adoption. That was a relief. At first, Tab wouldn't even consider it. Now they're talking about artificial insemination. That maybe her wife can carry a baby."

"It's a lot to swallow." Vanessa hurried up the two small steps in front of the main entrance to the wine bar and pulled the door open. "Being told you can't conceive. That if you do, odds are, you won't carry a baby to term. You have to grieve over that before you can consider a next step."

Mercedes eyed her closely as she stepped inside.

"I have a girlfriend who had trouble," Vanessa answered. Mercedes gave her a quick nod before looking away.

"This place is so cute!" Mercedes looked around the small, dimly lit room. The interior walls were a rustic brick; the bar itself a gorgeous cherry wood. Hanging copper light fixtures sent a warm glow through the room.

"Isn't it?" Vanessa waved at the bartender. She didn't know her well, but she and Journey had been here a time or two when Samantha worked.

"Hey!" Samantha flashed them a smile. "Sit wherever you like. I'll bring you a wine list."

Vanessa led the way to a high-top table at the front picture window.

"This okay?"

"This is great," Mercedes agreed. "I've never heard of this place."

"Welcome in." Samantha approached behind them. "Here's our wine list. And on the other side, we have a few cheese trays and chocolate trays if you're interested."

"Wait." Mercedes slid onto her barstool. "You have wine, cheese, *and* chocolate?"

Samantha laughed softly.

"Best kept secret ever," Mercedes mumbled.

"Do you need a minute?"

"I'll have a glass of cabernet sauvignon," Vanessa told Samantha.

"Me, too. And I'm gonna just throw all my hopes into this question. Do you have a combination cheese and chocolate platter?"

Samantha grinned and nodded. "It'll be right out."

"Oh my God." Mercedes rubbed her eyes as the girl walked away. "This place is incredible."

"There are times when it's so packed in here, you feel like clowns in a circus car."

"Nice."

"You okay?" Vanessa tipped her head.

Mercedes dropped her hands to the table and sighed. "I am, yes. Kiara came by. Earlier. It's just…"

"I am so curious about Kiara. And Nick."

Mercedes laughed and licked her lips. "She's really not that bad. Ya know? I mean, other than she doesn't want to be a mom. She doesn't know how to be a mother and doesn't care? I mean, she cares enough, I guess, that she likes that I'm there for them now. But I don't get that."

"Parker said she's career-oriented."

"She is," Mercedes said with a nod. "And I don't think there's anything wrong with that. Apparently, neither of them wanted kids when they got married. Or at least, Nick didn't think he did. I respect a woman's right to choose not to have children, so I certainly get that she was unhappy." Mercedes frowned. "But I don't know how you look at those adorable kids and not love the hell out of them."

"But maybe she does," Vanessa suggested. "In her own way? Enough to watch you step in and be to them the person she can't."

"Maybe." Mercedes nodded again. "She brought me a bridal magazine. I was sort of stunned."

"You guys aren't close?" Vanessa laughed. She looked up as Samantha returned with their wine.

"Back in a sec with the cheese and chocolate."

"We're not, no." Mercedes sipped her wine. "But things are easier between us now than they were. She's trying, I guess? I get the feeling she doesn't have a lot of girlfriends."

"Ew." Vanessa flinched. "We all need girlfriends."

"Right?" Mercedes agreed.

"So. Wedding stuff." Vanessa rubbed her hands

together. "Still sticking with the Saturday after Christmas?"

"We might be insane," Mercedes shrugged, "but, yes, we are."

"I love it. I hope it snows. I hope we get a beautiful fresh snow just for your wedding."

Mercedes flicked her eyes to Vanessa's and grinned. Samantha appeared again with their cheese and chocolate.

"I do, too," Mercedes admitted. She thanked Samantha and watched her walk away, and then she turned her head back to Vanessa. "So. Before we talk about wedding stuff."

Vanessa flinched. She hunched her shoulders and tipped her chin down to her chest.

"Hmm." She nodded, sucked in a deep breath, let it out slowly, and then looked up again to meet Mercedes' eyes. "Yeah."

"Okay, Parker would kill me." Mercedes grinned. "But you know about that whole thing with the test kiss before Nick and I figured out we were crazy about each other." She shrugged and tipped her head. "We've all just kind of been all up in each other's business since then."

Vanessa snorted a soft laugh, but she squirmed a bit in her seat, anticipating an interrogation. Her mouth and throat were dry, and she wasn't sure she could find words, so she waited for Mercedes to launch the first question.

But Mercedes only sipped her wine and then reached for a cube of cheddar.

"He's a great guy," she finally mumbled.

Unsure if she was supposed to agree here, or if Mercedes was just warming up to her argument, Vanessa hesitated. The cheese looked delicious, but if she had to answer questions about what she and Parker were doing, she was going straight to the good stuff. She picked up a square of dark chocolate and nibbled it, eyes on Mercedes.

"I mean." Mercedes drew in a deep breath. "Don't you think?"

"I do." Vanessa's voice was small and quiet, but Mercedes heard her.

"He said you're not interested in a relationship. You just want a baby."

Vanessa squirmed again and cleared her throat.

"The last guy I was with," she started and then hesitated. "Greg built the house where I'm living now. We were together long enough that I thought he was the one. I mean, I just assumed after living together for a while, we would get married and have kids."

"I'm guessing he had other ideas." Mercedes picked up another piece of cheese.

"Yep. He left me for an older woman. Try that on for your self-esteem. Bad enough to have a guy walk out for a college kid with a spring break body."

Mercedes winced. "I'm sorry."

"He's been gone for a while. I took some time to wallow. To wonder what the hell was wrong with me that he had to find something else. And then I went out on a date or two, and it was horrible. Like, excruciating to sit through dinner with a guy who drones on and on about going four-wheeling or hunting. Or a guy who talks about his job. Or guys who think that since they bought dinner, you owe them something at the end of the night."

"I'll drink to that." Mercedes lifted her glass and tapped it to Vanessa's. Vanessa picked hers up to sip.

"And so, I decided I don't need a man. I don't need a

relationship. I want a child. I'm in my thirties. I don't want to wait so long that I can't enjoy time with my child because I'm older. I want to do this now. I have a business. I have a house, although I would sell it to the first bidder just to get out and start over on my own."

Mercedes studied Vanessa over her glass.

"And so, enter Parker."

"Well, I mean, have you seen Parker Moore?" Vanessa grinned.

"Oh, I hear ya." Mercedes waggled her eyebrows. "He's a beautiful man."

"He is. And I know people who know him. Everyone likes him."

"Because he's a good guy," Mercedes said again.

"Yeah." Vanessa sighed.

"Is that a problem? That he's a good guy?"

Vanessa chuckled. "Kind of."

"Explain."

"I feel like I underestimated how good, how responsible he is. I wanted to sleep with him. Get pregnant. And cut the ties."

"And that's not Parker Moore," Mercedes whispered.

"No. He's too responsible, too respectful to do that."

"And so?" Mercedes coaxed her. She finally picked up a bite of chocolate and popped it in her mouth. "Oh, man. This is delicious. Perfect with that wine."

Vanessa nodded.

"Did you call it off?"

"Did Nick advise him to do that?"

"I honestly don't know what Nick said to him about it," Mercedes confessed. "The first night he ran the idea by us, Nick was pretty adamant that it was a really bad idea.

He was thinking about legal and financial ramifications. But I figured this is something they should talk about without my input."

"You just told me you've all been up in each other's business," Vanessa reminded her.

Mercedes ducked her head, but Vanessa saw the smile on her face.

"I've talked to Parker. And I'm sure Nick's talked to Parker, but I don't know everything they've said to each other. I swear."

"We didn't call it off." Vanessa watched an older man out on the sidewalk. He had a heavy-duty dog leash wrapped around his hand and a chocolate lab tugging on the other end.

"You didn't?" Mercedes yelped. "Really? So, you've done the deed?"

Vanessa smirked at Mercedes and looked back at the man and the dog. "We did the deed a few weeks ago. Parker suggested a trial run to break the ice."

"Smooth." Mercedes took another drink. "I actually know about that. Something about cookies on the kitchen floor."

Vanessa was glad she wasn't trying to swallow, because she might have choked.

"He told you that?"

"He alluded to it. No details. But I mean, bareback?"

"You're asking me if Parker and I have had unprotected sex?" Vanessa grabbed her glass now to take a big gulp.

"That's exactly what I'm asking. And if you say yes, the next thing I'm going to ask is how it was."

Vanessa dropped her head back and hooted with laughter.

"You're sleeping with his brother. How do you think it was?"

"I'm guessing you guys tore it up, and when he left you had a smile on your face."

"Mmm." Vanessa cleared her throat and nodded. "Yep. Pretty much that."

"So. How did you go from deciding he was too responsible to having unprotected sex?"

"He told me he wouldn't take my money." Vanessa mused as she stared into her glass. "And asked instead if we could just be friends."

Mercedes rolled her lips inward and studied Vanessa closely.

"What?"

"So, you've gone from business associates to friends."

"Yeah, I guess so."

Mercedes looked like she wanted to say more, but she finally lowered her gaze to the cheese tray again and plucked a piece of Havarti from it.

"So. I kind of want a small, casual wedding. What kind of hair style would you recommend?"

21

"And Mrs. Moany made him sit out of recess, Uncle Parker!" Maisy threw her hands in the air as if she couldn't get over the fact that a boy in her class had to miss recess.

"Mase, Jefferson hit a boy in first grade," Mercedes reminded her. "You can't do that."

"I didn't do it, Cedes! Jefferson did!" Maisy looked at Parker and rolled her eyes. Parker snorted and reached to tug Maisy into his lap.

"Parker." Mercedes stared at him over the top of the table. "You're not supposed to laugh. These are teaching moments."

"No, they're just pretty damned funny moments with my favorite niece." He kissed Maisy's cheek.

"I'm your favorite?" Maisy looked up at him with wide eyes.

"You are my very favorite niece," he promised her.

"What if Cedes and my daddy get a baby? Will I still be your favorite then?"

Parker held his breath, stunned by such a question coming out of Maisy's mouth. What did she know about getting or making babies? Surely, she hadn't overheard Nick and Cedes talk about it, because the two of them were careful not to show too much affection in front of the kids. And also, *yeah*. Of course, Nick and Mercedes were probably going to have babies. Surely, they would both want more. Parker knew Mercedes would be thrilled to have another baby, one she and Nick created together.

That thought was a kick in the gut. Here he was trying to get someone pregnant, and the idea that Nick might reach that finish line again before he did kind of left him frustrated. Not angry, but a little bit jealous. Because whether Nick beat him to it or not, Nick's baby story would end differently, wouldn't it? Nick would get to rock his baby to sleep and then go to bed with the woman who gave him that child.

His wife.

"Parker?" Mercedes cleared her throat. He gave himself a mental shake and found her watching him curiously. "You okay?"

"Yeah." He coughed and thumped his chest. "Why wouldn't I be?"

"You looked a little freaked out for a second."

Well, why wouldn't he be freaked out? Nick had been married before, and Parker hadn't felt a twinge of anything, except maybe relief that Nick was stuck with Kiara, meaning Parker would never have to deal with her. But now, Nick had these two little monsters that thought he was some kind of superhero and this woman who was desperately in love with him. And that woman was going to be Nick's wife, and this time, this marriage? Parker knew it was the real deal.

And hell yes, he was jealous.

Forget twinges. Parker's whole damned body was tense with envy. He wanted this. Not Mercedes or Nick's kids. But this *life.*

With Vanessa.

"I'm fine," he mumbled.

"Mase." Mercedes drummed her fingertips on the table. "Let's get this paper done, okay?"

Parker cut loose a sigh, relieved that she had directed Maisy back to her homework. He assumed Mercedes was about to send Maisy out of the room so she could interrogate him. What the hell would Cedes say if he told her he was in love with Vanessa?

What would his pain-in-the-ass, know-it-all big brother say?

"But what starts with D, Cedes?" Maisy climbed off his lap and rounded the table to sit with Mercedes.

"You tell me." Cedes pulled Maisy into her lap and tipped her head to watch when Maisy picked up her pencil.

"Ummm."

"So."

Nick would be home at any moment, so if Parker wanted to talk about Vanessa—just in general, not admit to Mercedes that he was thinking about touchy feely stuff he hadn't totally believed until just recently—now was the time.

"Tiger?" Maisy looked over her shoulder at Mercedes.

"They're only on D?" Parker tipped his head to study Maisy's worksheet.

"Really, Mase? Diger?" Cedes gave her a fake frown and glanced at Parker. "It's a review sheet."

Maisy giggled. "What about dog?"

"Yes."

"Do you think Daddy will get me and Eli a dog?"

"I think Daddy has a ton of stuff going on right now." Mercedes smoothed her hand over Maisy's back. "Like the wedding. Did you forget that?"

"No!" Maisy clapped her hands together.

"And Halloween will be here before you know it. Christmas is coming. I think we might be a little too busy to think about a dog for a while."

"So, Daddy will get me and Eli a dog after you get hitched?"

Parker propped his chin in his hand and covered his mouth with his fingers to stifle a laugh.

"Well, not right away, but maybe one day, he might."

"I want a gray dog," Maisy decided. "I'll name him Hambone."

"Hambone?" Cedes snickered. "Why Hambone?"

"I don't know, but that's his name," Maisy told her.

"Draw a dog." Mercedes tapped Maisy's D paper.

"Can it be Hambone?"

Mercedes glanced at Parker and grinned. "Sure."

"Have you talked to Vanessa?" Parker asked before he could lose his nerve.

"Mmm." Mercedes nodded. Her eyes were on Maisy's hand as she drew a kindergartner's version of a gray dog named Hambone. But Parker thought he saw the hint of a smirk on her face. And he knew damned well that was for him, not Mase.

"Is that a yes or no?"

"She's texted me a few times today. And I talked to her last night on the phone."

"Are you kidding me?"

"Does that bother you?"

"Cedes, what about a duck?"

"Yep, duck starts with a D," Mercedes answered Maisy, but she was looking at Parker. "Does it?"

"No." He shrugged and sat back in his chair. It did bother him, but he couldn't explain why. It didn't make him mad. It made him itchy. Like he wanted, needed, to know what they talked about. If they were talking about him. What Vanessa was thinking. Or maybe if they were friends now, if Vanessa was friends with Mercedes, maybe the girls talked about girl stuff, and it had nothing to do with him, and he had no right to wonder about it or be jealous about it.

"She sent me some pictures of hair styles," Mercedes told him.

"Because you went out for a drink that night last week to talk about wedding stuff," Parker said with a nod, but he still wasn't sure if he believed that, either.

"Yeah."

"What about daddy?" Mase asked without looking at either of them.

"Daddy does, but what the rest of us call Daddy doesn't."

"I know that!"

"Is it gonna be a problem if she and I are friends?"

"No." Parker shook his head. Hoped he sounded nonchalant but doubted it. His insides felt strung up like a poorly cast fishing line caught in tree branches. "No. Of course not."

"I like her, Parker." Mercedes shrugged. "She's fun."

"She is."

Mercedes rolled her eyes.

"What?" Parker asked quickly. "No. I wasn't thinking that. She is fun. We took a walk the other night through her neighborhood."

"Yeah?" Mercedes quirked an eyebrow. "Did you pull her in a wagon?"

"What does that mean?" He narrowed his eyes at her, wondering if that was some new euphemism for something sexual. God, had the girls really talked about that? In detail?

"A wagon, Uncle Parker." Maisy lifted her head to look at him like he was crazy. "Like you pulled Eli in at the park."

Parker bit his lip when Maisy rolled her eyes.

"Mase, did you learn to roll your eyes recently? At school?"

Mercedes laughed out loud.

"Maybe in gym class?"

Maisy screwed her face into a frown of confusion.

"We played Steal the Bacon in gym." Slowly, she looked away and turned her attention back to the picture she was drawing of Nick.

Parker met Mercedes' eyes and mouthed the words *steal the bacon*? But Mercedes only shrugged and shook her head.

"When we were walking," he told Mercedes, wondering if he should just stop talking and go home or go wake Eli up from his nap so he wasn't the only guy in the room. "We were like, playing a game."

"Like hotscot?" Maisy asked without looking at him.

Parker bit his lips together and closed his eyes.

"I'd love to play hotscot," Mercedes mumbled.

Parker narrowed his eyes at her but looked back at Maisy. "You mean hopscotch."

"Yep. That's what I said." Maisy sounded exasperated.

"No. We didn't play hopscotch. We were making up stories about the people that lived in the houses we walked past. And we had to follow the alphabet."

"Explain," Mercedes demanded.

"The first house was Alice and Bill. Alice is a mechanic, and Bill's a retired piano teacher."

Mercedes stared at him silently for a long moment.

"Who started the game?"

"I don't even know how it got started." He shrugged. "But when we got to O and P, I thought she was going to die, she was laughing so hard."

"Do tell."

"Otis and Polly. Otis is a funeral director, and Polly is a Vegas showgirl. She flies home two days a week."

Mercedes sighed and nodded. "Okay." She squeezed Maisy's shoulders and kissed the top of her head. "You done there, Mase?"

"Yep." Maisy brandished the paper for Mercedes to approve.

"I love it," Mercedes told her. "I especially like Daddy's muscles."

Maisy turned the paper for Parker to see it. Her drawing of Nick did have some big bicep muscles.

"Daddy can lift Cedes' car," she told him.

"Really." Parker raised his eyebrows as if he were impressed.

"He said he would if me or Eli got stuck under it."

Parker shot Mercedes a look, but she shook her head to hold off any questions.

"Can I wake Eli up now?" Maisy asked Mercedes. Parker noticed Maisy wrap her fingers around Mercedes' wrist as she looked up at her with big eyes. Cedes looked toward the microwave, probably wondering what time it was.

"You can go check on him," Mercedes told her. "Daddy should be home any minute, so it'll be supper time."

"Yay!" Maisy scrambled backwards to get off Mercedes' lap, but Cedes caught her and held onto her hand for a second.

"Mase, don't wake him up. You know how crabby he gets when you wake him from a nap."

"I won't. I promise." Maisy nodded and took off at a full sprint through the living room. Mercedes opened her mouth—probably to tell her not to run—but she thought better of it and looked at Parker with a tired smile.

"Staying for supper?"

"No. Thanks."

"Hot date?"

Parker nodded his head back and forth. "Um, yeah. Vanessa and I are going to a movie."

"A movie," Mercedes repeated. "Oh, Parker." She shook her head as she stood up.

"What does that mean?"

"You're in trouble, buddy," she announced as she leaned over to kiss the top of his head. "You're in so much trouble."

"What—?" He climbed to his feet as Mercedes crossed the room to open the fridge. She pulled a plate of thawed chicken strips out and set it on the counter. "Why am I in trouble?"

"This is how it starts," she said quietly.

"How what starts?"

The back door opened, and Nick strolled in. He put his bag on the counter and gathered Mercedes in his arms for a hug and a kiss.

"Pregnant yet?" He lifted his head to look at Parker. He was teasing him, Parker knew that, but the whole situation still didn't feel right for Parker, and he wasn't in the mood for teasing.

"No but practice sure the hell makes perfect." Parker pointed his finger at Nick like a gun.

"Don't I know it?" Nick turned back to Mercedes.

"See ya."

"Enjoy the movie," Mercedes called as he neared the door.

"What movie?" Nick asked her.

"Vanessa and Parker have a date tonight."

"It's not a date." Parker pulled the door open.

"They're going to a movie?" Nick asked Mercedes.

"Yep."

"That's a date," Nick hollered as Parker stepped into the garage.

"You haven't taken me to a movie."

"Well, maybe we should have made plans for a double date."

Parker rolled his eyes, called a goodbye over their flirty mumbles, and headed out through the garage.

22

Movies. Long walks in the evening. Holding hands. Kissing. Kissing all the time. Things with Parker had gone haywire, and Vanessa loved it too much to fight it. They had sex—bareback sex, as Parker liked to call it. Since that first awkward time— Parker had acted like a virgin, had treated her like a virgin, easing inside her with caution, as if a lack of condom meant it might hurt—they'd had a lot of unprotected sex.

She wasn't pregnant yet.

The first time she got her period after they started sleeping together, she was torn between feeling weepy and sweet relief. She wanted a baby. But right now, she wanted Parker more. The other things they were doing, the romantic things most real couples did, were addictive. Every moment spent with Parker was intoxicating. And it would all end if and when she got pregnant.

She wouldn't be paying Parker any hefty loads of cash. No severing ties. So, if she saw him outside next spring doing yardwork, it would be cool to walk out and say hi. If they ran into each other in the produce aisles at the grocery store, even if she were so big she looked like she had swallowed a watermelon, it would be okay to stand and catch up for a bit.

But there wouldn't be more movies. No holding hands. Definitely no more sex, no more kissing. Vanessa wasn't sure what she would miss the most. The sex was so intense—so tender and then so dirty the next time, Parker blew her mind every time he took her body. But the hand-holding. And the kisses—the ones that led to nothing more than more kissing. Like they were greedy just to breathe together, to let their mouths hover together—that alone sometimes drove her crazy.

"Hey."

Vanessa motioned Mercedes to come inside.

"Hey, Cedes," she greeted her friend and then squatted down to say hello to Maisy. "Hi Mase."

The little girl beamed at her and then looked around the living room Vanessa had grown to like a little bit again, since Parker was often part of the décor now.

"Hi Bandessa." Maisy put her hands on Vanessa's shoulders. "Is this your house?"

"Sure is."

"Does your daddy live here, too?"

Mercedes snorted and closed the door behind her.

"Nope. Just me." Vanessa tipped her head at Maisy. "You like it?"

"It's gia-gantic."

"Gigantic," Mercedes corrected her.

"Right?" Maisy looked up at Cedes and shrugged.

"You are a breath of fresh air," Vanessa mumbled as she stood again. "C'mon in."

"Thanks for having us here." Mercedes took Maisy's hand and followed Vanessa to the kitchen.

"I hope it wasn't inconvenient coming here." Vanessa glanced at them over her shoulder. "The girls are working at the shop today. I thought it would be quieter and easier to talk and maybe practice some stuff here."

"Not inconvenient at all," Mercedes said simply.

"Want something to drink?" Vanessa offered. "I have lemonade. And apple juice."

Vanessa didn't miss the wide-eyed look Maisy shot up at Mercedes.

"One of each, please."

Vanessa chuckled. "Have a seat."

"Does Uncle Parker live here now?" Maisy asked from the other side of the kitchen. Vanessa took a juice box from the fridge and carried it back to Maisy. Mercedes ducked her head and covered her face with her hand.

"No. Why do you ask?" Vanessa put the juice box on the table.

"Those are his shorts." Maisy pointed at a small stack of folded laundry at the opposite end of the table. Mercedes coughed and then pushed her fist to her mouth, but Vanessa could tell she was laughing.

"Mmm." Vanessa nodded. "They are. He does my yard-work. Like he mows and trims and works on my land-scaping stuff."

Maisy settled on the edge of a chair across the table from Mercedes and nodded as if to say she followed. Vanessa watched her pull the plastic-wrapped straw from the box.

"Need help?"

Maisy shook her head. "I got it."

"Sometimes, your Uncle Parker is just really hot and gross after working here. If he has somewhere else to go, he showers here and changes clothes."

Vanessa and Mercedes shared a look over the top of Maisy's head. Mercedes arched her eyebrows.

"Does his mower live here, too?"

"No." Vanessa went back to the cabinet to get glasses for lemonade. "When he works here, he uses my stuff. The mower and weedwhacker."

"My daddy says it's a we deeter."

"It is." Vanessa nodded as she filled the glasses and took them back to the table. "You're right."

"Thanks." Mercedes took the glass Vanessa offered.

"I should have made cookies," Vanessa mumbled as she sat down.

"No," Mercedes insisted. "We're fine."

"I like cookies," Maisy whispered.

"Mase." Mercedes cocked her head at the girl.

"So. Tomorrow's October." Vanessa tapped her knuckles on the table and grinned at Mercedes. "Three months to get this wedding planned."

"Oh, don't do that." Mercedes shook her head. "I keep thinking it's cool. I've got this. And then someone says something like that, and I get all freaked out."

Vanessa reached across the table and touched Cedes' wrist.

"I'm sure you've got things handled."

Mercedes sighed and rubbed her face. "Mase, are we getting this wedding stuff figured out?"

"Tab is going to be Cedes' mater of honor."

Vanessa's heart spilled gooey, sweet stuff in her chest. Her lungs so thick with love, with longing, she couldn't breathe for a moment.

"Matron of honor?" she asked Maisy.

"Yeah." Maisy nodded. "And Andrea's going to be a bridesmaid."

Maisy looked at Mercedes to see if she said it correctly. Mercedes nodded.

"So, Uncle Parker is going to be Daddy's…" She looked at Cedes again.

"Daddy's best man," Cedes told her. "And Eli will be a groomsman."

"What is that again?' Maisy asked her.

Vanessa sipped her lemonade. If she and Parker had a baby together, would she or he be as delightful as Nick Moore's kids? Surely, part of what made these kids so adorable was something they got from their father, right? Something that ran in Parker's blood, too?

"Eli will be in front of everyone. By Daddy. Wearing a suit and tie. He'll be there to support Daddy, like my friends will be there for me."

"And I get to scatter roses, right, Cedes?"

"Rose petals."

"That's a really important job," Vanessa told Maisy.

"I know!" Maisy nodded. "I can do it."

"Of course, you can."

"Cedes said you're going to do our hair."

"I am. If you want me to."

"I do." Maisy smiled. "I want it to look like yours or Cedes', because you're pretty."

"Aw." Vanessa gushed and tipped her head at the girl.

"Thank you, Mase. Let's go see what we can do. We'll do some styles and see what you like."

"Can we?" Maisy blinked at Mercedes.

"Yes. Of course."

Vanessa led them out of the room and to the stairs.

"More room up here." She led them into the master bath. "Okay, kiddo." She plugged a flat iron in. "Wanna sit up on the counter? Then I can reach you better."

"Yes."

Vanessa groaned inwardly as she pushed the box of tampons to the back of the counter. She had now lived through the first period while trying to get pregnant. Just hadn't put the new box of tampons away, and surely, that would invite questions.

She lifted Maisy up to the counter with ease.

"Cedes has them." Maisy whipped her head around to study the box. "She says they're just for big girls. And I don't have to worry about it yet."

"Cedes is right." Vanessa glanced at Cedes and met her eyes. She prayed Mercedes wouldn't say anything, so when she arched her eyebrows and shook her head, Vanessa simply shook hers and looked away.

"How do you curl hair with that?" Maisy asked. "It's flat."

"It'll curl," Vanessa assured her. "I'm gonna spray a tiny bit of stuff in your hair, okay? It's to protect from burning it."

"Would that hurt?"

"No. But the heat can damage our hair. So we have to protect it. And that's why we trim our hair regularly. To trim off the split ends and stuff."

"Can you make my hair purple?"

Mercedes snorted.

"Absolutely not!" Vanessa grinned. "Your daddy would be so upset if I colored your pretty hair."

Maisy giggled.

Vanessa took the heat protectant from the cabinet beneath the sink and then pulled a wide-toothed comb from the top drawer. Maisy closed her eyes as Vanessa sprayed and then combed her hair.

"Cedes braids my hair for school."

"I bet it's really pretty."

"Do you love my Uncle Parker?"

Vanessa flinched, but she did her best to keep her smile firmly in place.

"Mase." Mercedes frowned and shook her head. "That's not nice."

"It's not nice to love Uncle Parker?" Maisy raised her hands, palms up.

"It's not our business. It's not nice to ask that."

"Sorry." Maisy ducked her chin. Vanessa hooked her finger under the girl's chin and tilted her head up.

"It's okay." She winked. "It's hard to know what's okay to ask, huh? I like your Uncle Parker a whole lot, Mase."

"Maybe you guys can get hitched, too."

Vanessa avoided Mercedes' eyes as she smoothed the first chunk of Maisy's hair with the iron. She twisted the iron and flipped a longish wave back over Maisy's shoulder. These days, Vanessa did an awful lot of thinking about marriage. Being married to Parker, specifically. She told herself it was because she had been talking more to Mercedes about her wedding plans. Mercedes had shared that she booked a photographer and a small reception venue. Daydreaming about weddings was normal when a friend was planning a wedding. Didn't have to have anything to do with the way Parker made her feel special, loved, when they were together.

"Your uncle is gonna make someone a great husband someday," Vanessa agreed. "But Parker and I are just friends, Mase."

23

"Not pregnant yet?"

Parker held his breath for a moment. And another. Counted to three, slow and steady. Let it out in a long, controlled sigh. And finally turned to meet Nick's eyes. He dribbled the ball once and then propped it against his side.

"Why are you here?" he asked his brother.

"Thought we could shoot." Nick held his hands up for Parker to pass the basketball to him.

"Do you know that before Vanessa came into my life, you came to my house approximately twice? In the past year?"

"Before Vanessa came into your life?" Nick pursed his lips. Parker shot a crisp chest pass at him, which Nick caught easily. "Is she, though? Really?"

"Seriously, Nick." Parker sighed and shook his head.

"Trouble getting things done?"

"No." Parker gestured for Nick to shoot.

"So, you guys are knockin' boots okay but no baby yet? Is that it?"

Parker, stunned by his brother's question, watched Nick arc a perfect free throw shot. The ball swished through the bare hoop on the backboard above Parker's garage.

"Knockin' boots?" He grabbed the rebound and dribbled back out toward Nick. "Really? Did you just come from the saloon, or did you give Miss Cedes the old lust and thrust before headin' over, pardner?"

"Don't be a dick." Nick shook his head. "What's going on?"

"You're the one being a dick." Parker snapped. "First of all, don't stroll in here channeling your best Wyatt Earp impersonation. Second, have I ever disrespected your fiancé that way?"

Nick didn't answer him, but the way his eyebrows shot up and goosed his hairline, Parker knew he had stepped in it. One thing to defend his friend Vanessa. To defend what she wanted, what she had asked of Parker. Quite another to jump down Nick's throat about respecting her. Comparing his relationship with Vanessa to Nick's relationship with Mercedes.

"Did Cedes send you over?"

"Actually, no." Nick scrubbed his hands over his head. "Cedes and the kids are at home. When I left, they were playing tag in the backyard. Their plans included bath time and story books."

"So, why are you here?" Parker asked again.

"Cedes was over at Vanessa's last week."

Parker nodded. "I know. She texted me a picture of that fancy hairdo Nessa did for Mase."

"She said they talked."

"Jesus." Parker grunted. "Did they commiserate over periods or something?"

Nick offered him a reluctant shrug. "Cedes didn't say anything specific. Just that you guys are still trying to have a baby."

"This is so crazy." Still with the ball trapped at his side, Parker raised his free hand to rub his face and his eyes.

"You're tellin' me this is crazy, Parker? What would Mom think?"

"Mom would love her," Parker said simply. "And you know it."

Nick clamped his mouth shut and swung his gaze to the street as one of Parker's neighbors walked by with a poodle on a leash. "I know." He nodded curtly. "I don't even—" Nick cleared his throat. "I don't know how long it took. With Kiara. I mean. We never planned it. And we were being careful. So." He turned back to Parker with a dramatic shrug.

"Are you here to give me a pep talk? To get my girl pregnant?"

"She's not, though, Parker," Nick reminded him.

"Screw this." Parker shook his head. He winged the ball to the back corner of the garage and stomped inside. Unfortunately, Nick followed him.

"This is dangerous."

Parker yanked the refrigerator door open, grabbed two beers, and slammed the door shut so hard, he heard the rest of the six-pack rattle in the door.

"You? Being here to give me a pep talk? Or to lecture me on the nature of my relationship with Vanessa Mayne? Yep. Damned right, it is, Nick."

"You, playing around with a beautiful woman like that. That's what I'm talking about!" Nick twisted the top off his beer and chugged a long drink.

"And what does that mean?" Parker asked quietly. "Parker Moore is a fuckup playboy and doesn't deserve a woman like that?"

"What?" Nick shook his head. "No. Jesus, Parker, no. I'm worried about you—"

"I'm not taking her money," Parker announced. "We're friends. My friend desperately wants a child, so we're sleeping together. When—" He cleared his throat. "If she gets pregnant, we'll remain friends. No hard feelings. No tension."

"When," Nick said softly.

"What?"

"When she gets pregnant."

Parker studied Nick closely for a long moment, but he couldn't read his face, and he couldn't make heads or tales of what Nick was saying. Near as Parker could tell, Nick was talking out of both sides of his mouth right now. Frustrated, wishing Nick could just show up to shoot hoops with him without using it as a pretense to lecture him, Parker turned away from his brother. He twisted the top off his bottle and tossed it on the counter.

"Parker, you're blind, man."

"What?" He swallowed a mouthful of beer and leaned his elbows on the counter.

"She means something to you."

"I care about her," he finally answered with an insolent shrug. Nick's hard stare dared him to say more, but Parker kept his mouth shut.

"Do you want her to get pregnant?"

Parker coughed and laughed sarcastically. "What kind of a question is that?"

"Just answer me."

"I mean, are you asking if I want a child? No." Parker hated the way that word, that *lie* tasted in his mouth. Afraid Nick would see through him, he kept talking. "Do I want to give Vanessa what she wants? Yes."

"So, you want her to get pregnant."

Parker heaved a sigh and dropped his head back.

"No, Nick. I actually don't."

"Why not?" Nick's voice was gruff.

"Because as soon as she finds out she's pregnant, she won't need me anymore. Will she?"

"You're in love with her."

Parker rolled his eyes. "No. I'm not in love with her. Look at her, Nick. I get to touch that body, to taste that body any damned time I want right now. Would you want that to come to an end?"

"Didn't you just give me hell for making what you're doing with her all about sex?"

Parker took another long drink and stared his bottle down, rather than look at Nick.

"I get it." Nick's words were like a gunshot in the quiet kitchen. "I get to spend the rest of my life with Mercedes. Yeah, Parker, I get it. And that's why I'm worried about you."

"If she gets pregnant," Parker mumbled, "she won't need me anymore. Not like this." Worried about what Nick was thinking, Parker smoothed a worn spot on the counter with his thumb and avoided his brother's gaze. "And I don't even mean the sex. I love being with her, Nick. I love the way she laughs when she talks about her family. Your kids. I love the smell of her hair. The sound of her voice when we're outside in the evening. Waking up with her in my arms."

Parker waited for Nick to say something. He chanced a peek at him when he didn't, but Nick was staring at the wall, apparently lost in thought.

"I don't want to lose that." Parker cleared his throat. "And if she doesn't get pregnant? Soon?" He shrugged and cut loose a soft, bitter laugh. "Maybe she decides I'm not man enough to get the job done, and she moves on to find someone who can."

Nick stirred. He plopped onto a stool across the counter from Parker and frowned.

"I don't know, Parker." He finally spoke. His voice was strained, like it hurt him to speak. "She seems to like you. Cedes thinks so, too."

"Nope." Parker shut him down with a firm voice and a head shake. "Not even gonna go there. She's been adamant that she wants a child. No relationship. No marriage. She doesn't want someone to parent with her. She wants a child."

"And what? If you push that, if you try to woo her—"

"Whoa, whoa, whoa." Parker squeezed his eyes shut and pinched the bridge of his nose. "Nope. Don't say words like *woo*. Just don't. There's no romance going on with me and Nessa. We're friends. I'm not gonna make myself miserable hoping that changes."

"Okay." Nick waved his hands in surrender. "So, I have to ask."

Parker rolled his eyes.

"How's the sex?"

Parker stared at him without comment.

"With all of that conflicting shit going on in your head, how can you possibly be able to satisfy her? In your head, you're damned if you do and damned if you don't."

"Satisfying her isn't a problem," Parker informed him. "Jesus, Nick, the sex is fantastic."

"Is she charting her cycle?"

Parker flinched and doubled over like Nick sucker punched him. "Dude. You did not just say that to me. Please tell me you did not ask me that."

Nick shrugged. "You're my brother. The woman you're with wants to be pregnant. If you guys were married, we would—"

"Double date and do holidays together, but we would not have this conversation. Absolutely never are we going there."

"What if the girls do?"

"That's their business." Parker waved his hand at Nick. "They can talk about it—"

"Parker, I'm not sure you're ready to make a baby if you're not mature enough to talk about Vanessa's fertility cycle."

"Eeeeww. Dammit, you did it again." Parker cringed. "And I'm not making a baby for me. This is about her. Leave that stuff to Nessa and Cedes to figure out."

Nick drained his beer and stood.

"Okay, how about some hoops? If I get hot and sweaty, I'll have to take a shower. Maybe I can talk Cedes into washing my back."

"Nope. Double showers are like big boy beds, Nicholas."

"Shut up." Nick growled, but his words were followed by laughter.

"So, Kiara took the kids to a movie, huh?" Parker followed Nick back out to the garage.

"She did, yeah, a few weeks ago."

"And it went okay?"

"I think so." Nick kept his back to him as he rounded the front of Parker's truck to pick the ball up from the floor. "She mentioned wanting to do lunch with them."

"And?" Parker caught Nick's pass and dribbled back out to the driveway.

"You don't do lunch with a five and three-year-old." Nick shrugged.

"So, you're not gonna let her?"

"It's not about letting her." Nick watched Parker shoot and then scrambled after the ball when it bounced and shot off to the right. "I want her to spend time with them. But Mase can be picky. And Eli eats most things with his fingers. Even pudding sometimes."

Parker laughed softly. "He's a boy."

"Right?" Nick nodded. "But what if Kiara decides it means he's not developing right? Not developing motor skills. Or etiquette? What if she lashes out at Cedes again?"

"I think Cedes can handle herself, Nick." Parker rebounded Nick's layup. "But I get it if you're worried about Kiara being harsh with the kids."

Nick propped his hands on his hips and hung his head. "She's better with them than she used to be. But, I mean, she's their mother, and she's just so mechanical."

"Give it time."

"I could have said the same to you. About the baby stuff."

"You mean we could have avoided you telling me I'm

in love with a woman who doesn't love me back? Talking about her fertility cycle, and whether or not the sex is satisfying? Dude. Really?"

"Pig. Loser buys pizza this weekend." Nick threw the ball up in a ridiculous hook shot. Parker groaned when it crashed through the hoop.

24

Ray LaMontagne's voice surrounded them in her kitchen. Vanessa glanced at Parker as she twisted the corkscrew into the wine bottle. She gave a slight tug and noticed the impatient look on his face when the cork didn't pull free.

"What?" She rolled her eyes.

Parker sighed and shrugged. "Nothing."

"It's not nothing," she argued. "I can handle a bottle of wine."

"I didn't say you couldn't handle it. But you raced in here like it was a competition when we decided to open a bottle."

"So?"

Corkscrew still in the bottle, she closed her eyes and groaned out loud. She was exhausted. She hadn't slept well in a few nights. It had been a long day at work; she'd done three colors, a perm, and four guy haircuts, as well as answered the phone and booked six appointments for tomorrow for updos for an area homecoming dance. If she was tired tonight, she would be beat tomorrow.

"This music has to go." She tapped the screen of her iPad and "Supernova" instantly stopped and threw them into silence. A tense silence.

"You don't like Ray LaMontagne?"

"Not at the moment." She went back to the corkscrew and gave it another tug. The opener came out with half a cork. "Dammit." She squeezed her eyes closed when she saw the bottom half of the cork still in the bottle.

"Want me to get it?" Parker offered.

"No, Parker, I've got it."

"Of course, you do," he mumbled. Forgetting the wine, Vanessa turned on him, hands on her hips.

"What does that mean?"

"Forgot you don't need anything from me but my dick." He put his hands up as if to stop her from saying anything.

"That's not fair," she argued.

"Right. Because I'm good enough to fuck you. Good enough stock that you want to have my baby." He shrugged one shoulder. "But as for anything else, you don't need me."

Vanessa sucked in a deep breath and twisted the broken cork off the opener. She stuck the corkscrew back in the bottle again, but she flicked her eyes over to him.

"We do more than fuck, Parker."

"Well, okay. I'm good enough for sex."

"That's not what I meant." She rolled her eyes. "We go out. We have dinner together. We see movies. We watch TV. We played golf last Sunday, or have you forgotten that?"

Parker lifted his arms over his head and hooked his hands behind his neck.

"What're we doing?"

His grumble took her by surprise. She gave him another sharp look as she pulled the last of the cork from the bottle.

"I'm sorry." She tossed the opener down on the counter and reached to open a cabinet. She felt Parker's eyes on that spot where her top rode up from her jeans and bared her skin. "It's been a long day. I'm tired."

He nodded.

"Long week." He sighed.

"Yep." She set two glasses down a bit too hard and winced, praying they didn't break.

"It just frustrates me that the only thing you let me do for you is sex."

Vanessa splashed the cab in the glasses and then set the bottle down. She caught a spill on her thumb and licked it, careful to meet his eyes when she did.

"I have no complaints, Parker." She shrugged. "You're giving me the best sex of my life. What's wrong with that?"

"Nothing, but why can't you let me help you around here? Why take your car somewhere for an oil change? Why call a plumber to put a new faucet in the bathroom?"

"Because you're not a plumber. And I'm not going to take advantage of you being around here to get some home improvement stuff done. And you do my yard."

"You pay me for that," he reminded her. "If you recall, you wanted to pay me for sex."

She sipped her wine and studied his face over her glass.

"Why are you so pissed that I can handle things on my own?"

"Because I'm here. I'm capable. I want to help you with that stuff."

"You're not my boyfriend."

"Oh, believe me, I know." He nodded. "But I thought we were friends. I'm just saying you could let me do something. Since I…"

"Since you what?" She tipped her head. Parker shrugged and turned away from her.

"Since this isn't working," he said softly.

"Since what isn't working?"

"You're not pregnant."

"Nobody said it would happen immediately." She put her glass down again next to the one she had poured for him and he had yet to touch. "Are you bored with this, Parker? With me?"

"Nessa, no." He threw his hands up now in anger. "I just feel bad. That I haven't given you what you want."

"Parker."

"Nick didn't even *want* kids, and he got his wife pregnant and it blew up his marriage. I've had my dick in you every night for the past several weeks, and nothing's happening."

"Something's happening." The whisper slipped out before she could stop it, but she decided she was okay with that when Parker's lips tipped up in a small smile.

"Do I have a timeline?" he asked quietly.

Vanessa picked up the glasses and nodded for him to follow her.

"Red wine in your living room right now isn't a good idea," he argued.

"Follow me," she insisted, looking over her shoulder to make sure Parker followed her upstairs.

"Vanessa." He swallowed hard when she led him into her bedroom.

"C'mere." She stretched out across the bed and patted the spot beside her.

"More sex isn't gonna make me feel better right now."

"Really? Because sex with you always makes me feel good. No matter how bad I feel when we start."

"Why do you feel bad?" he whispered as he crawled across the bed to lie next to her.

"Well, one day I had a client give me hell because a hair stylist who wasn't me ruined her hair with a color. She came back to me to fix it, and her hair was fried. Not a quick, easy fix." She shrugged. "And one day, my mom and I got in an argument about my oldest niece."

"Why don't you tell me those things?"

"I don't know." She shrugged and stroked her fingers over his cheek. "Parker?"

"Hmm?"

"There's no timeline. No deadline."

"But you're not gonna want me in your bed forever."

She wouldn't mind it at all, but she didn't say so.

"And some hot little coed is gonna turn your head one of these days."

"I can't imagine," he answered, his voice gruff. She flipped over to lie on her back. Parker took a moment to appreciate her flat belly and her breasts, but he only smoothed his hand up her arm.

"I had a friend," she whispered, eyes locked with his. "She and her husband tried for years to get pregnant."

Parker's eyebrows jumped. "And what happened? Do

they have kids now?"

"They do, but they had to do artificial insemination."

"Oh."

Vanessa stroked her fingers over the severe grooves in his forehead.

"Well, that's not us." He shook his head. "And, if I'm the problem, you could visit a sperm bank. Don't forget that's an option."

"I'm not suggesting we should do artificial insemination. And I have no desire to go to a sperm bank. Not saying you're the problem. Maybe there isn't a problem." She pushed her fingers through his hair and cupped the back of his head to pull him closer. Parker gasped and parted his lips when she flicked her tongue over them.

"Then what?"

"Maybe we need to take a break," she suggested.

"What do you mean?" He wrapped his fingers around her wrist and kissed her again. "You mean, you want someone else to do this with you?"

"No." She licked her lips, afraid to spill too much and chase him off, but knowing she had to say something. She and Parker weren't even a real couple, and they were already going through the motions, feeling the pressure to conceive rather than enjoying each other's company, each other's bodies. "Parker, there's no one else I want to do this with."

"So, what are you saying?"

"Maybe we're trying too hard."

The flash of pain in his eyes was too real, too harsh for her to bear. She lowered her eyes to his lips and traced his full mouth with her thumb. "We've only been doing this for a few weeks, and we're not enjoying it—"

"You said this is the best sex of your life."

"It is. And I meant what I said. It was never like this with—"

"I don't wanna talk about Greg." Parker touched her lips and shook his head.

"All I'm saying is when we're together now, it's work. We go to bed thinking this is gonna be the night. And thinking everything has to be perfect."

"You're the one who read that doggie style is a good way to get pregnant," he reminded her.

She laughed softly. "I did. But you have to admit, it's different now."

Parker sighed and dropped to lie on his back.

"I just—I know you want a baby. I see how much you want a baby when you're around Nick's kids. You're so good with them. And it makes me angry, jealous that Nick has this incredible gift. This perfect life. Which makes me feel guilty, because it didn't start perfect for him, and it still isn't for his kids, because even as great as Mercedes is, moms should love their kids. And I don't wanna be a dick to my brother, but—"

"Maybe we take a week or two." She linked her fingers with his on the bed. "See what happens."

"Like a week or two without sex?"

"That. Maybe we don't see each other at all for a few days." Vanessa propped herself up on her elbow to study his face. "I like you, Parker. We're friends now. So, I don't wanna hurt our friendship because we're resenting each other for this taking longer than we expected."

"Okay." He brought her fingers to his lips "Okay. I get it."

25

"I don't get it." Parker ducked his head and plowed his fingers through his hair.

"You know, you could move in and live in the basement. Pay us rent."

"Nick." Mercedes chided him. "Not now."

"What? Why? What's going on?"

Parker sighed and lifted his head to find Nick and Mercedes in an embrace across the kitchen. Dressed for work in a shirt and tie, Nick watched Parker over Cedes' shoulder. Mercedes patted Nick's arm and eased away from him.

"Sit down. I made breakfast," she told him. Nick leaned on the counter at his back and eyed Parker silently. He took the cup of coffee Mercedes handed him and sipped from it as he made his way over to the table to join Parker.

"What's up? Trouble in Sin City?"

"Nick!" Mercedes sounded shocked.

Parker wasn't sure if he should be amused or embarrassed that Nick's girlfriend was fighting for him.

"Well, it's not paradise, is it?" Nick grumbled as he sat.

Parker flicked his gaze back to Mercedes and watched her plate Nick's eggs and freshly sliced fruit.

"You just come here to steal my coffee? Or are you stealing breakfast, too?"

"I ate at home." Parker studied the contents of his mug rather than meet Nick's eyes.

"So, what's up? Is she pregnant?"

Something snapped in him, like a taut rubber band inside, holding him together. Parker looked up, ready to launch himself over the table and take a swing at his brother. Mercedes chose that moment to deliver Nick's plate to the table. Parker watched her stroke the back of his brother's neck. The act catapulted him back to last weekend, waking up in Vanessa's bed. Only, he had slid out from under the sheet, pulled his jeans on, and tiptoed down to the kitchen to fix her coffee and breakfast.

Awake when he came back up with a steaming cup and a plate of French toast, Vanessa had gaped at him, surprised—later, he learned she was thrilled—as she scooched to sit up and recline on the headboard. She had fed him bites of her breakfast from her fork.

And now, suddenly, they were on a break.

"Where are the kids?" Parker looked around. He dreaded this conversation. There was no way he would start it if the kids were slinking around in the living room listening in.

"Mase is reading to Eli before I take her to school," Mercedes assured him.

"In his room?"

"Downstairs."

Parker huffed out another sigh.

"Parker?" Nick stared at him expectantly, fork in his hand, hot food forgotten.

"She's not pregnant," Parker mumbled. He groaned in misery when Mercedes winced.

"It's only been a few weeks," Nick reminded him. "It takes some people years to conceive."

"Thanks." Parker snapped his mouth closed before he could say more.

"Is she upset?" Mercedes pulled the chair out next to Nick so she could sit down. "She seemed okay the last time I saw her."

"She's okay." Parker hedged around the truth.

"But?" Nick finally scooped a bite of his eggs up. "So, what? You're worried about your manhood?"

"Do you have to be such a dick?" Parker dropped his hands to the table. "I'm not worried about my manhood."

"Parker, just tell us what happened. You texted me this morning with an SOS. Asked if we could talk."

Parker felt Nick's eyes on him when Mercedes reminded him he had requested a meeting.

"It's tense. Things between us are tense," he mumbled. "I know we haven't been doing this very long. And I know some couples really struggle with fertility. I get that. I have a whole new respect for them, and this situation is nowhere near what most couples who are desperate for a child go through."

"Have you guys been fighting?" Mercedes guessed.

Parker snorted. "For about three weeks straight, we've been all over each other. Sex every night. Afternoon quickies. Morning sex when I wake up at her house. Shower sex. Kitchen sex—"

"Got it." Nick nodded.

Parker gave him the side eye. "At least you don't have to watch it, man."

"He's got a point," Mercedes said softly.

"We don't do it in front of him," Nick scoffed.

"So, is it—" Mercedes cleared her throat. "Getting stale?"

"God, no." Parker shook his head and pinched the bridge of his nose. "She's incredible. But, things have just gotten a bit tense. Last night we got into a fight about opening a bottle of wine."

Parker stared at the smirk on Mercedes' face with disbelief.

"Seriously? I would expect that from him." He shot a thumb Nick's way.

"Parker, you guys are doing more than trying to make a baby," Mercedes insisted. "Don't you get that?"

"What do you mean?"

"You're in a relationship." Mercedes shrugged.

"No, we're not. She doesn't want—"

"But you are," Nick interrupted him. "You go places together. You do things together. You bring her here more often. The kids love her. She's met Tab and Andrea. You're having great sex with her. And you're *fighting* with her."

Parker slumped back in his chair.

"You're in a relationship, Parker," Mercedes spelled it out for him.

"Well, maybe now I'm not," he answered.

"What does that mean?" Nick asked quickly.

"First of all, let me remind you that Vanessa doesn't want a relationship. She doesn't want me. She wants my—"

"Whoa." Nick held his hand up and looked around as if

the kids might have snuck into the room during the conversation.

"Baby," Parker finished. "And last night, after we fought about the wine bottle, she decided maybe we need a break."

"A break," Nick repeated.

Parker nodded.

"Maybe she just means from sex."

"She suggested maybe we shouldn't see each other for a few days."

"You can't go a few days without seeing her?" Nick's eyebrows shot up in disbelief.

"Well, I can if I have to, and no, this is not me pissing and moaning about missing out on sex. I want to be where she is. I want to be with her. Even if we're cleaning out her gutters, I want to be there with her. She's all defensive, insisting she doesn't need my help with anything. I mean, I get it. She doesn't need anything from me but my dick."

"Uncle Parker!" Maisy squealed. Parker cringed and shot a quick glance at Nick before turning to watch Maisy and Eli run up the last couple of steps to cross the living room.

"Hey! How's my favorite niece and nephew?" Parker gathered both of them for hugs and kisses.

"I helped Eli write his name," she informed him.

"Well, that's pretty cool that you helped him, and he did it!" Parker held his hand out for fives.

"I gotta get to work." Nick finished his coffee and stood to carry his cleared plate to the sink. "Park?"

"What?"

"Is she gonna call you? You supposed to go see her when the break is over?"

"I don't know." Parker shrugged. "We left it at break."

Parker noticed the look of panic fly over Mercedes' face. If Vanessa's break worried Mercedes, then he was doomed.

"She'll call," Mercedes promised him. He climbed to his feet and picked his cup up, too. "Actually, I've got some free time—"

"No." Parker met Mercedes' eyes and shook his head. "Please, no, Cedes. She needs a break. Not pressure."

"Okay." Mercedes shrugged. "I promise."

"I gotta get to work, too." He ruffled Eli's hair and dropped a kiss on Maisy's head.

"Why don't you guys go out later?" she suggested as he followed Nick out the door to the garage. "Get a beer. Do whatever guys do when they go out for a beer."

"Sounds good." Nick moved around Parker and walked back to the open door where Cedes was standing. He kissed her goodbye. Parker called a goodbye over his shoulder and kept going. Nope, he wasn't going to grab a beer with his brother tonight. Between that look of panic on Cedes' face earlier and the giant pit in his stomach that only grew when he watched his brother with his woman, Parker was ready to go home and wallow.

Alone.

26

"Why are you wearing those shorts?" Journey stepped back on Vanessa's porch and eyed her attire critically. Vanessa rolled her eyes when Journey finally made eye contact again. "You've had them since seventh grade. You have food on your shirt. And when was the last time you washed your hair?"

"With friends like you, who needs enemies, Journey?" Vanessa mumbled as Journey came inside.

"What is that?" Journey reached out as if to touch the pink spot on Vanessa's T-shirt.

"Stop it."

"Is that ice cream?" Journey sounded horrified. "Are you eating *ice cream*?"

"It's yogurt." Vanessa twisted away and led her friend to the kitchen.

"This is about Parker." Journey dropped her keys on the table and eyed the open magazine there. Vanessa fought the urge to straighten up the small mess. For one thing, Journey had already busted her with a glass of wine, an empty container of yogurt, and an open bag of chips. Wasn't like Vanessa could erase the picture from her friend's mind even if she did clean things up.

She didn't argue that her crazy dinner and the sloppy, old shorts—which she *had not* had since seventh grade, but yeah, they were old and holey, for sure—weren't about Parker, either. Journey was too sharp to believe any lie she could weave, and Vanessa was too tired to make up a story anyway. Instead, she simply dropped back into her chair and took a deep breath, ready to endure her friend's lecture.

Journey sat down across from her and reached over the table to close the magazine. She eyed the cover and then looked up at Vanessa again.

"You're reading a tabloid?"

"First thing I saw in the checkout line, so I picked it up." Vanessa sounded defensive to her own ears.

"Van." Journey groaned. "What's going on? I thought things were good that night I was here. When I met him. What happened since then?"

"We're taking a break." Vanessa's whisper was thick with emotion. Before Journey could react, the doorbell rang again.

"If that's him," Journey stood, "I'm gonna deck him. And kick him in the nuts."

Vanessa held her breath as she watched Journey head back through the living room to get the door.

"This better be good." Journey pulled the door open. Vanessa chickened out and looked away at the last minute. She wanted it to be him. But she didn't want it to be him. And that volatile mix of emotions in her head, in her heart, made her dizzy and frustrated. This is why she'd propositioned the guy for sex, for a baby, in the first place. To skip through all of the bullshit red tape and heartache associated with relationships.

Now they weren't even *in a relationship*, and she was moping around and feeling as bad—worse, maybe?—than she had after Greg had left her.

"Um. I'm looking for Vanessa."

Vanessa's shoulders sagged with relief and maybe disappointment, too, when she heard Mercedes' voice.

"And you are—"

"It's okay, Journey," Vanessa called from her spot in the kitchen.

"Mercedes. I'm Parker's brother's fiancé."

Vanessa ducked her head and pushed her hair back from her face. It was one thing for Journey to catch her looking like this. She and Journey had lived a lot of breakups and bad days and loss together; Journey had seen her at her worst and loved her anyway. Now, as Mercedes followed Journey back to the kitchen, Vanessa wished she had taken a shower. That she had changed her shirt at the very least.

"Hey." Mercedes pressed her lips together. "You okay?"

Vanessa nodded. "Yep." The chipper answer was obviously fake, but it was the best she could do.

"Because he's not." The words slipped out on a whisper. "And I promised him I wouldn't do this. But I can't *not* do it."

"Do what?" Vanessa cleared her throat.

"What's going on?" Journey butted in. "Can we catch me up please?"

"Parker and I are taking a break."

"You said that," Journey nodded, "but why?"

"It's not that big of a deal," Vanessa insisted. "We've been going at it pretty hard. Nothing's happening, so it's getting kind of tense. So. We're just taking some time to ourselves."

"His choice?" Journey assumed.

"No." Vanessa shook her head. She met Mercedes' eyes. "But what's the point if we've already reached that extreme? Look at Shelly and Craig." She glanced at Journey. "Took them years to have kids. Almost ruined their marriage."

"What's the point?" Mercedes repeated with a frown.

"Is he seeing someone else yet?" Vanessa dreaded the answer to the question, but the fear over cutting him loose and not hearing anything at all from him was a hard knot in the pit of her stomach. Might as well as get it over with.

"Are you kidding me?" Mercedes tossed her hands up.

"Sit down." Vanessa waved her hand at Mercedes. "I feel like I'm in trouble at school."

"Vanessa." Mercedes groaned. She pulled a chair out and sat down. Vanessa watched her avoid her eyes as she set her keys and her phone face down on the table. "He's so wrapped up in you, he's lost without you right now."

"It's not like that," Vanessa insisted. "Parker and I aren't together like that, and if he thinks that's what's going on, it's better that we don't see each other again."

"That makes no sense," Mercedes argued.

"I think it sounds pretty reasonable." Journey wandered over to the cabinets. Vanessa watched her pluck two more glasses from the cabinet by the window and then snag the open bottle of wine from the counter. Journey held the bottle up to Mercedes in askance and poured two glasses when she nodded. "Van just came out of a bad relationship. She's not interested in making the same mistakes with Parker."

Mercedes stared at Journey with a frown, but Journey ignored the look and sat down again.

"Parker's such a good guy. Why do you have to assume he would be bad for Vanessa?"

"Because he's a guy, and it's pretty obvious he doesn't want to be tied down."

"You're asking a good man, a family man, to get you pregnant and walk away, Vanessa." Mercedes turned her attention back to Vanessa. "That's not fair. It's not fair to him, but you're cutting yourself short, too. Let him be here for you. Let him in."

"Her last boyfriend—"

"Journey." Vanessa patted her friend's hand. "I love you, but I can speak for myself."

"I warned you," Journey mumbled.

"What? You warned her off Parker?"

"Look, Mercedes," Vanessa took a deep breath and continued, "It's not Parker. It's me. I don't want to deal with relationships. I realize it was selfish of me to ask Parker—that's all water under the bridge. We figured that part out. But I don't want to get caught up in the messy emotions and the ups and downs of a relationship. He *is* a great guy. He deserves someone who wants everything with him."

"You're pushing him away now, because you guys are exactly where you didn't want to be," Mercedes said softly.

"What?"

"You're in a relationship. Lying to all of us, lying to

yourselves, but you're in a relationship. Nick and I fell in love in his kitchen. Over his kids. *You guys* are pretending you're having sex to make a baby, but you're both in over your heads and feeling all of these messy feelings anyway. The same damned things you said from the beginning you didn't want."

Journey nodded. "Yep."

"What?" Vanessa and Mercedes looked at Journey, surprised by her affirmation.

"She's not wrong." Journey shrugged. "I told you that you'd fall for him. That you would get hurt."

"I'm just—" Mercedes started and stopped herself. She rested her elbows on the table, combed her fingers back through her hair, and groaned out loud.

"What?"

"He would kill me if he knew I was here. I don't want to piss him off. But I don't want to see him get hurt."

"How's Vanessa gonna hurt Parker Moore?" Journey rolled her eyes.

"He's crazy about her!" Mercedes yelped. "Vanessa, he's miserable without you—"

"Without the sex," Journey clarified.

"No. Without Vanessa. He's at Nick's house moping every night. Right now. Either he's running his mouth nonstop about *Vanessa this* or *Vanessa that* or he's stewing and brooding and ready to hit something. The only people who've made him smile since you broke up with him are the kids."

"I didn't break up with him," Vanessa argued weakly. "Things were just really tense, and I suggested we take a few days away from each other. I don't want him to get bored with me."

"It's gonna break his heart if you get pregnant," Mercedes whispered. She bit her lip and covered her face with her hands. "Because all you want from him is his—"

"That's not true!" Vanessa snapped. "I love—"

"Van."

"I love being with him." Vanessa squeezed Journey's hand. "He makes me feel alive."

"Then what're you doing?" Mercedes tipped her head and stared at her with big eyes. "Tell him that."

"Do *not* tell him that." Journey turned their hands over and squeezed Vanessa's this time. "Do *not* tell him that. Do not give him that power."

"Power?" Mercedes laughed. "It's not about power. It's about—"

"Mercedes, we're not you and Nick," Vanessa said quietly. "You guys are a fairytale."

Mercedes looked like she wanted to say more. Vanessa squared her shoulders, prepared for more. But Mercedes simply shook her head. "Look, I like you. No matter what happens or doesn't happen with you and Parker, I consider you a friend. I just hate to see two stubborn people pushing each other away and hurting. And I feel the need to remind you that the next guy might hurt you. Or the next one." She shrugged. "Parker might love you. *He* might be *your fairytale*. Why not give him that chance?"

27

Nick advised Parker to stay away from Vanessa for a while, to use that break she offered him. He rattled on and on about thinking through this mess—Nick's word—before jumping right back in. Parker ignored Nick's advice.

After a five-day break, he texted her, which in his mind didn't make him guilty. He wasn't begging to see her or begging for sex. He just missed her, and he wanted her to know he was thinking about her. Simple. The fact that she texted him back, that they had a twenty-minute text conversation about everything and nothing at all was anything but simple.

Parker was totally fine talking about movies and Vanessa's landscaping project and her nephew's soccer team's winning record. But why couldn't they have that conversation in person? Why couldn't he just drop by and see her? Curl up with her on the patio and have a beer and talk about everything and nothing at all?

Why did every minute they spent together have to be

about a baby? Making a baby? Even when they went out—Mercedes and Nick were right. He and Vanessa might be calling it something different, but they had been dating, hadn't they?—the pressure of giving Vanessa what she wanted was always pushing in on his lungs and down on his shoulders and making him smaller and weaker. He had no idea if she thought about trying a different angle or if she thought sex first thing in the morning was better for conception when she was about to tee off on the first hole of the public golf course.

But he did.

After another three days of texting and not seeing her, Parker was in a foul mood and ready to punch a hole in the wall. Any wall, he wasn't picky. He wondered if she missed him. If she was seeing someone else. If she was thinking about finding someone else to experiment with. If the problem was him. If he should see a specialist. Mostly, he didn't think that. They hadn't been trying to conceive very long at all, compared to so many of the infertility stories he had read and studied. In the big scheme of things, he felt guilty for worrying about it. Couples actually divorced over this issue. Some went hundreds and thousands of dollars in debt with medical procedures to no avail. Worrying about his ability to father a child right now made him feel selfish and immature.

Because his biggest worry was losing Vanessa.

And he had never really had her to lose her.

Restless with life in general now that he was involved with Vanessa, Parker visited Lucas Hooper at City Trust and Savings to talk about a business loan. Come to find out, he was enjoying the landscaping project in Vanessa's yard, and he was ready to delve into that side of the lawn business. Not to mention, maybe if he had something more to show than a lawn mowing business and a tiny house and beat-up truck, a woman like Vanessa might want more from him than sex.

Parker wanted Vanessa to want him for a whole lot more than sex.

The following Monday—over a whole week since Vanessa suggested a break—Parker couldn't stand it any longer. The nine days since they'd been together had crawled by, and Parker was sick of his own company. He knew Nick and Mercedes had to be tired of his surly attitude. He went home after finishing his last yard, showered and dressed in jeans and a T-shirt, and then headed to Vanessa's salon.

He had driven by it a time or two, once on purpose, since they had been together. Looked like a nice little place, not that he knew much about salons or hair studios or whatever they were. The building was a neat-looking brick strip mall in a quiet, mostly residential area. Vanessa's place was between an optometrist's office and a children's boutique. He had flinched the first time he noticed that. Did that bother her?

Had she wanted to be pregnant with Greg? Like, had they tried with no luck? Was not having a baby something that would cause her grief for the rest of her life? Why hadn't he asked her that? Parker had assumed that after Greg moved out, Vanessa did some thinking and worried that she was getting too old to have a child—ridiculous, in his opinion—made the decision to shop around for a baby daddy. But what if that wasn't the case? What if she had been actively trying to get pregnant for years?

The thought nagged at him now as he parked down the street from her place. He should know how deep this need was. How desperately she wanted to be a mother. They had skipped so much when they started, and the fact that she had insisted on skipping those details, the emotions, made his head hurt.

Parker curved his fingers around the back of his neck as he reached to pull the door open with his free hand. The conversation inside stopped the second he walked in. Vanessa stood at the reception counter, a pen in hand, her face frozen with surprise. A young girl worked on an older woman's hair at the end station, two empty chairs between her and Vanessa.

"Are you busy?" he asked quietly.

Vanessa cleared her throat and glanced at the other girl.

"No." She set the pen carefully on the counter, as if it had wings and it might fly away when she let go of it. "What's up?"

"I was hoping you could give me a trim."

She blinked at him silently. Parker looked around the space again, noticed two pedicure chairs on the west wall. The chairs made him think about the last time he had Vanessa naked, and she had wrapped her thighs around his waist. Her toenails had been some sort of smoky gray then. He glanced at her feet now as she stepped out from behind the counter. Her legs were covered in tight denim. Her toes hidden in green ballet flats.

"You want me to cut your hair?" She sounded skeptical.

"Yes."

"Why?"

He wondered if she asked every potential client the same thing. But he wouldn't make a scene in front of the other women here.

"I'm looking at expanding the business a little." He shrugged. "I'm thinking I might need to do some advertising."

"Like TV stuff?"

"I don't know."

"What kind of expanding?"

"More landscaping," he answered simply.

"You never mentioned it."

"You never asked." He drew in a deep breath and arched his eyebrows. "You have time?"

"Of course." She nodded him toward the first empty chair. Parker moved with ease to the chair. When he noticed in the mirror that the other women were looking at him, he offered them a smile and said hello.

"Did Alexander's team win their game Saturday?" he asked of her nephew's soccer team.

"Yeah. He scored two goals."

"That's great." He nodded. Vanessa moved around him, careful not to touch him as she put a black vinyl cape over him and snapped it as his neck.

"How're Maisy and Eli?" Her voice was soft and quiet. She leaned around him to pick up a comb and a spray bottle full of water.

"Good." He met her eyes in the mirror. "They miss you."

She swallowed hard and tore her gaze from his.

"So, Mercedes found her dress?"

Parker had hoped coming to see her like this would melt all that tension away. That they would remember how good it felt to spend time together and call it quits on that break. Instead, making conversation with her now felt like running into an ex who had moved on when he was still in love.

"No idea."

Vanessa pumped the spray bottle to wet his hair. The other girl and the woman talked softly as the girl unsnapped her cape and helped the woman to her feet. Parker watched in the mirror as the girl led the woman to the counter.

"You haven't talked to her?"

"Not for a few days."

"Why not?" Vanessa asked quietly. "You're always over there."

"Haven't been lately."

She put the bottle down in exchange for her scissors. Parker watched deep lines appear in her forehead, as she concentrated on cutting his hair. She looked upset. Did she miss him? Or was she just angry with him for showing up?

"Have you talked to Greg lately?"

"Why would I talk to Greg?" she asked with a frown.

The older woman called a goodbye, drawing Vanessa's attention. Parker felt a stab in the heart when Vanessa turned and flashed her happy smile at the client. The other girl returned to her station to clean up.

Vanessa worked quietly while her coworker finished cleaning up her station. The girl disappeared into the back and returned a few moments later with a jacket and a purse.

"See you tomorrow, Van."

"Goodnight, Lanie," Vanessa said with that big smile. It vanished the second the door closed, and they were alone.

"Are you angry with me?" He broke the silence a few moments later.

"Why would I be angry?"

"For coming here."

"No."

"I miss you, Nessa."

She hesitated for a second and rested her hands on his shoulders. Their eyes met in the mirror.

"Hasn't been that long," she reminded him.

"After being with you nearly every night for the month of September, it feels like forever since I've seen you."

Vanessa chose to ignore his comment. She put her scissors on her counter and combed through his hair. Parker glanced at himself in the mirror, but he was more interested in looking at her.

"What've you been up to?" she asked him. When she unsnapped the cape and tugged it away, Parker stood to tug his wallet from his pocket.

"Nothing. What do I owe you?"

Vanessa flicked her eyes up to meet his. "I'm not gonna charge you for that."

"Why wouldn't you?"

"Why would I? We're friends. It took me less than fifteen minutes."

Parker considered pointing out all the things he had offered to do for her around her house, things that would take no time at all. But he didn't want to jump right back into that argument.

"So, we are friends."

"Of course we are." She frowned. She shook her head,

moved to the door to flip the lock, and then stepped around him to clean up her own station. "Seriously, what've you been doing with yourself if you're not seeing me and you aren't hanging out at Nick's?"

Parker watched her sweep up the hair under her chair. When she grabbed a couple of towels and the capes to carry them to the back room, her followed her.

"For the record, I would love to see you more. Again." He propped his shoulder in the doorway and watched her pull a load of towels from the dryer. "You're the one who suggested some time apart."

He watched with interest the way her shoulders climbed and then lowered as she took a deep breath. Was he making her nervous? If he was, why? Because she wanted things back the way they were? Or because she was done with him for good and didn't know how to tell him that?

"Are you seeing other women?"

"Jesus, Vanessa, no." He groaned and dropped his head back. Squeezing his eyes closed, he lifted a hand to shove his hair off his forehead. "I'm still reeling, trying to figure out what the hell happened with us."

"Nothing happened with us, because there is no us," she whispered.

"Right." He nodded. "Forgot. So, just to be clear."

She glanced at him.

"Are we done? Are we still taking some time to ourselves?"

"What do you want, Parker?" She turned to him and folded her arms over her chest.

He wanted her.

All of her. Which included her heart. Her soul. Her dreams. Her disappointments.

If he couldn't have everything, he didn't want anything. Not anymore. No more pretending.

"You know what I want, Nessa," he said quietly and turned to leave. "I'll let myself out."

28

Vanessa's hand shook as she folded the towels. She heard the lock turn on the door and imagined his hands holding her keys. Her heart climbed to her throat when she heard him set her keys on the counter again, and then the door opened, and he was gone.

She didn't know what to make of his visit. His decision to expand his business thrilled her, and not just because the thought of advertising had driven him to her for a haircut. She was happy for him, excited that he was ready to take the next step and grow his business and clientele. Parker was a good guy; Mercedes had nailed that, no question. Vanessa wanted him to be happy; of course she did. She just wished she could be part of his happiness. As more than a friend.

Even though she was relieved at his exasperation when she asked if he was seeing other women—his reaction was much too sincere to doubt him—she hated that he was apparently spending time alone. Why wasn't he hanging out with Nick and Mercedes? Why would he put space between himself and his brother? What about the kids?

Finished with the towels, she locked up the shop and headed for home, heart still hurting for Parker. She missed him. Again. Still. Even though she had been the one to suggest taking some time apart, she wanted to see him, to call him and ask him to grab a pizza and bring it over. She wanted to sit side by side with him in a golf cart and ride over the rolling green hills at the public course. Just the two of them in the autumn sun, playing golf badly and loving every minute of being together.

When Parker texted her last week, she was thrilled to hear from him. It felt natural. Talking through texts about every little thing that really added up to nothing and everything at the same time. No, a discussion about Maisy and her teacher and elephant starting with the letter E didn't mean anything in the big scheme of things. Telling Parker about running into an old high school classmate at the grocery store wasn't important.

But sharing the little meaningless things added up to big things. In Vanessa's heart. When Parker had walked into the salon, her heart had climbed to her throat, and she had struggled to breathe around it. She had hoped he was there to say he had it all wrong, that they had everything wrong, and they should be together first because they loved each other and then to have a baby together.

Instead, their conversation had been stilted and hard, and when he left, she wasn't just sad. She was scared. His goodbye had sounded so final. The ironic thing now was that she didn't want a baby, if she didn't have Parker. She didn't want another guy. She didn't want to have Parker's baby alone. She wanted everything with him. Or nothing at all.

How the hell did she tell him that? This was probably one of the blazing red flags Nick had waved at Parker in the beginning. He had probably warned Parker that someone crazy enough to ask a complete stranger to make a baby with her was probably crazy enough to turn into a stalker.

———

"You have a date, right?"

Journey nudged her elbow with her toes when she didn't answer her. Vanessa stirred and glanced at her friend at the opposite end of the couch. She blinked Journey into focus. The blood-curdling screams from the TV were distant and fake, and Vanessa realized she had been thinking about Parker since the movie started.

Horror movies. Journey insisted they watch as many as possible once the month of October started. Normally, Vanessa was all-in, even if Journey only watched them to give a running commentary on how stupid the female characters were. Tonight, Vanessa found herself wishing for Parker's company, rather than her best friend.

"What?"

"What're you thinking about?" Journey asked her.

"Why girls are so dumb in these movies."

"No, you're not."

"Mm-hmm." Vanessa nodded. "I think we should write a screenplay. About stupid frat guys getting slashed by an undead prom queen or something."

Journey studied her face for a moment. "Interesting, but no, I don't believe you."

"I'm tired," Vanessa mumbled by way of explanation. She huffed a deep breath and glanced at the TV. "We should watch *The Shining*."

"Sure." Journey shrugged. "You're pregnant, aren't you? You haven't touched that wine, and I've downed four beers."

"No." Vanessa pressed her lips together and shook her head. "I'm not."

Journey sat up suddenly and reached for the remote. Vanessa frowned, surprised when she turned the TV off. "What's going on? Tell me what's wrong."

Vanessa stared at Journey for a moment, weighing her need to talk about Parker with her desire to skip another lecture from her well-meaning best friend.

"Parker came by the salon a couple of days ago. For a haircut."

"And?" Journey tipped her head.

"It was horrible."

"What? Why?" Journey pulled her legs up to sit on them and twisted around to face Vanessa. "Did you guys fight?"

"No," Vanessa admitted. "We talked. But it was that... awkward, post-breakup kind of talk."

"You didn't break up, though."

"I know, but it feels like it, Journey. This is worse than Greg."

Journey nodded. "I know it is. Because you're in way over your head with Parker Moore."

Vanessa closed her eyes and dipped her chin to her chest. "Please don't say I told you so."

"What kind of friend would I be if I said that?" Journey asked softly. Vanessa blinked her eyes open to find Journey watching her closely. "So, how did you leave it? Are you still taking a break? Will you call him?"

"I don't know." Vanessa shook her head. "He wants sex. I don't know; maybe he's jazzed about having a kid now. I mean, we decided to have a baby together and be friends. Raising a baby with him wouldn't be bad."

"Are you kidding me?" Journey snapped. "Vanessa, that would be terrible."

"What?" Vanessa drew back as if Journey had slapped her.

"You're in love with him. You can't be friends. You can't co-parent with him if he's going to be seeing other women. It'll break you. I'm not gonna let that happen."

"Well, it's probably not gonna happen anyway, so there's nothing—"

"You could still get pregnant. There's no physical reason you can't—"

"Except that I need him, and I don't know what to do now. He wants sex. I think. I want him." Vanessa dabbed at her eyes, embarrassed to be crying over him. "What if he thinks I'm just crazy? What if he's over it, and he's moved on, and I call him? And he's seeing someone else? Then I'm that psycho who asked him to—"

"What if you tell him how you feel?"

"You are the last person I expected to push me on this, Journey."

Journey reached for Vanessa's wine glass and took a big gulp.

"I know, right?" She shrugged. "I've seen you guys together, Vanessa. You've got something worth keeping."

"We've got nothing, because it all started with a paid proposition."

"I'm gonna have to side with Mercedes on this. You're in a relationship with him, whether you want to admit it or not. Stop being stubborn and fix it."

"You're drunk." Vanessa narrowed her eyes at Journey.

"I'm not drunk. I'm right."

Vanessa looked around the room, desperate to change the subject. Or to conjure Parker up from nothing.

"I don't know how to fix it."

"I do."

"You do?" Vanessa laughed softly, but when she looked back at Journey, she dabbed at her eyes again.

"Invite him to the party."

"What?"

"Ask him to be your date for my dad's party, Van."

"How's that gonna change anything?"

"That alone won't," Journey agreed. "But if you come to the party together, you'll leave the party together."

"More sex isn't the answer."

"No, but you could talk to him, Vanessa. You can tell him you're in love with him."

29

"No monkey suit? Really?" Parker tipped his head and eyed Mercedes with suspicion.

"Why do guys think that?" She shook her head and lifted her hands from her lap as Eli crawled over the couch to sit on her.

"Think what?" Nick asked without looking up from the book he and Maisy were reading.

"That a tux is a monkey suit."

"You're gonna be a monkey?" Maisy twisted her head to look up at Nick and then at Parker. "Why are you being monkeys? For Halloween?"

"That's what guys call tuxedos," Mercedes explained.

"What's a tuxedo?" Maisy flattened her hand over Nick's so he couldn't turn the page.

"A monkey suit," Parker said simply.

"It's a nice suit that guys wear to weddings," Mercedes told her. "Very fancy. They look really nice when they wear them."

"My daddy's always nice." Maisy's face twisted in a frown.

"He is."

Mercedes' smile hit Parker square in the heart. He looked away, wondering what Vanessa was doing tonight.

"Guys hate wearing suits," Nick told Maisy. "They're hot. And ties are uncomfortable. And the collars on dress shirts are all starchy, and they make your neck hurt."

"And you think wedding dresses are comfortable?"

"How often have you worn a wedding dress?" Nick asked Mercedes.

She laughed softly. "Okay, dresses. You think dresses are comfortable? And heels?"

"You could wear yoga pants and be the most beautiful bride I'll ever see," Nick told her.

"Okay." Parker took a deep breath. "And with that—"

"Stop it." Mercedes shot him a stern look. "No tux. But you do have a suit, right?"

"Believe it or not, I do."

"And it fits you?" Nick asked him.

"Don't be a jackass." Parker shook his head.

"Uncle Parker!" Maisy leaned back into Nick. "That's a swear!"

"You're right, Mase. Sorry." He nodded. "Mercedes, I do have a nice suit. It's black. It fits. I have a nice, fitted white dress shirt. And I'll even wear a tie without whining about it."

"Doubtful," Nick mumbled. "Mase. Are we still reading this book?"

"Can we have popcorn?" Maisy looked up at Nick.

"Popcorn's for movies."

"Can we watch a movie? Like *Scooby Doo*? Cuz it's Halloween time. And I like Scooby."

"Too scary for Eli," Nick told her.

"Daddy!"

Parker's phone buzzed in his pocket.

"Eli, you're not scared of Scooby, are you?"

"I like Scooby." Eli rested his head on Mercedes' shoulder. "Can we have popcorn, Cedes?"

Parker pulled his phone from his pocket when Mercedes and Nick exchanged a look. Vanessa's number flashed on the screen. As much as he wanted to talk to her, he didn't want to do it while sitting in the middle of Nick's living room floor with four sets of eyes on him. He ignored the call, but he did climb to his feet.

"Where're you going?" Nick watched him dig his keys from his pocket.

"Home."

"Why?"

"Because you guys are gonna watch Scooby Doo, and those ghosts scare me."

Maisy giggled and slapped her book shut.

"But you're gonna trick-or-treat with me, right?"

"Of course I am!" Parker tossed his hands up as if to ask her what else he would do. "You and Eli."

"Daddy's coming, too," Eli announced.

"What about Cedes?"

"She has to stay home to give out candy to other trick-or-treaters."

"That's no fun. She should go with us."

"But who would hand out the candy then?" Maisy shook her head.

"You're right." Parker offered her his fist for a quick

bump and laughed when she tapped her little knuckles against his.

"You're leaving?" Mercedes asked him.

"Yeah."

"Daddy?" Maisy asked again. "Can we have popcorn?"

"I'll get it." Cedes stood with Eli in her arms and carried him to the kitchen. To Parker's frustration, Maisy followed her, leaving Nick free to walk him to the door.

"Still nothing?"

Nick and Mercedes knew Parker had gone to see Vanessa for a trim because he had inquired about a loan to expand his business. That he was considering some advertising. That he and Vanessa had talked, but Parker hadn't said anything more than that.

Because honestly? Parker had no idea what they were doing now. He wasn't even sure they were friends, and it had been a couple of weeks since they had been together. Not that Parker had confessed that to Nick or Mercedes.

"Nope." He shrugged like it didn't matter, but Nick was paying too much attention to him these days, so he knew he was lying.

"But you guys are friends. Right? At least you're friends."

"Yeah. We're friends," Parker mumbled, hoping it wasn't a lie. "What's the plan for Halloween, anyway?

"Cedes is gonna make chili. We can eat when the kids are done trick-or-treating."

"'kay. See ya later, man."

"Parker—"

"I'm not up for a lecture, Nick, okay? Maybe you think I made a mistake with Vanessa. With the whole baby thing. But if I hadn't said yes to that, I wouldn't have had anything with her at all."

Nick made a noise—a frustrated grunt—but he still followed Parker out the door and into the garage. Behind him, Parker heard the kids yakking at Mercedes excitedly, ready for popcorn and a movie. As much as he loved his niece and nephew, he needed to walk away for a while and go home alone. What he had said to Nick was true. If he hadn't agreed to Vanessa's outlandish proposition, he wouldn't have had anything with her at all. He would never have known what loving Vanessa Mayne was like.

But if he hadn't agreed to father her child, he wouldn't have this ridiculous yearning for a kid, for a wife, a family, nagging at him. He wouldn't be here, hanging around his brother's house, his family, on a weekend, pining away over something he had no idea he wanted. He would be out with another woman, having a good time.

Parker didn't miss partying. He didn't miss or want another woman.

But wishing for something bigger with Vanessa wasn't going to get him anywhere, either.

"Tell her."

"What?" Parker froze at the overhead door of the garage. The night was cool and still out there. He eyed his truck, the skeleton hanging from the awning of the porch across the street, and finally turned to look back at his brother.

"Tell her how you feel." Nick's eyes flashed to meet his briefly, but he didn't hold the eye contact.

Done pretending to Nick and Cedes, to himself, Parker sighed in defeat. He was one hundred percent wrapped up in Vanessa Mayne.

"She doesn't care."

"What've you got to lose at this point?" Nick's voice was gruff with emotion. Parker looked around, ready to scram, uncomfortable with this sort of conversation.

"Everything."

"And nothing," Nick reminded him. "You gonna wait forever for her to get how you feel?"

Their eyes met again. Nick looked as uncomfortable as Parker felt. Rather than drag the conversation on, Parker nodded and headed out to his truck. He had no intention of telling Vanessa he was in love with her. But he had to get Nick off his back. It was one thing to talk about sex with his brother—still not super comfortable, but better than talking about feelings and love and all that crap.

He considered calling her back when he was in his truck, but he waited. Considered driving by her house, but he didn't. He didn't trust himself to keep his mouth shut, to keep all that crap bottled up inside, if he saw her right now. Not after hanging out with Nick and Cedes, watching them love each other with just a touch of his hand on her arm and the way she trailed her fingers over the back of his neck when she walked by him.

Once he was at home, alone and a little bit surly and pissy, he settled into his recliner and dialed her number. The phone rang four times, and he was just about to give up. Wasn't going to leave a message, not the way he felt right now.

But just as he pulled the phone away from his ear, he heard her voice.

"Hey."

"Hi." His heart sprinted away from him, but he reminded himself to get a grip. That he was being dumb.

"Were you busy?"

"Just got home," he told her.

"Mmm." She sounded sad. "Are you alone?"

"I was at Nick's," he told her.

"How're the kids?"

"Right about now they're having popcorn and watching *Scooby Doo*."

"Oh! My favorite."

"You okay?" he asked her when what he wanted to say was *what happened? Why did things change? What're we doing?*

"I miss you."

"You do?"

"Mmm. I keep hoping you'll come by."

He thought about reminding her that she hadn't invited him, but he didn't want to argue.

"Ness—"

"No." She cleared her throat. "It's okay. I um—I wanted to ask you something."

"Okay."

"A favor, I guess. I mean, I know—we're not—we haven't—so maybe you're seeing other women, but—"

"Are you—" He snapped his teeth together and seethed quietly. Is that what she really thought of him? That just because they hadn't been sexually active in a couple of weeks, that he would take their break and run off to be with someone else? "I'm not, Vanessa. I'm not—"

"I need a date." She plowed right through his denials, her voice soft but determined. "For Journey's dad's party. It's um—it's fancy. Like suit and tie fancy. And I just—do you wanna?"

Stunned at the invitation—even as sloppy as it was—
Parker was speechless.

"I get it. If you can't. If you have a date. If you just
don't wanna go—"

"I'd love to be your date, Vanessa."

"I mean, just, you know, as friends."

"Absolutely."

"So, really? You'll go?"

"Yes. I'll go. I'll wear a suit and tie." He fought down
the urge to tell her about Maisy and the monkey suit
conversation. "I'll pick you up. I can borrow Cedes' car, if
you don't wanna climb in and out of my truck with a
dress on."

"Your truck's fine, Parker," she sounded exasperated.
"I'm not a snob."

He wanted to know more about the party. If there
would be music. Dancing. He wanted to hold her in his
arms and dance with her just once before she called
everything with him quits. Before they officially quit
trying to get pregnant and walked away as friends and
then rarely saw each other.

But he didn't ask.

"It's the night after Halloween," she told him.

"Okay."

"You don't have plans?"

"No. I don't."

"What about Halloween?"

"Going trick-or-treating with Mase and Eli."

"Bring them over here."

"We will."

30

"Do you like my costume, Uncle Parker?" Maisy tugged at his hand. He eyed her curiously for a moment, not sure what she was dressed as. No doubt she looked adorable, but then, his niece always looked adorable.

"Doc McStuffins," Mercedes said to Maisy, though Parker knew she was throwing him a life jacket. "Do you have all of your stuff? Your jacket in case you get cold?"

"Doc McStuffins doesn't wear a jacket," Maisy whined. "Do you like it?" She turned her face back to Parker. "Mercedes and I picked it out, and I got to wear it to school today. For a party. Did you have Halloween parties at school when you were a kid, Uncle Parker?"

Parker raised his eyebrows, gave himself a mental shake, and glanced at Mercedes, hoping she saw his appreciation in his gaze.

"I really like your costume," he told her. "But, Doc McStuffins is a doc, and so, if she were to get cold, I'm pretty sure she would wear a jacket."

Maisy sighed, clearly frustrated with Parker for siding with Mercedes.

"Grab it. You don't have to put it on yet," Mercedes said softly.

"So, I'm guessing she's had some sugar already."

Mercedes snorted.

"I did my part." She pinched the bridge of her nose and shook her head. "Pretty sure I ate my weight in chocolate on the drive home from school."

Parker grinned. "Thanks for the save."

"Thanks for hanging with Nick and the kids."

"You sure you don't want to go? I can stay here and hand out candy."

"I would love to." She tipped her head. "But on the other hand, I'm kind of excited about being here in this gorgeous house on a fun night like this. Seeing the kids. Hanging out candy."

"Okay." Parker nodded. "You can have Nick if you want. I like the kids better."

Mercedes laughed again. "You're just scared of him."

"I am," he agreed. "More afraid of lectures from my big brother than I am of witches and ghosts. Lectures that will go on all night because I can't get away from him."

"He's just concerned, Parker."

"I've got a dad."

"Oh, come on." Mercedes nudged his side with her elbow. "You wouldn't be worried about Nick if it were him in this situation?"

"Um, Nick was married to Kiara. This thing with Vanessa is all lollipops and rainbows compared to that disaster."

"And you weren't concerned about him then? About his happiness?"

"I didn't lecture him."

"Nice costume," Nick said as he entered the kitchen. "Let me guess. Homeless guy?"

"And you're sure I can't talk you out of marrying him?" Parker glanced at Mercedes.

She shook her and shrugged. "He's ruined me for any other man."

"You can snag a girl like this with lame kisses, and I can't hook one who *asked* me to sleep with her."

"Nobody said life was fair," Nick reminded him. He took a drink from a water bottle and flashed Mercedes a sloppy smile. "And I don't think there was anything lame about those last kisses we shared."

Parker shook his head.

"When your kids nap, you get a little afternoon—"

"No." Parker cleared his throat. "I don't wanna know why you were home from work early, and I don't wanna know about your afternoon stuff." He wandered out of the kitchen to wait in the living room for Maisy. "Where's Eli?"

"Coming," Eli answered as he moseyed down the hallway.

"Dude." Parker held his hand up for a high five. "Peter Pan in the flesh."

Eli grinned at him. He carried his empty plastic pumpkin in his hand, but as far as Parker could see, he didn't have a jacket.

"Nick, grab Eli's jacket," Mercedes told him.

Maisy reappeared when Nick went back through the house to get Eli's jacket from his room. Her jacket was thrown over her shoulder, and she held her plastic pumpkin in one hand and a book in the other.

"Mase." Mercedes reached for the book.

"But it's my favorite!" Maisy tucked the book behind her back and looked at Mercedes with sad eyes.

"Maisy, sweetie, you're going trick-or-treating," Mercedes reminded her. "You're not gonna have time to read a book."

"Will you read it to me when we get back?"

"Of course, I will." Mercedes offered Maisy a big smile and reached again to take the book from her.

"You ready, munchkin?" Parker asked Maisy.

"It's Doc McStuffins," Maisy corrected him.

"Right. Sorry. Doc and Peter Pan. You ready to get this party started?"

"It's not a party, Uncle Parker." Maisy rolled her eyes.

"Yes, it is!" he argued. "Fun costumes and free candy!"

"Daddy!" Maisy called. "Are you ready to party?"

Parker coughed to hide his laugh as Nick joined them again, Eli's jacket in hand.

"Party?" Nick repeated. He narrowed his eyes at Parker, but before he could say a word, Mercedes slipped up close to him and pressed a chaste kiss to his lips.

The action made Parker think of Vanessa. The fact that he didn't just want sex with her. He wanted those sweet little chaste kisses, too. He wanted to be around if and when she got pregnant. He wanted to be with her when she gave birth. He wanted these little family moments. Everything. He wanted every. Damned. Thing. With Vanessa Mayne.

"Love you," Mercedes told Nick. "Have fun, guys!"

Grateful to Mercedes for pushing them out the door, Parker followed Eli out through the garage.

"How many houses are we going to, Daddy?" Maisy gushed behind him. "I wanna get lots of candy!"

"I think you already had lots of candy, Mase." Nick told her.

"What's your favorite kind, Uncle Parker?"

His mind on Vanessa, he bit his tongue before he could say her name. Might be true—he'd never tasted anything so sweet and rich—but he couldn't imagine explaining that to Maisy.

"Snicker bars."

"You can have all of mine!" Maisy announced.

"Hey!" Nick yelped. "I like Snickers, Mase."

"It's a deal!" Parker turned to walk backwards and reached out to knuckle Maisy.

"Okay. What do you say at every house?"

"Trick-or-treat," Eli said matter-of-factly.

"Yes, but what do you say when they give you candy?" Nick asked as they walked up the street.

"We say thank you!" Maisy bounced up and down on her toes.

"Yes!" Nick high fived both kids. "Okay. You guys get to do the fun stuff. Me and Uncle Parker will wait on the driveway, okay?"

Maisy nodded. Eli looked a bit uncertain, but Maisy grabbed his hand and led him up the driveway to the sidewalk.

"Vanessa asked me to bring the kids by tonight." Parker watched Maisy reach up to ring the doorbell. When he felt Nick's eyes on him, he looked away and made a show of looking around the neighborhood street.

Normally quiet, tonight it was already buzzing with groups of trick-or-treaters, some younger children with moms and dads and some older kids, out on their own for the evening.

"Okay." Nick agreed without asking questions. Parker had been ready for Nick to launch an inquisition again, so the simple okay left him feeling a little off. He shoved his hands in his pockets and debated on letting it go or saying more. For instance, he really wanted to tell Nick that Vanessa had asked him to be her date for that party.

But did he? Did he really want to invite more of Nick's opinions? Comments?

Not really.

But he did want to talk about Vanessa. Just saying her name sent a thrill through him, a little bit like the freefall side of a Ferris wheel.

"She asked me to go with her to a party." His mouth moved before his brain could stop it.

"Cool."

From the corner of his eye, he saw Nick nod.

"Halloween party?"

"No." Parker cleared his throat. "Um. Something for her friend's dad. Like a fancy birthday party."

"Fancy?"

"Yeah. Suit and tie." Parker shot a quick peek at Nick, and they shared a laugh.

"Wow." Nick arched his eyebrows. "That's something. Right?"

"Maybe." Parker shrugged.

He stopped talking when Maisy and Eli chimed their thanks and scrambled down the drive where he and Nick waited.

"What'd you get?" Parker leaned over to peek into their pumpkins.

"Skittles!"

Parker and Nick followed just behind the kids as they made their way to the next house.

"Why is it only maybe something?" Nick asked him once they were alone again.

"I knew about this party a while ago. I was there when she and her friend were talking about it. I didn't get an invite that night."

"So, what?" Nick asked quietly. "You think she had a date, and he cancelled on her?"

"Possible, isn't it?"

"I guess so." Nick studied Parker with a heavy frown.

"What?"

"She doesn't seem like that kind of woman. Someone who would get hot and dirty with you and date someone else at the same time. Why would she do that? If she was dating someone else, why wouldn't she just sleep with that person and hope to get pregnant?"

"Maybe she likes suits. I don't have a lot to offer her, Nick. I have a lawn cutting business."

"Bullshit. Your business is successful. You're looking to expand. You're currently debt free. You're marginally good-looking." Nick shrugged. "I mean, yeah, I got the lions' share of the looks in the family, but you're not bad."

Parker laughed and rolled his eyes.

"You're a hardworking guy. You're compassionate and loyal. Except when you're kissing my woman."

"Once," Parker reminded him. "One time. And that was before you claimed her."

"I know." Nick nodded. "I know you would never do

that, Parker. That's what I'm saying. You're a good guy. She's blind if she doesn't see that."

Uncomfortable under Nick's heavy stare, Parker cleared his throat and looked up at the house as Maisy and Eli hurried back down the drive.

"Here, Uncle Parker!" Maisy fished a snack size Snicker bar from her pumpkin and waved it at him.

"Mase!" Nick tossed his hands up. "I'm your daddy. You're supposed to share your candy with me."

"But you say you have all the sweets you want with Mercedes," Maisy said innocently. "Uncle Parker doesn't have sweets."

Parker clenched his teeth, still smiling, but hating the situation he had gotten himself into. He was beyond backing out of anything now. No way he could just walk away from Vanessa Mayne and pretend that none of it had happened. Nope. He was going to have to tell her. Tomorrow night, at the party, after the party—whenever —he had to tell her how he felt, damn the consequences.

He ripped open the candy bar wrapper with his teeth and then peeled it back to take a bite.

"When we're done on our street and after we see Grandpa, do you guys wanna trick-or-treat at Vanessa's house?"

"I love Bandessa." Maisy nodded. "Oh. I'm posed to call her Van, right, Uncle Parker? Why can't she be your sweets like Cedes is Daddy's?"

"How much candy did you eat today, Mase?" Parker asked her. Nick snorted.

"Two bags of Skittles," she answered seriously. "Except the green ones. I don't like them."

"You could give the green Skittles to Daddy," Parker

suggested, knowing full well that Nick preferred chocolate candy.

"That's a good idea!"

They wandered through the neighborhood for a while,
Nick and Parker discussing sports and movies and things
that didn't revolve around Vanessa and Mercedes. Parker
was grateful for the reprieve. Once Nick realized how
much candy Maisy and Eli were stockpiling, he suggested
going to Vanessa's. A ripple of excitement put a little
bounce in Parker's step and made him feel like one of the
kids as they turned around to head for home and
Nick's SUV.

———

The porch light was on at Vanessa's. Parker eyed a devil,
Captain America, and a pirate as they made their way to
the front door. Nick walked Maisy and Eli up the drive,
but Parker hesitated. When Vanessa opened the door with
a big orange and black bowl in her hands, he huffed out a
breath he didn't realize he was holding. Vanessa wore her
hair pinned up in a messy twist. She would say she looked
homeless, but Parker thought the black yoga pants and
long-sleeved orange T-shirt was a perfect mix of sexy and
sweet.

She didn't notice Parker and Nick, so he watched her
toss candy into the trick-or-treaters' bags. Her voice
carried to him as she asked them about their night, if they
were getting lots of candy. Her laugh felt like home. As
happy as he was to be with his niece and nephew, Parker
wished he could stay here when Nick left.

When the kids at the door turned to leave, Vanessa

lifted her gaze and saw him in the drive. He snapped his jaw closed, worried that she might flinch or falter, but she stepped out to the porch and smiled bigger when their eyes met.

Didn't that mean something?

"Maisy and Eli!" Vanessa called as she turned her attention to the kids. Maisy wiggled free from Nick's grasp and ran to throw her arms around Vanessa's legs. "Doc McStuffins! Ohmygosh! Way cool, Mase."

"How did she know what her costume was?" Parker grumbled as he joined Nick.

"What?" Nick gave Eli a nudge and glanced at Parker, but Parker only shook his head.

"Are you guys havin' fun?" Vanessa asked the kids. "Let me see how much candy you have."

"She's a natural with kids," Nick told him. "You need to give her babies, Parker."

Parker spared Nick a quick look, but he clenched his teeth together rather than remind his brother that he wanted nothing more than to give Vanessa babies. Well, okay, not true. He wanted to give her babies and be around to help her raise them.

"Wow!" Bent over the kids to better appraise their haul, Vanessa peeked at Parker when he approached. "These guys are gonna be on a two-week sugar bender!"

"Not if Mercedes beats them to it," Nick mumbled.

Vanessa chuckled. "C'mon in. I have something special for you guys."

Parker held his breath again when Vanessa led them all inside. He felt like he floated over the porch. Vanessa's TV was tuned to a Halloween movie, but her friend Journey quickly turned it off once they were inside.

"Hey." Journey climbed to her feet and offered them a smile. She tossed the remote to the couch and moseyed closer to the kids to eye their candy. "Holy smokes! You guys are winning Halloween!"

"How do you win Halloween?" Maisy tipped her head and stared at Journey with a frown.

"She just means you have a ton of candy," Vanessa explained. "And you're about to get more!"

"I like candy," Eli announced.

Vanessa glanced at Parker and grinned.

They were having a girls' night, Parker realized. Nice for them, but he was jealous as hell that Vanessa wanted Journey here and not him. Journey snagged her glass of wine from the coffee table and took a sip. Vanessa disappeared into the kitchen, taking Parker's heart with her. Maisy chatted at Journey, but Eli hung back, fingers wrapped tightly around Nick's.

"Here we go!" Vanessa sang as she returned with fancy little packages for each of the kids. Parker didn't dare glance at Nick as she tucked the cute little brown bags decorated with pumpkin stickers and orange ribbon into the kids' pumpkins. "Save those from Daddy and Cedes, okay? Because they're super special from me."

Jesus. The woman was trying to kill him.

"I'm giving my Snickers to Uncle Parker," Maisy told Vanessa.

"There's no Snickers in my bags," Vanessa promised. "And I actually have something for Daddy and Uncle Parker, too."

Parker gave himself a mental shake and met Vanessa's eyes again. Special treats for his niece and nephew. Okay, they were adorable kids, so who could blame her for that?

But did any of it have anything to do with him? Did she feel anything for him, or was this just another reminder how badly Vanessa wanted children?

"C'mere."

Surprised by her summons, Parker blinked at her silently and followed her to the kitchen. The kids chattered to each other about candy. Parker heard Nick say something about the number of people out. Journey answered, but their voices faded when he was alone in the kitchen with Vanessa.

"What've you got for me?" While he wanted her, he decided to keep it fun, lighthearted. No sense in coming undone right now when they had an audience in the other room.

Rather than answer him, Vanessa moved in closer and stood on her tiptoes to kiss him. Parker opened his mouth to her searching tongue, thrilled to taste her again.

"Happy Halloween," she whispered when she pulled back from the kiss.

"It is now," he agreed with a smirk. "But I hope that's not what you have for Nick."

"Nope. I made cookies for you guys."

"You made—? Cookies? You made cookies? For us?"

"Yep. Figured the kids would rather have candy, since it is Halloween. Cookies for you and Nick."

Parker whooshed out a deep breath and nodded.

"Still gonna be my date tomorrow night?" Vanessa nibbled on her lip as she waited for his answer.

"I can't wait for tomorrow night, Vanessa." He leaned in close to kiss her again. In the gamble of pushing his luck or pushing her away, he was ready to push his luck.

"Uncle Parker!" Maisy hollered. "Uncle—"

Vanessa dipped her head when Maisy gasped, clearly surprised to find them kissing. Parker laughed, kissed Vanessa's cheek, and turned his attention to Maisy.

"Hey, Mase."

"Van is your sweets." Maisy's smile tugged at his heart. "Like Cedes and Daddy."

31

The trouble with the party being for Journey's dad was that Vanessa couldn't call her friend to obsess over what she was wearing, which shoes paired better with the emerald green dress she chose, and whether the hoop earrings or diamond studs were the better choice. Because Journey's relationship with her mother was tenuous at best, Vanessa had to suck it up and talk herself through the nerves.

It wasn't really the dress or the shoes. Parker wouldn't give a damn if she wore the hoops or the studs. The way he looked at her, she figured she could probably wear coveralls, and he would still want her later tonight.

She wasn't particularly worried about Parker showing up dressed all wrong, either. She had seen the guy in casual clothes, and she had no reason to believe he couldn't rock a suit and tie the same way he did denim and a button-down.

Nope. She was nervous about Parker. Telling Parker that she had fallen in love with him.

She eyed the sparkly black heel critically. The shoes themselves were works of art, and they made her legs look pretty hot. She met her eyes in the full-length mirror in her closet and laughed softly. But were they going to be comfortable, or would she be miserable after an evening of standing and dancing in the heels?

Dancing.

Would Parker dance with her? Would he like Journey's family? What if he was bored? What if he wanted to leave early? Leaving early wouldn't matter to Journey's parents, but Journey might kill her.

If they danced, she might prefer a more sensible heel. Vanessa leaned over to slide the shoe off, but the doorbell rang.

"Sensible," she muttered as she hurried down the steps. Who was she kidding? She needed the sexy heels the same way she needed the thong and the tiny silk cups that barely covered her nipples. She was fighting to hold Parker's attention, not trying to herd him out of her life. The doorbell rang again just as she sidled up to stand in front of the door. She took a moment to breathe, smoothed her hands over her hips, and pulled the door open.

She melted. And not because the man at her door wore a simple, yet elegant black suit with a white shirt and a gold and black tie. No, she melted because that man was watching her with stars in his eyes. If only he wanted more than sex. She could live with him forever. She wanted to. She had never planned to fall in love with him when she propositioned him, but here she was, desperate to hold on to him.

"You look beautiful." His tone was almost reverent.

"Thank you." Vanessa felt her pulse beating rapidly in

her throat. His lustful gaze paralyzed her; when he finally dragged his eyes up to meet hers, she cleared her throat and tipped her head. "You look..." At a loss for words, she gave him a tiny shrug and stepped back for him to come inside.

"Presentable?"

She chuckled softly. "You look incredible, Parker." Her whisper was a bit shaky, so she turned away hoping he didn't notice. She would grab her things so they could go. Journey was probably already there, and odds were, she and Lenore had probably already gone a few rounds.

Parker caught her hand in his and pulled her around with a gentle tug.

"But then you already know that," she mumbled when she found herself tugged in tight against his chest.

"Why would you say that?" He tipped his head and studied her face with an intensity that made her squirm.

"You're not the one who had to offer someone money for a date," she reminded him. Her stomach was twisted in knots. Nervous about the conversation she wanted to have later, she patted Parker's chest and tried to free herself of his arms.

"If I remember correctly, you offered me money to get you pregnant," he corrected her.

There was no venom in his tone, but his words bit her just the same. She fought to hold eye contact with him, worried that he would see through her and know she was hiding something from him now.

"And while we aren't holding to that original deal, I'm pretty sure this is a date, Vanessa."

"A date?" She arched her eyebrows. "I thought it was just a friend helping another friend out."

Parker stroked the back of his knuckles over her cheek.

"Nope. I think this is a real date."

"A real date," she repeated.

"That okay with you?"

"Yes."

He leaned in closer to her and rested his forehead against hers. "I have to tell you that I really want to kiss you right now. But I don't wanna mess up your lipstick."

When he tilted his head back and fixed his gaze on her lips, Vanessa parted them for a tiny sigh.

"I could always fix it," she said softly.

"Yeah? So, it's okay?"

The hint of a smile played on his mouth. All thoughts of Journey waiting on her, arguing with her mother, wishing Vanessa was there to rescue her went out the window. Parker cupped her chin in his hand and leaned in closer to kiss her.

It was just a soft kiss, probably not even enough to mess with her lipstick, but she felt it on her heart. In her belly. Maybe even her knees. When Parker backed away a bit, she hung onto the lapels of his jacket to steady herself.

"Still beautiful." He grinned.

"It's a good color on you."

With a frown, Parker lifted his hand to smooth his fingers over his lips. Vanessa laughed out loud and slipped away from him when he grabbed for her again.

"Let me get my purse," she told him.

"So, give me the scoop," he called after her.

"Sherwin's birthday," she answered simply. She heard his footsteps on the stairs behind her as she entered her room.

"Obviously." He stood in the doorway of her bedroom, hands in his pockets, looking for all the world like it didn't bother him to think of all the times they had made love there in her bed the last several weeks.

"Um. Journey does not get along well with her mom at all." Her voice was all wrong, breathy and a bit high pitched. Because seeing Parker standing there in her bedroom, waiting for her so they could go out on a date most certainly did bother her. In all the right ways, but it would do no good if she was the only one feeling this way.

"Why not?"

"Good question," she mumbled. "Lenore got pregnant at seventeen."

"So, is Sherwin her real father?"

"Oh yeah." Vanessa looked up at Parker and then looked back at her shoe. Still not sure which to choose. "They didn't get married until Journey was five. Lenore got pregnant with Kendric then. She dotes on him. But Journey can't do much right as far as her mom is concerned."

"And what's she do?"

"She's the manager at Signed and Delivered."

"What're you doing?" Parker stepped further into her room and eyed the shoe she was worrying over.

"Trying to decide which shoes to wear."

"What's the other contestant?" he asked. "Is Journey involved?"

Vanessa snorted. "Nope. The day that woman settles down with someone will be the end of the world. She hates relationships. Commitment." She held up a much tamer, simpler black pump.

316 | TRACY BROEMMER

"Well, those are pretty, and they look more comfortable." Parker took the shoe from her.

"'kay." Vanessa snatched it back and tossed it in the closet. "I'm ready."

"Wait." He laughed and shook his head. "You're not going to change?"

"I would love to be comfortable," she told him. "But I'd rather be so sexy, you don't forget this date for the rest of your life."

Parker's eyes flared with heat. "Vanessa, I won't forget anything about you and being with you for the rest of my life."

It was a nice thing to say, sure, but it only made her nerves flare up worse. He might not forget her, but he hadn't said he wanted to spend the rest of his life with her.

"And if we're going to make it to that party," he stepped away from her and shoved his hands in his pockets again, "we should go now. Because I very much want to strip you down to whatever sexy things you have on under that dress and lay you down on that bed and make you forget your own name."

Vanessa swallowed hard.

"Maybe we could do that after the party?"

"I sure hope so."

———

They weren't late, but because Lenore and Sherwin were Lenore and Sherwin, the party was already in full swing by the time Vanessa led Parker into the event hall. Decorated in muted silvers and burgundies, the place was a mix of elegant and festive at the same time. Vanessa slipped out of her wrap and let Parker take it as she eyed the bouquets of white roses and the flickering battery-operated candles that served as centerpieces on the tables. Something quiet and jazzy played in the background; Vanessa knew it was probably causing Journey to break out in hives.

"There you are!"

Vanessa spun around as Journey pulled her into a hug and clung to her out of sheer desperation.

"You okay?"

"Hmm." Journey pulled away from her and looked at Parker over her shoulder. "I shot a sixpack before I even got here. Not even close to a buzz."

"You did not." Vanessa rolled her eyes. "Journey, you remember Parker?"

Journey tipped her head and grinned at him. "Like I'm ever gonna forget Parker Moore and what he is to you."

Vanessa flinched at the second reminder of the night that she had propositioned the guy beside her to get her pregnant. If it made her feel guilty to be reminded of that, how did it make him feel?

"Parker—"

"Hi, Journey." Parker leaned around Vanessa to give her best friend a quick hug. "It's good to see you again."

"Thanks for coming," Journey said softly, turning her attention back to Vanessa.

"Where's Lenore?"

"No idea." Journey shrugged. "I'm doing my best to steer clear of her. She ripped me apart this morning because the bouquets are wrong."

"How do you get white roses wrong?"

"Apparently, there's supposed to be a second flower in them. I don't know, Vanessa, because you know me. I don't *do* flowers. I had nothing to do with ordering the flowers. I was not here when they were delivered, but it's my fault that they're wrong."

"Take it easy." Vanessa rested her hand on Journey's shoulder. "Deep breath."

"Not to mention."

"Mention what?"

But something behind Vanessa and Parker caught Journey's eye. She frowned and excused herself with a gentle pat on Vanessa's hand and an absent smile for Parker.

"Everything okay?" Parker asked as Vanessa twisted around to watch her friend. When Journey met a guy in the middle of the dance floor and let him slide his arm around her, Vanessa turned to Parker with a frown.

"I don't know," she mumbled. "That's Bryant Abbott."

"What?"

"The guy she's with." Vanessa shook her head.

"She wasn't supposed to bring a date?"

"Well, actually, her mother demanded she bring a date, but I'm shocked that she brought him."

"Who is he?"

"She knows him through work. They're sort of not really friends. He's probably the exact kind of guy Lenore would want her to date."

"Which is why you're surprised she's with him."

Vanessa met Parker's eyes and nodded.

"Okay." He raised his eyebrows. "Got it."

"You don't, really. Because no one understands Lenore. Except Kendric and Sherwin."

Parker stepped closer to her. "How about a drink?"

"Please."

Goosebumps prickled her skin when Parker rested his hand on her lower back and ushered her ahead of him to go to the bar. It shouldn't come as a surprise to her that he was such a gentleman; he had never treated her with anything less than respect. But this felt different. Vanessa had asked for a favor, but Parker had called tonight a date.

"What do you feel like?" he asked her as they neared the short line of people at the bar. He moved his hand from her back to her hip. The weight of his arm around her was comforting. In fact, it felt like home, and that was dangerous. Maybe this was a date, but Parker had dated a lot of other women, so there was no reason to think she was special. Maybe he would spend the night with her again, but nothing was going to come of these crazy feelings she couldn't fight anymore.

"Chardonnay," she told him and moved with him again, a step closer to the bar.

"Do you have to be available to Journey all night, or do I get you to myself?"

Before Vanessa could reply, they were at the bar. She waited quietly while Parker asked for her wine and a shot of bourbon for himself. Once they had their drinks, they wandered away from the bar in the general direction of the dance floor.

"Should we find a table?" He took a sip and looked at her over his glass.

"Yes." Vanessa nodded. "But there's seriously no one here I want to sit with other than you and Journey."

Parker's grin sent a thrill through her heart so intense it made her shiver.

"You think she saved us seats, or is she at the head table? Is this like a reception? Is she going to have to toast her father?"

Vanessa laughed softly. "At least she and her dad get along well."

"Hey."

Vanessa turned at the familiar voice and found herself smiling at Journey's little brother, Kendric.

"Kendric!" Careful not to spill her wine, she hugged him as if he were her own younger brother. "Hey. Long time no see."

"No kidding, stranger." He nodded. "And we live in the same town."

"Such is life, right?" Vanessa tipped her head toward Parker. "Kendric, this is Parker Moore. Parker, this is Journey's brother, Kendric."

"Nice to meet you." Parker reached to shake hands, but Vanessa noticed the hard set of his mouth. Way to blow a good night, Vanessa. She could have at least introduced him as a friend. Instead, she had simply shared his name, as if he was no more to her than the guy she had asked to get her pregnant. Nice of her, especially after Journey's comment a few moments ago.

"Is that Dalton McKenzie?" She spotted Kendric's old friend as the guy stepped into the event hall. She hadn't seen him in years, and yes, he had changed a lot, but his big, solid frame and his blond crew cut hair remained the same.

"Yep." Kendric spun around to watch his buddy make his way over to say hello to Lenore and Sherwin. "Just moved back from Texas."

"Wow." Vanessa shook her head. "Flash from the past. I think you guys were eighteen the last time I saw you."

"Should you say hello to the man of the hour?" Parker asked when Kendric made his way to the next guest to greet.

"Yeah." She had been avoiding that, but Parker was right. Vanessa liked Sherwin a lot, and she liked Lenore okay until the woman started nitpicking her own daughter to Vanessa. Families were odd, she decided as she led the way across the room. Good thing she and Parker weren't seriously involved. If they were only ever going to be friends, she wouldn't have to worry about introducing him to her family.

Then again, she liked her family, and the more time she spent with Parker, the more she knew they would like him.

32

P arker didn't mind crowds, and he didn't mind elegant affairs, and he didn't mind meeting people. In fact, he liked that Vanessa had dragged him along with her to say hello to Journey's parents, to wish her father a happy birthday. He wouldn't mind meeting Vanessa's family one day, but at the rate they were going, it didn't seem likely. They had slept together, and they had changed it from a business arrangement to friendship early on in the game. But Vanessa still seemed hesitant to call him that. She had introduced him to Lenore and Sherwin as a friend, but not Kendric. And not his friend Dalton. Nope. Both times she had introduced him to guys closer to her age, guys she could conceivably date, she had simply introduced him by name.

That seemed telling.

Didn't mean he wasn't going to be the most attentive, pleasant, fun date she would ever have before his one big chance at changing her mind was over. At dinner, he offered to carry her plate for her, so she wouldn't have to juggle her wine and her food. He had done the gestures—pulling out her chair for her, standing when she left the table earlier to go to the ladies' room. When her wine glass was empty, he had gone for another. When she turned down dessert and then made eyes at his piece of cake, he shared it with her.

When they finally joined the small crowd on the dance floor, Parker held her close without being too possessive or too physical. Of course, his mind was on the curves under his hands and the smooth skin of her breasts pressed just a touch against him. He liked to dance, and he loved dancing with her, and while he hoped there was more between them later, Parker had no desire to rush through this experience with her.

"Do your feet hurt?" he asked her after three songs in a row. With her cheek pressed close to his, her laugh was like music so close to his ear.

"Of course."

"Worth it?"

She pulled back to look at him, her soft smile lighting him up inside.

"Yes." She nodded. "Where did you learn to dance like this?"

"My mom," he told her. "She taught me and Nick both so we wouldn't stand around at high school dances and look like jerks who stood their dates up."

Vanessa tipped her head appreciatively. "Way to go, Mom," she said softly. "Did you dance at high school dances?"

"Not much," he admitted. "I was either inhaling snacks and watching girls. Or making out with girls in the corners."

"Was Nick ever like that?"

"Nope."

"Your mom would be proud of the man you are now, Parker."

Taken aback by her words, Parker swallowed his heart as she pressed her cheek to his again. He had told her his mom had passed away, and they had talked some about his dad. Parker secretly hoped he would get to introduce her to his dad someday, though he didn't believe it would happen.

"You would be the sexiest woman here even in the other shoes," he told her. He felt rather than heard her laughter.

Later, after more dancing and more wine, Vanessa helped a bit with the cleanup, until Lenore insisted they had hired help to take care of the mess. Parker sipped another shot of bourbon and watched Vanessa and Journey in a whispered exchange. He wondered if they were talking about him. Or if they were talking about Journey's date. The guy seemed fine to Parker, but he couldn't say there appeared to be much chemistry between him and Journey.

And maybe, they were talking smack about Lenore again. Parker found it interesting that Lenore and Journey didn't get along, but Vanessa seemed at ease with Journey's mom. The whole situation made him think about Nick's ex-wife and her tenuous relationships with Maisy and Eli. Would they eventually be close, or was this stutter-step attempt at motherhood going to end up doing them more harm than good?

"You ready?"

Parker blinked Vanessa into view. He gave himself a mental shake and nodded. "Yeah. Ready if you are."

"What's wrong?" she asked as they made their way to the coat rack.

"Thinking about Maisy and Eli." He laid her wrap over her shoulders and led her to the front door. "Wondering what their relationship with Kiara will be like when they're older."

Vanessa nodded, but she didn't reply. Parker reached for her hand as they walked to his truck. Where they would go from here? Was this the end of their arrangement? He had no doubt they could still be friends, but things hadn't gone as they had planned. Parker had done a lot of research on pregnancy. And attempting to get pregnant and infertility, and he knew they had barely scratched the surface. Some couples tried for years to have children, only to be told it was never going to happen. He and Vanessa hadn't put in the time or the heartache those couples did, but on the other hand, Vanessa hadn't asked him to become a permanent fixture in her life. There would come a time when she was ready to move on and find someone, try with someone new.

He eyed his truck critically as he helped her climb in. It served him well for the job, but maybe he should get a second vehicle. Something a bit newer, a bit nicer. For nights like this when he really wanted to impress his date.

"Parker?"

He glanced at Vanessa as he buckled his own seatbelt and started the engine. She sat with her legs crossed, but she rested her head on the seat with her eyes closed.

"What?"

"I have a favor to ask."

She opened her eyes when he chuckled.

"Isn't that how we started?"

She rolled her eyes.

"Anything, Vanessa," he told her.

"I want to see your house."

"My house?" He couldn't have been more surprised by her request. "Why?"

"I don't know," she answered simply. "Maybe I just want to leave part of myself there."

That sounded ominous. She was planning to end things tonight. One last night together. If the dancing hadn't done it, making love to her one more time wouldn't make her want to stay, either. She knew that side of him well enough, she should know his touch by heart now.

"Okay."

She talked about the party as he drove, enough so that he knew she had enjoyed herself. No matter what happened between them, Parker had enjoyed the night as well. He was happy to have spent a little more time with Journey. He liked Kendric and Dalton. And Bryant, even though Vanessa swore the guy was all wrong for Journey. He listened to a three-minute rant about how Journey was going to sleep with him tonight. That Vanessa wished Journey would let someone catch up with her and love her. Tried not to think about Journey and her date having sex in his car or on her front porch, as according to Vanessa, Journey often did because having sex in a bed leaned a little too closely to commitment.

"My house can probably fit inside yours three or four times," he announced when he pulled into his short driveway. Vanessa leaned forward in the truck to look at the front of his place. With no lights on and the only street-light two houses down, she couldn't possibly see much. But she turned to him with a smile.

"I like it."

He rolled his eyes, but the little note of excitement in her voice made him happy.

"You haven't seen it yet," he reminded her as hopped down from the cab and rounded the front of the truck to give her a hand.

"Greg didn't build it," she mumbled.

Parker slipped his arm around her as they made their way to the door.

"Haven't we exorcised Greg's ghost from your house yet?" He unlocked the door and ushered her inside.

"I feel much more of you in the house than I do Greg." She tossed her wrap aside and glanced at him. "But. He built it. He makes the payments. I want something different."

What did that mean? Was she going to start looking at houses? Did she want to be roommates?

"Show me." She tilted her head and looked at him with a shy smile when he turned a lamp on.

"There's really not much to see, Nessa," he told her. "Living room and kitchen. My bedroom. A tiny second bedroom that probably isn't as big as your closet. And a bathroom about the same size."

Vanessa licked her lips and stepped closer to him.

"Parker." She rested her hands on his chest. He waited for her to look up, but she kept her gaze on her fingers. "It's not just the house I need to see. It's you. It's your house. It's your life. I want to see what you're doing when you're not with me. I want to look at your living room and picture you here."

"Are you asking me if I'm seeing other women when we're not together? Because I promised—"

"No." She sighed and shook her head. He reached for her when she started to pull her hands away from him and gently cuffed her wrists in his hands.

"What're you thinking?" His voice was gruff. "Is this it? Time's up?"

"I'm not pregnant," she whispered. "And I might never get pregnant."

"Van—"

She shook her head and pulled one hand from his grasp. Parker sighed when she pressed her fingers to his lips.

"That's okay. Parker, it's okay."

"Dammit." He dropped her other hand and backed away from her. "The irony here is that Nick didn't think he wanted kids. And he got Kiara pregnant twice—and she definitely didn't want kids. And here I am with you, wishing like hell I could give you what you want. And I haven't yet."

He paced away from her and turned his back to her.

"I don't want Nick." Her whisper shook with emotion. "That's what I'm trying to tell you. I don't...want...If I don't get pregnant, I'll..."

"What?" He turned to look at her. "Don't tell me you'll adopt, because this isn't about—"

Vanessa sighed and closed her eyes.

"I don't know what I'll do about it. Yes, I would like to have a baby, Parker, but I'm trying to tell you I don't want to lose you."

Parker stared at her, stunned at her confession.

"What did you say?"

"I want you," she whispered. "With or without a baby. I want you. I want to be with you."

"As we are? As friends? Sleeping together? Hoping for the best?"

She shook her head and paced away from him instead of toward him. Parker balled his hands into fists and took a deep breath.

"I know I said it was all about a baby." She spoke quietly, but Parker heard the hitch in her voice. "And it was. At first, it was."

"But?"

"You're a great guy, Parker—"

His stomach dropped at what sounded like a dismissal.

"And I fell in love with you, and now, I'm afraid to be with you."

"Afraid?" He moved then. Crossed the room and took her hands in his. "Why are you afraid of me?"

"Not afraid of you," she corrected him. "I'm afraid to be with you. To love you. And lose you."

"Why would you lose me?"

"You didn't sign on for this. For the long haul. For commitment. I'm the fool who fell in love with a hook-up."

"Nessa." Parker drew her in and held her close. He kissed the top of her head. "Has being with me ever felt like a meaningless hook-up?"

She shook her head against his cheek. "No."

"I'm crazy about you, and I've been racking my brain on how to make you stay with me. How to get you to fall for me."

"Here's how you do that." She drew back to look him in the eyes. "You tell me you don't want money to get me pregnant. You practice making love to me before we try to make a baby. You introduce me to your family. To those damned adorable kids. You eat frozen pizza with me, and you take me to movies, and you come to me for a haircut because you just want to see me."

Parker cupped her chin in his hand.

"And you dance with me. And bring me to your home. And let me in."

"I love you."

"I still want a baby. With you," she whispered. "But I want us to be together first. And always."

"And if we don't—"

"Always," she repeated.

Thank you for reading Hookin' Up! If you enjoyed it, please consider leaving a review on the retail site where you purchased the book or on Goodreads or Bookbub!

Turn the page for a sneak peek at Holdin' On, the H Books, Book 2.5, Journey and Dalton's story.

"Did you sleep with him?"

Journey Ryan froze in the act of pulling her black hair up off her neck. Felt like Dalton had the heat up to crackling, and she had already shed her coat and her hoodie. She glanced at him now, a little bit stunned by his question. Surely, she'd heard him wrong.

"What?" Slowly, she tugged her ponytail through the elastic band and lowered her hands to stare at her little brother's friend. To his credit, Dalton kept his eye on the road ahead of them, his right hand relaxed on the wheel.

"Abbott." He glanced at her. "Isn't that his name? That guy you were with at your dad's party?"

Journey fidgeted with the oversized silver band she wore on her right middle finger as she considered how to answer him. Dalton McKenzie used to be a staple in her house, like a second little brother. Back in those days, Journey had mostly thought of him as another pain in her ass, yet another kid for her parents to like better than her. At least someone to keep her brother, Kendric, busy most of the time.

Dalton had left town for school. Before her father's party, she hadn't seen him in years—at least five. She had no idea how to take his question. True, she had talked to him for a while at the party. She'd even danced with him a few times. But even that had been over a month ago.

"What?" she said again.

When he reached to turn the radio down, Journey's eyes followed his hand, but she locked eyes with him again when he lifted his gaze to hers.

"What're you doing?"

"I dunno." He shrugged. "Can you not hear me? Did you sleep with Bryant Abbot?"

Journey leaned sideways and turned the radio up. She didn't love Dalton's music choice, at least not today. For Pete's sake, they were on the way to Kristophe House for a Christmas getaway. It was the second weekend in December. Was it too much to ask to hear some holiday music? When she had said that to Dalton earlier, he'd narrowed his eyes at her and stared at her like she had morphed into a short green alien.

"Really?" He tipped his head at her and rolled his eyes. "An hour ago, you were griping about Aerosmith."

"I wasn't griping about Aerosmith," she corrected him. She liked Aerosmith. Particularly "Janie Got a Gun." But hello? December? Fun trip? Festive music? "I just asked if we could listen to Christmas music."

"Tell ya what."

She didn't like the sound of that. Rather than watch Dalton drive—the guy was huge, big surprise he'd played Division I football in school—she turned to look out the windshield at the snowflakes that swirled in a whirlpool pattern in the beams of his SUV's headlights.

"I'll give you full control of the music."

Looked like it was coming down harder now. Faster. Thicker. Something. She wasn't particularly worried about getting to the bed and breakfast. She was worried, however, about the rest of the gang. They'd all agreed on a later start, since everyone was working at least until five.

"If you tell me if you slept with him."

At this rate, Journey was kind of sorry she hadn't just waited. She could have caught a ride with Vanessa and Parker. For some reason—most likely temporary insanity

—she had been all in when Dalton suggested they head on up and get the lay of the land.

"I saw Aerosmith in concert once," she told him, eyes still straight ahead. "Did I tell you that?"

"No."

She wondered if he would let it go now. She hadn't slept with Bryant Abbott. Ever. And it wasn't that big of a deal, but she wasn't sure why Dalton needed to know. They were friends years ago, sure, but they had never been the kinds of friends to share popsicles or secrets. More like Journey snorted and made fun of Dalton and her brother for their celebrity crushes and Dalton and Kendric made snide comments as she left the house to go out on dates.

"Dric said you didn't date him for very long."

She huffed out a sigh. Nope. Apparently, Dalton wasn't going to let it go.

"I didn't date him."

"But he was your date for the party."

"Lenore threw a ridiculously extravagant party for my father. And she instructed me to bring a date. Bryant and I know each other through work. We're friends."

Well. Sort of. Maybe not so much. After the party. When Bryant thought they were going to take things to the next level. Again, Journey didn't really want to discuss it with Dalton. In fact, she had talked—vented—to Vanessa and Mercedes, another friend, and it happened over a month ago, so there was no point in digging it back up.

"You danced with him."

Journey turned to look at Dalton. "Danced with you, too. But I didn't sleep with you."

"So, you did sleep with him."

"Why?" She rested her head on the seat behind her and closed her eyes. "Why does it matter?"

"I was gone for several years, Journey. Just trying to get caught up on things."

"Why don't you wanna catch up on my job? Or on who Dric's dating now, or if I still like skiing, or if I prefer crunchy peanut butter to smooth?"

"Speaking of jobs." He tapped his fingers to the rhythm on the wheel and glanced at her again. "I heard your dad's talking about retiring."

She nodded. "Yeah. It's a little early, but I think he and Lenore are going to do some traveling."

"Why do you call her Lenore? Kendric doesn't."

"Kendric is her favorite child. Lenore and I tolerate each other."

"Bullshit."

Journey rolled her head his way on the seat and blinked her eyes open.

"It's complicated," she said quietly.

"You look like her."

"Biology." Journey cleared her throat. "Lots of nature. Not a lot of nurture."

"She still smoke weed?"

"Yep."

"More nature, huh?"

Journey snorted and shook her head. "Yeah, I guess so."

Back to the snowflakes. Fatter and thicker, still.

"So, did you?"

"No. I *did not* sleep with Bryant Abbott the night of my dad's party. Nor have I ever in my life slept with Bryant Abbott, nor do I have any desire to sleep with him. Ever."

Dalton was silent in the wake of her outburst.

Expecting him to—well, hell, if she knew, but she'd expected SOME kind of response after he'd asked the question several times—she finally turned to look at him again. Inside the SUV, his sparse, buzz cut hair looked dark, but she knew in real daylight, it was a nice honey blonde. The kind women paid her best friend Vanessa to do for them.

Dalton finally nodded, thoughtfully, as if he was going over lines in a play.

"Hmm."

Journey flinched as if he had slapped her.

"Wait." She tipped her head to study him closely. "That's it? That's all you have to say?"

Dalton shrugged. He opened his mouth to answer her, but Journey cut him off.

"No, no, no. No. Wait. You didn't even *say* anything. You *harrumphed* me. What the hell, Dalton? That sounded like something my grandfather would do."

"I asked, you answered."

He sounded so damned nonchalant; Journey's fingers twitched with the need to slap him.

"But."

Irritated now, ready to dig into this conversation, Journey unbuckled her seatbelt, scooched around to sit sideways, and glanced out the windshield once more as she reached blindly to click the buckle again.

"It's getting slick."

Journey eyed him silently for a moment. What guy admitted to slick roads when he was driving? None she knew. The men in her life—brother, father, losers she'd dated—all acted like they were smarter than the weather and women, too, and could handle driving blindfolded with a hand tied behind their backs through a hurricane of snow and farm animals blowing around them.

"How much farther do we have to go?"

She still wasn't worried about getting to Kristophe House. Now, she was worried that she might be stuck overnight with just Dalton if the rest of the gang waited until tomorrow to get on the road.

"Mmm." Dalton pursed his lips in thought.

She watched his eyes move to the clock radio and back to the road. It was just after five, but darkness had slammed them pretty quickly once they got on the road. Her feet were hot now. Dear God, was this big brute of a guy coldblooded?

"Maybe an hour?" He kind of wiggled his lips a bit.

Journey leaned sideways to tug her Uggs off.

"Jesus, Journey, what's next? Your jeans? Or your T-shirt?"

"Why do you have the heat on full blast?" she griped. "It's hotter than the surface of the sun in here."

"I thought you were cold."

She laughed softly when he reached to turn the heat down.

"Thank you." She wiggled her toes, relieved to get the boots off.

"Hmm."

"What?"

"Maybe you should take off your shirt or your jeans."

"What?"

"Do you wear underwear?"

"What?" She shook her head. "Dalton, did you have

one too many head injuries in football? What the hell are you talking about?"

"Your feet are bare in your shoes. Just sayin'..."

Realization dawning on her, she cut loose with a hearty laugh. "You wish."

"Maybe." He grinned.

His playlist started over. Journey barely held in a groan as she leaned forward to snap the power button off.

"What're you doing?"

"Only so many times I can hear 'Dude Looks Like a Lady.'" She stared at him boldly, daring him to argue. "Besides, I answered your question, so I should get to choose what we listen to now."

"Just know that if you put Bing on my radio, I'm not responsible for what might happen."

"Do you mean that in a good way or bad? Like are you pro-Bing or not?"

"Not."

"Interesting." She turned the radio on and tapped through the XM stations until she recognized Ella Fitzgerald singing "Sleigh Ride."

"Why is that interesting?"

"How can you not like Bing?"

"I don't love Bing," he answered with an exaggerated shrug. "Why didn't you sleep with Bryant Abbott?"

"That's hardly the same thing. It's not even a relevant question. It doesn't make sense."

"Just answer me."

"Dalton—" Journey sighed and rubbed her eyes. "I never thought I'd say this, but I miss the pain-in-the-ass twelve-year-old version of you."

"Not true." He shook his head. "We had fun at your

dad's party. And we had fun a lot of nights when I was home during college."

Point, Dalton. They weren't close, but Journey and her brother were. So, yes, she saw Dalton when he was home from school, and they partied together, with at least 50 other people around.

"His lips were too red."

Again, her comment was met with silence from Dalton. Ella Fitzgerald's voice segued into Elton John singing "Step Into Christmas."

"What?"

When Dalton did finally turn to look at her, the amused look on his face made her wish she could take it back. Why had she opened her mouth?

"You heard me," she mumbled as she turned her face away from him. If he was going to laugh about that, he would really tease her for blushing now.

"His lips," Dalton started. "Right? His lips? His lips were too red?"

"Yep."

"Journey, what does that even mean?"

"I just don't like it."

"But I mean. How? How are a guy's lips too red? Like lipstick red?"

"Some guys are just kind of pale. Almost vampiric. And they're sort of...posh-looking. Soft. And because of that, their lips look too red."

Journey didn't look at him this time. She was content to ride the rest of the way to Kristophe House in silence. A gross, uncomfortable silence, but still.

"There's just so much there, I don't know where to start."

His comment came out of left field at least ten minutes later. Three songs had played and changed between her announcement and his comment.

"Let's just not." She turned to him and offered him a sweet smile.

"So. Okay, first. Posh-looking. What? What is that? What does that mean?"

Journey jumped when her phone rang. Dalton gave her a look when her holiday ringtone blared in his SUV.

"Seriously? You don't strike me as such a festive person."

"What does that mean?"

She was curious what he meant, but when she pulled her phone from her purse, she looked down at the screen to find that Vanessa Mayne was calling her.

If you'd like to keep reading Holdin' On, click here:
books2read.com/holdin-on

Turn the page for a sneak peek at Plus One, the newest contemporary romance!

SNEAK PEEK AT PLUS ONE

C ait

The last time I flew across the country to California I was with my sister and her family. We were heading to Disneyland for my niece's birthday, because turning five is apparently a big deal nowadays. I think I got a new doll and my sister's hand-me-down bike for my fifth birthday, but whatever. The whole family enjoyed Stella's birthday, so there's that, I guess.

Anyway, back to the fact that I'm stuck in Row 17, on Southwest Flight 472, bound for wine country. Sounds perfect, right? I mean, given a choice, I'd rather be in like, *Row 6*, but still—wine country! If your destination is wine country, that makes up for any inconveniences on your flight, right?

Well, no. Not really.

The only thing worse than my current situation is that I could be sitting in the middle seat, stuck between my best friend Teagan and her guy, Derrick—lovey-dovey newlyweds—instead of in the window seat on the flight to my other bestie's destination wedding in wine country.

Well, I mean, I guess I could be flying to, like, Detroit for a destination wedding. Or anything, really, other than wine country.

I like my wine. Brynna, Teagan, and I all like our wine. Sure, we started our drinking career many years ago—maybe when we were underage, but I won't confirm that. Anyway, we started our careers with the cheap beer pretty much every high school—strike that—every young person starts with. Because first of all, it's cheap, and when you need to spend your money on jeans and shoes and cute tops, who has cash leftover for beer? Second? Well, none of us liked the taste of beer back then, so why would we want to pass up a new pair of gladiator sandals or Miss Me bootcuts for something we didn't even like?

From beer, we tiptoed into whiskey, but let me tell you, that stuff was way worse than beer. Then again, maybe some of that reflects on our mixologists. Show me a high school kid—I mean, a younger, inexperienced drinker—who can make a mean Old Fashioned, and I'm calling bullshit. We all took our turns doing the mixing, and yeah, we were all equally bad. Maybe part of that was because when you're young, the sole purpose of drinking is to get blitzed and be stupid, right? Not to enjoy the *taste* of something.

We didn't venture into wine until we were in our early twenties, definitely of age. And those first forays into the wine world were box wines and the two buck chuck stuff that tasted either like Kool-Aid or cough medicine. I'll never forget the first time Teagan killed a bottle of that stuff on her own. Teag loves to talk, and when you add alcohol, you seriously can't get her to stop talking. Pretty sure she recited the entire preamble to the Constitution that night. But she did it with a bunch of corny, badly done accents.

Teagan taps my arm now. I pause the music on my phone and take an ear bud out as I turn to her.

"You brought the stuff, right?"

"Yep."

She nods. "But. I mean. You brought everything. Right?"

"Got it," I promise her. By stuff, she's referring to the few gag gifts and bachelorette sorts of things she and I got for Brynna, our friend who would be a beautiful bride in just four days.

"Okay." She smiles and relaxes back into her seat.

The three of us met in first grade. Teagan was the chatterbox, the most outgoing of all of us, and the one who had to write *I will not talk in class* at least five times a year starting in fourth grade. In first grade, she had a bowl haircut, and her smile was missing a front tooth. Took forever for that tooth to grow in because it didn't come out naturally. She and her older brother—River's a year older than we are—were wrestling in their living room, and River knocked Teagan face first into the coffee table. Knocked her tooth out. She's gorgeous now with short, spiky dark hair and a friendly smile, but if you know what you're looking for, you can see that her tooth didn't grow in as perfectly as the rest of them.

"But." She leans forward again and curls her fingers

around my wrist. I eye her thick white gold wedding band and lift my eyes to hers. "Did you remember the body paint?"

"Teag." I tip my head at her. "It's all under control."

She studies my face to make sure she can trust me. Because normally, I am the forgetful one. I can make a long list of things to pack for a trip, and you better believe, I'm still going to forget something. Every. Time.

Not this time, though. I made sure to pack every last fun little gift we got for Brynna: from the slinky, sexy stuff to the kinky, funny stuff, to the actual real gifts we had picked out for our friend. I even have a gorgeous wine-colored gift bag that says *Bride to Be* in silver sparkles. The whole lot of it is the first thing I packed for the trip.

"'Kay." She smiles. Drags her front teeth—the right one is just a tiny bit shorter than the other one—over her lip. And then she snorts this cute little giggle that makes Brynna nuts. "She's gonna die."

Die of embarrassment, she means.

"Well, either that, or she'll kill us." I shrug.

Teagan closes her eyes, that smile still on her lips. I look past her to Derrick, who has his nose stuck in a Dean Koontz book. Like always. Not that I don't love a good Dean Koontz book, too. Derrick must feel my eye roll—about their joined hands resting on Teag's leg, not because of the book—because he takes a quick peek at me.

Don't get me wrong. Love the guy. He's the perfect match for Teagan. He's the calm to her crazy. The quiet to her loud. The thought to her impulsiveness. They started dating when we were seniors in college. Brynna and I wondered if maybe they were shooting for a longest dating relationship before they got married last year.

So, yeah, okay. Boxed wine.

Well, I mean, thank God we graduated from that stuff. Some of us have experimented and found we actually like craft beers, and by some of us I mean Teagan and me. Give Brynna any kind of beer, and she'll just turn her nose up and go in search of good wine. Teag and I have taken to some mixed drinks, too, and an occasional shot of bourbon or whiskey.

But the three of us definitely love our wine.

Now that we're grownups, we've traded in the two buck chuck stuff for real-deal California wines. Brynna's aunt and uncle moved to wine country when we were first learning the ropes of drinking and sucking on pennies to get the alcohol off our breath so we could hide that we were breaking parental rules and real laws. The three of us have always been sort of family fluid, so on any given weekend, one of our houses could have all three of us there, leaving the other two families without their daughters.

Well, in my case, without their youngest daughter.

Don't take it the wrong way, but through the years, we were so close, that our parents were interchangeable. I was just as used to waking up in Brynna or Teagan's room as mine. My mom did their laundry. Teag's mom helped Brynna and me with our science homework. Brynna's parents took us along on several family vacations. To the beach. To amusement parks.

And finally, to wine country. We were eighteen the first time we went. It was for Brynna's high school graduation, and even though we couldn't legally drink at the wineries, Brynna's aunt and uncle had quite a personal wine collection, and we were allowed to taste the good stuff under their watchful adult eyes.

And we might have pilfered a bottle or two through the years when we visited. Brynna's Uncle Tom marked the value on the bottom of each bottle with a silver pen. We were careful not to take anything we thought was too expensive. And we were careful tiptoeing down the steps of their house and sneaking out to the patio to sip wine and rehash old times and share our hopes and dreams.

Brynna was the most sentimental of the three of us. When we were twelve, she was in love with Henry Mason. I mean, it was almost comical the way her eyes bugged out of her head when he walked by us in the halls at school. She wrote his name on the inside of all of her notebooks in eighth grade. Drew hearts with his initials in them. Henry was clueless. He was kind of a dumb jock, though. Taller than most of the boys, and even then, he was almost twice as wide as most of them. Not fat wide, but football player wide.

Brynna loved a lot of guys through the years. Some of them loved her back. And one of them—Theo Garvey—really loved her back. They dated from the beginning of sophomore year until they went away for college. Theo found someone else before college freshmen orientation was over. He was a nice guy, but girl code clearly states that you never say that around the bestie that he dumped. So. Theo became the jerk that we didn't name. Brynna was broken-hearted. It took her a long time to date again.

Even then, she wanted us to find our guys. Or, as she started saying when we were older, our person. She's always been a flowery, sweet, feminine girl, and she loves romance, and she's always happy. She sees the good in everyone, and she wants happiness for everyone, so she tends to be a bit heavy-handed with dating advice and arranging for meet cutes for all of her friends.

Well, Teag doesn't have to deal with that anymore, right? We all thought Brynna would be the first down the aisle, but Teagan shocked us and did the *I dos* and so now, it's just me, fortunate enough to get all of my best friends' attention and set ups.

Really. It's just me.

Like, at midnight last night, my boyfriend Ryan was supposed to hop a different flight this morning—he's been in Boston the past few days—to meet me in Sonoma for the wedding. And this morning, just before Derrick beeped the horn of their Honda Passport to let me know he and Teagan were waiting in the drive to head for the airport, Ryan called and let me know he couldn't make it.

Yep.

Just like that.

Hey, Cait, listen, I'm sorry. But I can't make the wedding. Give Brynn and Adam my best.

To read more of Plus One, click here:
books2read.com/plus-one

ABOUT THE AUTHOR

Tracy Broemmer is the author of several contemporary romance novels including The Mississippi Queen Trilogy, the H Books, and Wedding Day Shenanigans. Tracy also writes women's fiction and is the author of the Williams Legacy series as well as several stand-alone titles.

Tracy's books have been called gripping, emotional, and timely, and readers describe her characters as real and relatable.

Tracy lives in Midwestern Illinois with her husband of 29 years.

For more information on Tracy's books, go to www.broemmerbooks.com

ALSO BY TRACY BROEMMER

Women's Fiction Novels:

Luther's Cross (Writing as Therese Kinkaide)

Luther's Cross 10th Anniversary Edition (Tracy Broemmer)

Fairytale (Writing as Therese Kinkaide)

Just Like Them (Writing as Therese Kinkaide)

Small Hours (Writing as Therese Kinkaide)

Picket Fences

Two Story Home

Green-Eyed Girl

Say Everything

Come Home For Christmas

Sketching Litchfield Lake

Ever, Again

Safe as Houses

Damsel

Every Little Thing, Lorelei Bluffs, Book 1

Two A.M., Lorelei Bluffs, Book 2

Blind, Lorelei Bluffs, Book 3

Leaving July, Lorelei Bluffs, Book 4

Hesitation Marks, Lorelei Bluffs, Book 5

Four Letter Words, Lorelei Bluffs, Book 6

See Kate, Lorelei Bluffs, Book 7

Loved You More, Lorelei Bluffs, Book 8

A Lorelei Ending, Lorelei Bluffs, Book 9

I Do, Lorelei Bluffs, Book 10

Truth Is, The Williams Legacy, Book 1

Other People's Ugly, The Williams Legacy, Book 2

Omissions, The Williams Legacy, Book 3

Contemporary Romance Novels:

Destiny's Calling: Your Future Is Waiting

Wedding Day Shenanigans

Holiday Fling

The Kiss Off

Something Like Love

Love, Nashville, The Mississippi Queen Trilogy, Book 1

Forever, Duncan, The Mississippi Queen Trilogy, Book 2

Always, Jess, The Mississippi Queen Trilogy, Book 3

Getting' Hitched, The H Books, Book 1

Contemporary Romance Novellas:

Indian Summer, A Novella

Dear Jaclyn Perris, A Novella

French Stuff, A Novella, originally published in the newsletter
builder anthology, Just Coffee

Boone's Girl, A Novella, originally published in the Aced, Back
to School anthology

Contemporary Romance Short Stories:

Perfect Pictures, The Wine Tasting Series, Traminette

Coming Home, The Wine Tasting Series, Edelweiss

Save Me Every Dance, The Wine Tasting Series, Rosé

Marry Me, The Wine Tasting Series, Shiraz

Birthday Wishes, The Wine Tasting Series, Muscat

Dad Jeans, The Wine Tasting Series, Vignoles